EXPRESSION

EXPRESSION

E. G. WILSON

Atthis Arts, LLC

EXPRESSION

Text copyright ©2017 by E.G. Wilson

This is a work of fiction. Any names, characters, places, events, or incidents are either the product of the author's imagination or are used fictitiously. Any similarities or resemblance to actual persons, living or dead, events, or places, is entirely coincidental.

Cover design copyright ©2017 Jennifer Zemanek, Seedlings Design Studio
Editorial services by Catherine Jones Payne, Quill Pen Editorial
Proofreading by Bob Michiels, Sarah Savage, and C.T. Templeton

All rights reserved. Except as permitted under the US Copyright Act of 1976, no part of this publication may be reproduced, stored in a retrieval system, or transmitted in any form or by any means electronic, mechanical, photocopying, recording, or otherwise, without written permission of the author.

Published by Atthis Arts, LLC
Centerville, Ohio
www.atthisarts.com

ISBN 978-1-945009-10-5

Library of Congress Control Number: 2017951011

For Nikki,
who asked what happened next.

CHAPTER ONE

Theo Te Ngawai was twenty-seven when he graduated from Richard Pearse University with a Ph.D. in mechalectrical engineering. His first order of business when he got home was to scrub his hands through his hair, restoring it from its abnormal sleekness to his usual mop of dark curls. That was better. He felt more himself, now.

His shoes and socks landed in a heap in the corner. Graduation cloaks were certainly impressive, but they were also heavy; he hung his on a nearby hook, ready to be returned the next day. That done, he rolled his shoulders, loosened his tie, and padded on bare feet down the hall to the kitchen.

Maunga was nowhere to be seen. Working upstairs in the office? Maybe.

Now ... food. The after-party had been rather lacking in anything more substantial than a canapé. He made a sandwich, double cheese on thick seven-seed rye, and took it over to the sofa. His book lay upside down on the coffee table, its cover splayed.

Memory intruded. With it came the pain, a sickly twisting in his gut that pounded in urgent double-time with his heartbeat.

"You monster," the memory of Addy said. Her brown eyes flashed in mock anger. *"How could you, Theo? It's a poor defenceless book, and you've broken its spine. Fix it."*

Ever the defender of the weak, his little sister. Addy hadn't spoken since she was thirteen. He hadn't seen her since she was sixteen. She'd be twenty-two, now. Nearly twenty-three. He stroked the cracked spine of the book.

Fix it, Theo.

He was destroyer and creator, breaker and restorer . . . but there were some things even he could not fix. Some things, once broken, remained broken; once lost, they remained lost.

She would not be one of them. Not if he had anything to say about it.

He demolished the sandwich and skimmed through two chapters before a hand on his shoulder lifted him from his thoughts.

"Hello, husband," said a warm voice in his ear.

When had Maunga come in? Theo waited for her to sit beside him, then slipped an arm around her waist and kissed her thoroughly. "Hello, wife."

"Anyone would think you'd missed me."

"Don't be daft. I saw you five hours ago across a crowded auditorium." The first hairpin was easy to find; he pulled it free and unravelled the small braid it had held in place. "Busy day?"

He swung a leg up onto the couch and patted the empty cushion in front of him in silent invitation. Maunga melted back against his chest with a sigh.

"You know how I caught up with Dmitri yesterday? He said management's been in talks with NZPsycSoc since the Fairbank incident. We had a staff-wide conference call this morning to discuss it. Mostly it sounds like there's going to be more paperwork . . ."

Theo listened, putting in a question here and there and combing out her hair with his fingers as he unwound the braids. There were only a few braids left to unpin when she finished.

"How was your day?" she asked, glancing over her shoulder at him.

"Also busy. I spent the whole morning organising people and catching up with friends. Hardly got time for lunch before we had to meet for the walk to East Hall. And guess what? Hamish actually remembered this year. He was wearing a grey cross-checked shirt with a blue striped jacket, but he was ready on time."

Maunga's jaw dropped in mocking astonishment. "A checked

shirt with a striped jacket? How dare he! Did you eat anything?" she added, veering straight back onto a topic he'd hoped to avoid.

"A bit." Half a scone and a few sips of scalding hot coffee, if he was honest.

She let it go. "I suppose the whole campus was out in force."

"Mmm. Bumped into Autumn. She's expecting again."

"Expecting what, to look like a whale, *again?* They'll need a bank loan just to pay school fees at the rate they're going."

The words were acerbic, but only reflexively. Theo unwound the last braid, pulled her close against his chest, and dropped a kiss on her head. Neither of them particularly wanted kids, but that didn't mean the news they'd received last year had been welcome.

"Did you make the call?" he asked, deliberately changing the subject.

"I did. That's what I was doing upstairs just now."

"And?"

"We have an appointment with the principal in three weeks."

"It was that easy?"

"Certainly was." She grinned. "East Cape Finishing School, here we come."

He drummed his fingers on her arm. "Three weeks to plan, that's good."

Maunga reached across and stilled his hand. "We've been planning for years. Building contacts, training, sourcing supplies. This is just another stage in the game."

"The final stage." The words provoked an anxious fluttering in his gut.

"Yes. We can do this, Theo. We'll get her back."

He bowed his head to the nape of her neck. His words emerged muffled. "Of course we will."

But in what state?

The question remained unasked. He'd spent countless sleepless nights pondering it. Maunga would wake to see him silhouetted against the windows of their room, washed in the grey light of dawn, staring out at the city with blank eyes. Some nights he was frozen by his own fear and doubt. Could they do it?

Caroline moved premises without warning—what if they lost the trail? Other nights it was unadulterated terror: he was terrified that Caroline would always be one step ahead, terrified that even if they found Addy, she might be in no fit state to leave.

It had been six years, after all. Nearly seven. Who knew what Caroline had done to her in that time? Physically, she could be a wreck. Broken bones, amputations, festering infections danced in his mind's eye. She'd had no voice last time he saw her; this time, would she have no eyes? Or it could be worse. She might be physically present but mentally gone. What if she had no memory of him? No memory of *herself?*

The thoughts drove him back to bed, trembling beneath the weight of his own mind, weeping at imagined horrors; back to Maunga's arms and her fierce reassurances.

We'll find her, Theo. We'll bring her home. And if she's broken, we'll fix her.

Maunga's dark nights were vastly different from his. She had nightmares, for one thing—blood-drenched dreams of violence and death. Sometimes she watched Seth as he committed suicide at seventeen. Other times she took his place. Sometimes Caroline's blackmail went too far and she woke gasping, adrenaline surging through her system and nausea following on its heels.

She told Theo about the dreams once, in ghastly detail, down to every unwilling movement of her body, the gleam of metal in her hand, the rasp of rope around her neck. He held her, heart aching, as she painted the visions in clinical, detached strokes. They slept with the light on that night—and for the two nights following.

He remembered Addy's dreams before she left. She'd started seeking him out when she couldn't sleep. He'd tried not to notice her shaking. Tried not to look at her tearstained face. He wished he'd said something, now. He should have made some sort of gesture to show that he cared—that he'd even noticed—instead of tactfully ignoring it. What sort of a brother ignored his sister's tears?

A poor one.

But he already knew that. He'd long since faced the fact that it had only been when she lost her voice that she'd become interesting to him.

"We will," he said again, trying to sound confident and failing miserably. "We'll get her back."

He had that promise, too: that she was, at least, alive.

Caroline had visited him not long after Addy left. She'd talked in circles, leaving him to read between the lines: One, she knew Addy had recorded the events of her Breach session in writing; two, she knew Addy had given that record to Theo; and three, Theo would not like the consequences if he chose to make the record public. She had Addy. And she could make life very . . . difficult . . . for her. You wouldn't want your little sister getting hurt, would you?

Theo met her smirk for smirk. Caroline had Addy, yes. But he had the record of events. And he could make life difficult for Caroline in return. For example, the media could find out that she was behind the creation and spread of Vox Pox. He hadn't put it that overtly, of course. There was no telling what recording devices she had hidden on her. In the whole conversation that ensued, offers and counter-offers, there was nothing that any jury could use to convict either of them of blackmail.

Nonetheless, mutual blackmail it was. They came away in a stalemate, and in that stalemate he had lived for almost seven years now. Theo would hide the record, would not breathe a word of it to anyone. And Caroline would keep Addy alive.

It was precious little, he'd known that. *Alive* was such a broad state. But it meant that when the time came to rescue her, at least there would be something to rescue.

So he had buried the record deep, where no one else would find it. He'd hidden it from his own restless hands; he'd even hidden it from his own memory. The knowledge faded, growing indistinct. He knew the broad strokes, but the detail had been lost.

And then, a year after they started dating, he proposed to Maunga. She told him everything: the way she infected Addy with Vox Pox, the way she manipulated her into joining the TheraRPG session, the way she led her straight to Caroline in hopes of selling her out.

It had ripped the wound clean open.

Maunga frowned at his change in mood. She sat up and looked at him closely, and then her eyes softened. Her hands came up to cradle his temples. She leaned forward, pressing forehead to forehead and nose to nose in an intimate hongi. "You think too much."

Theo curled two fingers around her wrist and let her gaze anchor him in the present. "Yes." They had covered this ground many times.

"I'm here," she said.

"I know."

"Not going anywhere."

"I know." If nothing else, he had that: the promise that she would never leave him to drown in his thoughts.

"Be here. Now. With me. Don't worry about next week."

He had to. He had to explore the branches of the path ahead, the twists and turns of the trail. He had to know where the cliff edges were. A single misstep could spell ruin.

"Think," she said. "Plan. Scheme. But don't *worry*. We'll find her."

He nodded, nose bumping against nose. She had so much conviction. Fighting her was like fighting a flood. And she was right. He let go and drifted with the tide, borrowing her strength. "Of course we will."

Addy.

They had to find her. The alternative was . . . unthinkable.

It scared Maunga, he knew, the way he retreated into his mind, barring the gates against all entry. For the most part, he could come back at any time. But sometimes he couldn't. Sometimes a newly explored tunnel revealed unthought horrors and caved in around him, leaving him suffocating under the weight of his mind. He left the back door on the latch for her, and she always found a way to pull him out before it became too much.

"Stay with me," she whispered.

On the flip side, her violence scared him. He understood revenge, the payment of like with like, and he understood justice, Caroline getting what she deserved. But he would never understand the bloodlust of her dreams, the way her mind slid so easily into ugly paths of torture and brutality. Repaying like with like wasn't enough for her; she needed *more.*

She fought it, the same way he fought being overwhelmed by his thoughts. And in the end, it was only another sort of darkness. She had her bloody violence. He had his thoughts, churning and spinning out of control. Addy had had darkness of another sort, a deep depression that sapped all energy and emotion from the world. She'd never talked to him about it. Looking back, he didn't know if she'd even recognised it for what it was.

"I'm here," he said. "Not going anywhere."

Maunga drew back, exhaling a little. "Good."

The impulse to apologise was there. He resisted. She'd broken him of that habit. *Don't apologise for being yourself.* He rubbed the soft brown skin of her wrist, thinking.

"What is it?" she asked.

"We should get the gang together."

"That would be the logical next step. Everyone?"

They'd need all the help they could muster. "It's the endgame. Everyone."

"Okay. When?"

"How does Saturday suit you?"

"I'm out for either brunch or tea with my husband; not sure

which. But I'll be free after that." She was watching him with a half-smile and a quizzical look, as if he'd unexpectedly missed a step in some elementary formula.

Theo paused, mentally scrambling. What was the date today? And Saturday?

Blast.

"Brunch," he said. "If you'd like. At the Arboretum." No need to overdo it; it was only their keeking five-year wedding anniversary.

The half-smile grew to a full grin. "That sounds lovely."

Their anniversary. *Keek.* And now he'd practically made plans for that night. Was it too late to back out? "The meeting doesn't need to be Saturday."

"You can always send a message out and see when people are available."

"Good idea."

"I do have them occasionally."

"So we want Tuku, Tarata and Manatu, Dave, Challa . . . "

"Te Kaha and Kimbell . . . "

"And Liam."

Caroline hadn't needed to tell him not to involve the police. He'd known for years that any rescue attempt would be up to him alone. But their friends were as committed to the cause as he and Maunga, and he wasn't too proud to admit they could do with the help. He'd rather he hadn't inadvertently booked the meeting for Saturday, though. "We always have that night free."

"Well." She looked at him through her lashes. "If you're so worried about missing Saturday, you could make it up to me tonight."

Mmm, now there was an idea. "Thought you were tired?"

"Not too tired." She trailed a finger over the bare skin showing at the open neck of his shirt and smirked at his involuntary shiver.

He pressed a kiss to the corner of her mouth. "Minx."

"You love it."

And then to the other corner. "You're incorrigible."

"Is that a yes?"

He groaned as she slid a warm hand up under his shirt, palm skimming over his stomach. "Yes," he murmured, and kissed her full on the mouth.

CHAPTER TWO

They rescheduled the meeting. The Saturday after their anniversary found all ten of them seated around the massive table in Theo and Maunga's dining room. Tea finished, the Johnson twins cleared dishes while Te Kaha took charge of the coffee machine. Once they were settled, well supplied with drinks and snacks, Theo spoke from his seat at the head of the table.

"Welcome, everyone. We're glad you could make it."

"Glad to be here," Tuku said. "You guys make good kai."

A ripple of laughter spread around the table.

There was no sign of vulnerability in Theo now, no crippling doubt in his eyes, no slumping shoulders. But that was Theo all over, Maunga thought. Give him a team and he was the consummate leader—charismatic, passionate, vivacious. As long as someone was looking to him for strength, he would be strong. It was only when he was alone—or alone with Maunga—that he could let himself be subject to human weakness.

Theo grinned. "Thanks, Tuku." He hesitated. "I was going to launch straight in, but it occurs to me that we haven't met for over a year, and there have been some significant additions to our team in that time. We'll start with introductions. Hi, I'm Theo Te Ngawai."

"Hi, Theo," the three Johnsons chorused.

"I have a doctorate in science—engineering—and I'm married to Maunga. I founded this team five years ago, about six months after I learned exactly what Addy had done."

Maunga had told him the night he proposed, a year after they started dating and fifteen months after they'd last seen Addy.

The anguish and the helpless rage in his eyes would stay with her forever.

"To sum up," he continued, "for anyone who doesn't know the whole story: At thirteen, Addy contracted Vox Pox. At sixteen, she embarked on a TheraRPG session with the aim of finding a cure. She succeeded. But she bargained with the best thing she had left: herself.

"Caroline York released the cures and ended the Vox Pox research in return for Addy as a live test subject, 24/7, with no end date. Addy left home soon after, supposedly to take part in an extended trial at Breach. We haven't seen her since."

He paused. "In short, I am here because Adelaide Te Ngawai is my little sister, and I would very much like her back."

"Amen to that," murmured Challa.

"Tuku." Theo nodded to his left. "Your turn."

Tuku lived down south on Stewart Island. She'd dyed her hair almost pure white, and the effect of the trailing tendrils against her dark skin was striking. She spoke of being in Addy's class at school and touched on everything important—that her dad was a higher-up at Breach, that she'd organised Addy's papers for the TheraRPG session, that Theo had asked her to join the rescue group—before handing off to Tarata.

The twins had kept their natural dark hair. They'd been in Maunga's class at school; these days they worked at Breach, Tarata in payroll and Manatu in tech system management.

Soft-spoken Liam Chatham was an old friend of the Johnsons. He worked as a paramedic for St. John. Theo had appointed him team medic for the rescue op.

Te Kaha Irvine, dreadlocked, tattooed, and heavily muscled, owned Addy's favourite cafe, The Dusky Moose. He'd made contact through Tuku after Addy disappeared and had brought Kimbell Aranui, freelance trader and supplier of all things semi-legal, along for the ride.

Dave, the newest member of their team, was next.

"Kia ora, everyone." He flicked shaggy, chestnut hair out of his eyes. "I'm David Rathbone—Dave."

"Welcome," said Tuku.

"Thanks. Glad to be here." He rubbed a hand across the back of his neck. "I am—was, rather—a research assistant at Breach Laboratories. Worked with Caro York on the TheraRPG programme."

The attention of the room abruptly, intently focused on him.

"It occurred to me a couple of months ago that it'd been a few years since I'd gone under to see my virtual clone. So I set up a private session and went in. The assimilation was . . . painful." He sipped his coffee, brows beetled over dark blue eyes. "Thankfully, my clone was able to guide me to the most important events. The disappearance of more than half the clones was one milestone. My counterpart was offered a choice at that time, too: he could remain in the programme, or he was free to leave. To be erased. Permanently."

Maunga had no doubt that Seth had chosen to leave. He was free—finally, he was free of the system.

"When was this?" Tarata asked.

"I don't know exactly. In-system time uses a vastly different metric from real-world time. I believe it was after Adelaide's session. Perhaps a week afterward, maybe as long as six months."

"So Addy might have had something to do with it?"

"Yes." Dave's gaze flickered to Maunga and back to Tarata. "She did. It was one of her three conditions."

"What do you mean, *conditions?*" Challa asked.

"Adelaide set three conditions on her exchange. She wanted the cures for Vox Pox, the closure of the Vox Pox programme—which meant that no new cases would be created—and the release of the ghosts, or in-system clones."

Te Kaha spoke up. "How do you know this?"

"My clone had interacted with Adelaide during her session. It was a simple matter of going back in the records and then following her through the remainder of the three hours."

"We have a recording of Addy's meeting with Caroline," Theo added. "We can watch it later if everybody's in favour of that."

A murmur of agreement spread around the table.

Manatu frowned. "Why can't you just tell us?" she asked Dave.

"Because it's not my place."

"Then whose place is it?"

"Mine," said Maunga. She stared Manatu down until the twin looked away.

"I copied the pertinent records," Dave continued after a moment. "They found out, of course. I came back from lunch one day to find my office had been searched. They called me into a disciplinary meeting. I made up some excuse and handed the records back. Luckily I'd already moved the backups to a secure location away from work."

"And then?" Kim asked.

"Officially, I resigned two weeks later. To pursue my dream of becoming an actor, was the reason they put on record."

"And unofficially?"

"I'd been compromised. They couldn't keep me on. There may have been some small amount of . . . pressure . . . to quit before they were forced to fire me."

Kim winced. "That's rough. I'm sorry."

"There are worse things in the world than leaving a bad job. I'd seen Maunga on the recording with Adelaide, so I thought she'd be a good place to start. Looked her up one night, and here we are."

Looked her up, indeed, Maunga thought. Dave was the reason they knew where to find Addy; he'd turned up on their doorstep five weeks ago, haggard and with bruises under his eyes from lack of sleep.

"I want to help," he'd blurted, brandishing a cloth bag with shaking hands. "Here. I brought the recordings—and I can find out where she is now. I want to help rescue her."

"And that's me," he finished.

There was a long silence.

"Challa," said Theo. "You're up."

Challa Molesworth was a ground reporter for the *Herald,* and Addy's former best friend. And, she confessed, she still didn't understand why Theo included her in this business.

"She took the picture," he murmured.

"She—what?"

"That picture of you and her that she'd had above her bed for years. Addy took it with her when she left."

He retrieved a small metal pyramid and pushed it toward the middle of the table, then tapped his wrist holo. "Here."

The holo trijector lit up, blue screen unfurling to show an image of Challa and Addy at twelve years old, arms around each other, laughing into the viewer.

Challa groaned. "That *hair*—!"

"I'll send you a copy," Theo said with a sneaking grin. "Hang on, there's a more recent one of her . . . "

The image changed to show Addy and Theo sitting on his bed. Maunga leaned forward, intrigued. She hadn't seen this one before.

A much-younger Theo frowned at a book, clearly not reading a word of it. His expression was easier to interpret without the beard—he had that look of half-aborted curiosity, like there was a question on the tip of his tongue but he wasn't quite willing to ask it. Beside him, Addy curled up under a blanket. Her head was tipped back against the wall, chin lifted, nostrils flared; she gazed at the far wall as if staring down her nightmares.

How could someone look so scared and so defiant at the same time?

The angle of the shot placed them somewhere between three-quarter and full profile, with Addy nearest to the viewer. As close as they were, Maunga saw the resemblance easily—the line of the nose, the straight eyebrows, the resolute chin.

"That's Addy at sixteen," Theo said. The picture disappeared. "But we're getting sidetracked. Maunga."

Maunga set her mug down with a click. "Maunga Richards. Married to Theo, went to school with Manatu and Tarata, vaguely knew Addy and Tuku and Challa. I'm a trauma psychologist." Backing out was a tempting thought, but she didn't entertain it seriously. "What I'm about to tell you will surprise you. Hear me out. Please."

Te Kaha raised his eyebrows. "You make it sound like you've done something unforgivable."

"Not recently," she said with a ghost of a grim smile.

"Go ahead." Challa didn't look up from refilling her scotch glass. "We'll reserve judgement until you're done, mate."

"It'll make more sense once you see the recording of Addy's talk with Caroline because you'll get to see me, too—me from seven years ago. I wasn't a nice person."

"You can say that again." Tuku started guiltily as Tarata elbowed her. "Sorry."

"It's the truth," Maunga said. "I admit it. But I'm starting in the wrong place. When I was fifteen, I dated a guy called Seth. I loved him, as much as you can love anyone at that age. He came down with Vox Pox two months before my sixteenth birthday. Two weeks *after* my sixteenth, he took his life."

The wound was long healed, but the memory still hurt.

"A couple of weeks after *that,*" she continued, making deliberate eye contact with the horrified faces around the table, "I was approached by Caroline York. She expressed her sympathies and said it would be a shame if something like that happened to me. I wasn't in the healthiest frame of mind, as you might imagine. I agreed to her terms: infect one person with Vox Pox within the next four weeks or be infected myself. When I was assigned to tutor some girls from the ninth, the decision was almost too easy. Caroline had given me a few different options for infecting my target, depending on age, sex, and so on. I sent Challa back to class and was left alone with the last girl: Adelaide Te Ngawai."

The table erupted.

Theo held up a hand, his face neutral. "Let her finish."

"So I infected her," Maunga said as the noise died down. "Caroline used that first incident against me; Addy wasn't anywhere near the last person I infected. When the TheraRPG programme became available to the public, I entered a session and found Seth's ghost waiting for me. We made plans."

"Plans for what?" Manatu burst out.

"Plans to be free of Caroline. Seth's clone carried all his memories; it wasn't a pleasant existence. And I wanted out from under her thumb. Knew we couldn't do it by ourselves, so I leaked information through the twins to Tuku and on to Addy. She showed up to the session, I explained the situation, and together we confronted Caroline. The result of that little meeting, you already know."

"That's it?" Kim asked.

"In essentials, yes."

"You stole Addy's voice," Challa said, low and angry.

"But you helped her find the cure," Tuku said. "That counts for something."

"It counts for a lot," said Te Kaha with a long look down the table at Theo.

"My motives weren't altruistic at all," Maunga said. "I'd been planning to use Addy as a bargaining chip. She could easily have returned the favour. But no, she had to do the heroic thing and use *herself*." She snorted. "I told her she was too keeking selfless. Guess she took it to heart."

Manatu drew herself up, looking indignant. "You were going to sell her out?"

"Told you I wasn't a nice person. I'm still not, really."

"I disagree," Theo murmured.

"Yeah, but you're biased."

He shrugged. "Doesn't make it untrue. But moving on—"

"Hang on," Manatu said. "What about Maunga?"

"What about me?" Maunga asked.

"You stole Addy's voice. You were going to sell her out. And you expect us to still trust you?"

Ugh. She was so self-righteous, it hurt. "Yes."

Manatu blinked. "What?"

"Yes. I do expect you to trust me."

"Why?"

"Because people change. I'm not the same person I was six years ago. I'm not claiming to be as angelic as Addy, but doesn't the fact that I'm sitting here scheming to rescue her suggest something to you?"

Manatu opened her mouth, gaped, and closed it again. She nodded.

Good. They had enough to get through without her theatrics.

"On to the next point on the agenda." Maunga consulted the list in front of Theo. "Our objective. We're keeking well rescuing Adelaide Te Ngawai." She ticked that point off, aware of Challa's mouth twitching. "Timeframe. Dave."

Dave cleared his throat. "You know Adelaide's being moved to a different facility once a year on average. She was moved again four weeks ago, and this time we know where she is. I'd recommend going in soon, before Caroline gets wind of what we're up to."

"How do you know where she is?" Kim asked.

"Theo hacked the records I stole from Breach. If I may?" Dave clicked his fingers. The trijector extended spindly legs and skittered down the table to sit in front of him.

"Thank you." He synced his wrist holo and brought up a familiar view. "The current testing facility. It's in the same location as the original facility, oddly enough."

"That's . . ." Liam leaned forward, frowning. "Is that a *school*?"

"It is," said Theo. "East Cape Finishing School for Ladies. They supposedly bought the place from Breach four years ago. Caroline sent out an official letter claiming that Breach moved the trial facility to another, top-secret, location. The other nine in the testing group have long since been cured, of course. Addy's the only one left."

"Very convenient," Challa muttered.

"Isn't it?" Dave said. "We hacked into the original blueprints of that block. The testing facility is joined to an obscure sub-basement, and the best way in is through the school."

"How—?"

"We have an appointment with the principal on Thursday," Theo said. "To discuss future placement for our fictional daughter."

Te Kaha straightened in his seat. "We're not all going?"

"Ten strangers barging in on an elite girls' finishing school?" Maunga arched her eyebrows. "Yeah, that'd go down well."

"Only three of us will be going." Theo raised a hand, checking the uproar. "The fewer people we take, the less conspicuous we'll be. We'll have one group in the field and another group at home base running ICL: Intelligence, Communications, and Logistics. Te Kaha has volunteered the rooms above the cafe for that. Anyone with other commitments—"

"Like what?" Manatu protested. "What's more important than rescuing Addy?"

"Other commitments," he said mildly, "like going to work—are free to maintain their alibis as needed."

"We can call in sick," said Tarata.

"And have no one at Breach to run interference for us?" Maunga snorted. "Great idea."

"The rest of us can, then," said Kim.

But Theo shook his head. "Three of us in the field, that leaves seven people. We need the twins at Breach, which leaves five. Te Kaha will be downstairs. Tuku?"

"Sorry. I'm booked up down south. I can remote in on the day."

"Thanks. Anyone else have prior commitments on Thursday?"

Dave shook his head. So did Kimbell.

"I'm off shift at six that morning," Liam said. "But that's it."

Challa grimaced. "I should be at work, but I'm not missing this. I'll be there."

The three Johnsons and Te Kaha were out of the picture. That left six people to be divided between the home and field teams.

Tuku asked the question they were all thinking. "Who's going in to get her?"

"I am," Theo said. "And Maunga."

Manatu opened her mouth and then winced. Tuku's serene gaze didn't waver.

"And the third person?" Te Kaha asked.

"Dave. He knows the maps best."

Even Kimbell frowned at that. Maunga understood. They wanted to be in at the frontline, not stuck in the back running support. For the guys who had been involved since day one, ceding the coveted third field position to the newest member of the team grated.

"Which leaves Kimbell, Challa, and Liam to run ICL," Theo said.

"Order of command?" Liam asked.

"I'll head up the field unit. Challa, you're in charge of home base."

"Me?" Challa looked surprised. "But—"

"You're Addy's oldest friend. Except myself and maybe Maunga, you know her best. Share the load with Liam and Kim all you like, but if it goes south, remember you're in charge—and responsible for your team."

Challa nodded and made a quick note on her holo.

"Now that that's out of the way—trijector? Thanks—we'll watch that very enlightening conversation Addy had with Caroline. And then we can go through the plan for Thursday. Sounds good? Alright. Here we go . . ."

CHAPTER THREE

Here they went, Theo thought five days later. He eyed his reflection in the mirror and frowned. The cuffs of his grey silk shirt were crooked. He tugged them straight. There. Was that everything? He needed to make a strong first impression.

Shoes: black leather, polished until they shone and then scuff-brushed, just a little, to make it look like he had more important things to do than worry about his wardrobe. Trousers: black moleskin, not as formal as suit trousers but not as casual as jeans. His belt was black, of course. Wearing a brown belt with black trousers had been a fad a few years back, but he'd never taken it up. It had gone out of fashion again before long.

He'd hidden a green merino t-shirt under his collared shirt. Who knew what sort of environment they'd find in the testing facility? It could be snowing, for all they knew. The collared shirt had a distinct herringbone weave, a mark of one particular high-end tailor. He hadn't gone for anything as pretentious as cufflinks, though. Buttons were perfectly functional.

Now, what was he missing . . . his wedding ring remained safely on his hand. The brown leather strap of his everyday holo was fine. The contrast with the careful coordination of the rest of his outfit would add the right touch of casual indifference.

A jersey, he needed a jersey. A quick rummage in his wardrobe turned up a blue v-neck in a mohair/merino blend. That would do. He slipped it on and straightened his collar before adjusting the cuffs with automatic movements. Good. Was he ready? He thought he was ready.

"Stop fussing," Maunga said, poking her head around the door. "You look fine."

"Think they'll buy it?"

"Of course they will." She padded into the room in her tights, carrying her boots. "Expensive, high-quality clothing mixed with scuffed shoes and a well-worn holo band? They can't *not* buy it."

"Hmm." He hoped so. "You're looking good."

She grinned and twirled in place. "Think they'll buy it?"

"Will they *what.* My brain's short-circuiting just looking at you."

Her hair was swept back and coiled in an elegant variation on her signature mohawk braid. The mustard-yellow dress set her skin off to perfection. Fitted enough to show off her figure but not so tight that it restricted movement, its asymmetric hemline hung lower at one knee than the other, and—Theo tilted his head—were those *pockets*?

They were, too. Clever. One on each hip, trimmed in matching leather. With the addition of the low boots and the black leather jacket, they lifted the outfit from mere good taste to peerless styling.

"They'll buy it," he said.

"Excellent." Maunga pulled on her boots and strapped them shut. "Ready to go?"

"Just need to clean my teeth. Might be a while before we get a chance to do that again."

"Slacker," she said cheerfully. "I cleaned mine ten minutes ago."

"Why don't you bring the car around?" he asked. "While I'm scrubbing my fangs to within an inch of their lives."

Kim's voice came clear and quiet through his earpiece. "Half an hour, you two. You'll have to be out of the house in the next five minutes if you want to be on time."

"Will do," Maunga said. She kissed Theo and vanished out the bedroom door.

Theo gave his teeth a thorough cleaning and slipped a pack of breath mint capsules from the cabinet as an afterthought. One last glance in the mirror, and he was down the stairs and out the front door. Maunga waited in the courtyard with the private hovercar. He locked the house and slid into the passenger seat.

He reached for the seat's safety field and activated it. "Where's your bag?"

"Behind your seat." Maunga eased out into the morning traffic.

He groped behind him, found the handbag, and pulled it around onto his lap. It was one of those massive leather contrivances that always seemed twice as big on the inside, with a dozen pockets and zips and hidden compartments. Maunga somehow knew exactly what was in the bag and where it was; he hadn't a clue, but if he kept it simple, he should at least be able to find these again. The pack of capsules went into an end pocket.

"Nervous?" Maunga asked.

"A bit. I'll be better once we're through the front door. It's the waiting that gets me."

"Performance anxiety is perfectly normal." She took a hand from the wheel to reach over and pat his knee. "Your dominant response under this sort of stress is to throw up a wall bricked with intelligence and mortared with arrogance—which, not coincidentally, is pretty near the image we want to portray. You'll be fine."

Five years of marriage had taught him a little about basic psychological theory. He might not understand what she'd said, but he understood what she meant.

"Hands," he said.

"Don't you trust my driving?" Her eyes stayed fixed on the road ahead. A smile ghosted across her lips. Her hand didn't budge from his thigh.

"I trust your driving. I don't trust theirs." He nodded to the car in front, a nine-seater Crowdshifter that sported glowing yellow L-plates. It was making rather jerky progress along the road, and the left side of the car was dangerously close to intruding into the next lane.

"We're turning off soon, anyway."

As they approached a three-lane roundabout, the Crowdshifter slowed and then abruptly sped up again.

"Watch it," Theo muttered at the unknown learner driver. The Crowdshifter's AI hadn't seized control of the car yet. Theo hoped the learner hadn't turned it off. Keek knew he hated automated driving, himself, but the shaky control of the learner driver was crying out for it.

Maunga opened her mouth, but before she could speak, the Crowdshifter pulled a hard stop just short of the entry to the roundabout. She braked and caught Theo's wrist as he flung out a hand to grab the wheel. Throwing a lightning look in the side holocam, she indicated and veered around the Crowdshifter, still with only one hand on the wheel, and they slid through the roundabout without a problem.

"See?" she said, letting his hand go. "No worries."

"For us, maybe." His heart was beating rather faster than it had been a minute ago. He twisted his head to look at the far side of the intersection. The Crowdshifter hadn't made any progress, but it had at least pulled off the road into the parking lane. The L plate had changed colour from yellow to white, signalling the AI takeover. Finally.

Maunga squeezed his leg and put her hand back on the wheel. "Interesting."

"What?" It was one of the perils of being married to a psychologist: having to put up with occasional backseat analyses of actions and reactions when her client-brain came to the fore.

"Six years of driving together and you still lunge for the wheel when you think we might be trouble."

He snorted. "Habit. Don't read anything into it. I do the same when I'm driving with Mum and Dad." No doubt he would have with Addy, too, but she hadn't been old enough to learn to drive before she went off with Caroline.

He and Maunga owned a serviceable old Ford; it came out a

few times a week but otherwise lived in the garage at home. They'd hired this car from one of the more discreet rental places. The sleek Jag gleamed in blue-grey metal, its engine noise replicator sounding somewhere between a purr and a growl. First impressions, as Maunga often reminded him, were everything.

Stereotyping, he thought. And confirmation bias. Or was it the mere exposure effect? He wasn't sure.

She liked pushing his boundaries, Maunga did. Not maliciously, just enough to stretch his comfort zone a little. Like turning a potential car crash into a test of trust. Really, every day with her was a trust test. But then, so was marriage. So was life itself.

They picked Dave up as they swung through Ashbury, and before long they were out on the reclaimed land of the Cape, away from the worst of the inner-city traffic.

"Who's on Comms at the moment?" Dave asked, slipping his earpiece into place.

"I am," said Kim. "Challa's right beside me."

The dashboard beeped. At the same time, the Jag's AI said in a smooth voice, "Roadworks ahead. Turn left to avoid them."

Theo braced himself against the dash as Maunga took the turn a little fast. "And Liam?"

"Asleep on the sofa," Kim said. "He started his shift at six last night and was meant to be off at six this morning, but they had another callout at quarter to. He didn't get here until close to nine."

"Told us to wake him at eleven," Challa added. "We'll see how we go. He's pretty zonked."

"Alright," Theo said. "Keep us informed."

"Will do."

The East Cape Finishing School for Ladies was only two blocks from the main thoroughfare—far enough to mute the worst of the noise but not so far that it was hard to find.

"There's a small carpark," Maunga said, turning into a private lane. "I warned them we'd be bringing the car, so they're expecting us at the back entrance."

"Back entrance?" Theo affected a wounded look. "What are we, tradesmen?"

"Yes, dear. Didn't you know? We're just here to check the basement."

The carpark was signposted with small brass plaques: *East Cape Finishing School for Ladies. Staff Parks Only; Visitors By Appointment.* Maunga backed the Jag into an empty space and switched the engine off.

"Two minutes to ten," Kim said. "Good timing."

Theo hopped out of the car and eyed the rear of the school. It loomed above them, all antique window mouldings and modern paint—and quite a few cameras, he noted. The fact that the holo-cams could be seen with the naked eye meant the school *wanted* them to be seen. It was either an effective scare tactic or another way of showing off. Or perhaps both.

Yeah. Probably both.

"See them?" Dave muttered at his shoulder.

"The cameras?" Theo asked, making no attempt to hide the conversation from any audio recorders. "I see them. But you'd expect it for a swanky place like this, wouldn't you?"

Maunga came to his side, tucking the keys into her bag and shouldering it. Her voice, when she spoke, was slower and smoother than usual. It wasn't so pronounced as to be obvious, but he certainly noticed it. Her words were crisper, too. "Ready to go in?"

"Ready." He pressed a hand to the small of her back.

They ascended the steps to the closed timber doors and rang the bell. A few seconds passed before a voice spoke from the comms box beside the door frame.

"Welcome to the East Cape Finishing School for Ladies, how may I help you?"

"Good morning, I'm Maunga Richards. I'm here to see Principal Benvenue."

"Very well. Do you have an appointment this morning?"

"I do. It's for ten o'clock, and I'd prefer not to be late, if you don't mind."

There was a short, muffled discussion and then the voice returned. "Ms. Benvenue will be out to greet you shortly. Please make yourself comfortable in the foyer."

"Thank you."

The doors swung inward, and they walked through.

Dave whistled. "No expense spared, eh?"

"Only the best for Emma," Theo said. Dave had volunteered his teenaged daughter for future placement here. Theo had agreed to the change without protest. It saved them the hassle of making up a fictional child.

They waited on the low leather couches for perhaps five minutes before Theo heard the click of heels approaching from within. The door at the far end of the foyer opened and a woman stepped through. The first thing he noted was her height: even in heels, she didn't reach much past his chin. Brown frizzy hair, cut short and blunt at the shoulders. Just enough makeup to be noticeable. Cream stovepipe trousers. And a navy blazer hanging open to show a black turtleneck.

Who wore turtlenecks these days? It made her look like she had no neck at all.

"Ms. Richards?" the principal said, extending a hand to Maunga. "I'm Tracey Benvenue. Sorry for the wait."

"Mrs.," Maunga corrected her. Theo knew she usually preferred to shake with her left hand, but in this case, she met Tracey right-for-right. "Pleased to meet you. Call me Maunga. May I introduce my husband Theo and his brother David?"

Tracey's expression was so open even Theo could read it. The title correction threw her off balance; the firm handshake let her regain her equilibrium; and now she was mentally labelling them, quite incorrectly, as *The Richards*. Let her think that. It made things easier for them if anyone from Breach came around asking about Theo Te Ngawai or Dave Rathbone.

"Pleasure," she said, shaking hands with Theo and Dave in turn. "If you'll come this way? My office is on this level, on the far side of the building."

"You aren't related to one of my colleagues, by any chance?" Theo asked as they walked down a white-panelled corridor. "I lecture engineering at the university with Bethwyn Benvenue."

Tracey shook her head. "No relation of mine, I'm afraid. It's a common enough surname."

"Hmm, true." The pronunciation was idiosyncratic—Ben-ve-noo-ey rather than Ben-ve-noo—and had long been a way of telling true Te Maruvians from out-of-towners. "There are a few other Benvenues in the department, but I suppose you're no relation to them, either."

"None whatsoever," she said, smiling, and changed the subject.

"Now," Tracey said once they were seated in her office, "I understand you're here to discuss placement for your daughter?"

"I am." Dave took the lead. "Emma's only fourteen, so it's early enough, but from what I hear your waiting list is fairly long?"

"It is, yes. We've become very high demand in the last two years. Our current waiting list is sitting at just below one hundred names, I believe."

"And your intake per year is . . . ?"

"We take on four classes of ten ladies each at the beginning of the year, although I wouldn't be surprised if that had grown to six classes by the time your daughter is old enough to join us. We've been looking at expanding. The usual enrolment age is sixteen or seventeen, and the standard length of time to obtain our diploma is two years."

"Emma's very bright," Dave said. "And I say that not just as a father but as an observer with a doctorate in cognitive neuroscience. She's smart, very intuitive, hardworking to the point of obsession when it's something she's passionate about, and completely science-mad. She takes after me," he added with a self-deprecatory look.

"I'm sure she does," Tracey said warmly. "We generally require the ladies to have a high school leaver's certificate before being allowed entrance, but if the lady in question has proved fully capable, we do make allowances. Of course, there is a standard protocol for such exceptions to the rule; they are still required to take an entrance exam and so on."

"Of course, no, I understand completely. Wouldn't expect anything less. As I said, it's early days yet. I'm really just putting feelers out, seeing where she might fit in best, which schools will challenge her and push her to the best of her abilities instead of letting her coast."

"Well, we certainly do that. Challenge the ladies, I mean, not let them coast."

She produced a syllabus and took them through it, outlining class structures and weekly timetables. After ten minutes, her desk holo chimed a warning. She checked it and grimaced. "I'm afraid I have another meeting to be at soon. If you'd like to see the school, I've taken the liberty of arranging for one of our second-years to give you a tour."

"Thank you. We won't take her away from her studies for long."

They waited at reception, and soon a slim girl stepped through from the hall. Theo took in the uniform: black skirt, white blouse, maroon cardigan to match the knee-high socks, and tidy black shoes. No tie, which surprised him. She wore it neatly but without the fastidiousness he'd expected, given the vaguely pretentious tone of the school.

The girl herself was of average height, button-nosed, her brown eyes sharp and not unfriendly. He took in the details automatically: black hair brushed back in the traditional schoolgirl braid and tied with a maroon ribbon, no makeup, a single silver ring in each earlobe. No other jewellery.

Conclusion: a girl who took pride in her school, and a school that took pride in appearances.

The girl stepped forward, eyes darting from Theo to Dave

to Maunga. "I'm Cynthia. I'm here to give you a tour of the school . . . ?"

Maunga offered her hand—the left, Theo noticed with a private grin. "Maunga Richards. Pleased to meet you, Cynthia. This is my husband Theo and his brother David."

"Pleasure," Cynthia said, shaking hands. "Is there anything in particular you'd like to see, or are you happy with a general tour?"

"Oh, I think the general tour will be fine," Theo said. "For a start, anyway. We'll let you know when there's something we want a closer look at."

Cynthia nodded and turned back to the door. "That's fine. We'll start at this level and work our way upward."

Out in the hall, Maunga lost no time in sparking up a conversation: how did Cynthia find the workload, what were her teachers like, what was her favourite subject?

"Gym," Cynthia said.

"The bane of school kids' existences everywhere? Why's that?"

"Because it's not just running laps on a hoar-frosted field in the dead of winter. There is a bit of that, because ladies should show decorum even under the most extreme circumstances, and of course trials build character—"

"Of course," Theo murmured.

"But it's not all we do. Our teachers believe in holistic learning: even in something as physical as gym, they find ways to work in anatomy lessons and strategy studies and history and nutrition and leadership."

"That sounds fairly comprehensive," Dave said.

"It is. This is the elocution classroom," she added as they passed a closed door from behind which issued a hubbub of noise. "If there are any classes where you'd like to stop in and see what they're doing, please don't hesitate to let me know."

"Thank you," Maunga said. "Perhaps later."

They passed holocam after holocam, an etiquette class, more cameras, and then a home economics room.

"It does involve a fair amount of cooking," Cynthia said, "but also a lot of, you know, actual economics. We have to make a budget and plan a menu for a week for the whole school and then go out and buy the ingredients. It's always fun when the teachers invent some sort of crisis at the food market, and we find our supplies have been cut in half . . ."

As they came to the stairs and started up the first flight, Theo hesitated. "Could you show us the gymnasium? I'd like to see what sort of setup you've got. And the library after that?"

Maunga made a show of checking the time. "We've got half an hour before we have to leave. Is that long enough?"

"Oh." Cynthia looked startled. "You're on a tight schedule? Of course we can see the gym. Down this way."

"We've got another appointment in the city," Maunga said as they went back down the stairs and turned along another hall. "We need to leave by quarter past eleven at the latest."

"That's not a problem. I'll take you to the gym, and then we'll head upstairs to the library. Was there anything else you particularly wanted to see?"

There were cameras *everywhere*. "Actually," Theo said, "I don't suppose there's a bathroom nearby?"

"Just along the hall from the gym. I'll show you the door on our way past."

He would have seen it even without their guide pointing it out; the brass plaque said simply *Men's Room.* The others went on ahead, and he ducked inside.

A casual glance didn't reveal any cameras, but just because he couldn't see them didn't mean they weren't there. Under the guise of washing his hands, he ran water in the sink and then grabbed a paper towel and faked a sneeze.

"Kim," he muttered, holding the towel in front of his mouth, "we've got cameras dogging our every step. Can you do something about that?"

"Working on it," came the calm reply. "No guarantees for the wider area, but we'll get you a dead zone from the intersection by the basement entrance at least. Give us ten minutes to get it sorted."

"Thanks."

He finished the sneeze, binned the towel, and rejoined the others. They *oohed* and *aahed* over the equipment and the facilities for a few minutes before declining a visit to the adjacent classroom.

"Time's pressing," Dave said apologetically. "If you could show us the library . . . ? And then we should be going."

Upstairs and along a couple of winding corridors, they came to the library.

Dave whistled. Theo was rather inclined to agree with him.

The room was at least as large as the gymnasium and just as high. Narrow lead-lighted windows looked out onto a balcony, which itself overlooked a grassy courtyard. A shallow staircase, gleaming in polished rimu, rose to a midlevel gallery, turned, and leaped upward again to the topmost floor. The ambient lighting was a diffused golden-white; no doubt it would be fed through UV filters to prevent damage to the books. Shelves stretched forever, groaning under the weight of hardbacks and digital books alike. He could see couches scattered on all levels along with study nooks, information displays, and even private, glassed-in cubicles.

"Impressive," Maunga said.

They took their time, exploring everything from the help desk to the upper levels and quizzing Cynthia extensively.

"We keep the archives locked down as a matter of course," she said. "Anyone can apply for entry through the librarians. No visitors, I'm afraid, otherwise I'd show you. Staff and students only. But of course, if you were to ask your daughter—"

"Niece, actually," Theo said.

"If you were to ask your niece to borrow a book on your behalf, there's no objection to that. The librarians wouldn't even know."

Cynthia grinned. "Not that I'd know from personal experience or anything."

"Of course not," he agreed, lips twitching.

Kim's voice came through the comm channel. "Okay, we've looped the cameras. The approach to the basement is clear from Point C; you've got fifteen minutes."

Point C. The intersection just before the main hallway on the route from the library to the rear entrance. Good.

"Theo!" Maunga strode up behind Cynthia. "Sorry to interrupt. Time to go. We don't want to be late."

He checked his wrist holo. "It's after eleven already? Sorry, Cynthia. We'll have to cut the tour short."

"No worries," she said. "Do you need me to show you the way out?"

"No, we'll see ourselves out, thank you. It's just downstairs and then left and left again to the main hallway, yes?"

"That's the one."

They left the library together. Cynthia turned right and vanished around the corner while Theo, Maunga, and Dave turned left toward the stairs.

Theo dropped back and let Dave take the lead as they came to the bottom of the flight. He hadn't been lying when he'd told the team that Dave knew the maps best. The older man had spent hours poring over them, memorising the layout of the school, the location of the basement, the best approaches and escape routes—and the half-klick radius showing on the testing facility blueprints.

It hadn't seemed much then, and it seemed pitifully inadequate now. They simply had no idea what they'd be facing.

But as Maunga would say, what was life without a challenge? It was one thing they understood about each other very well: the need to keep themselves challenged, to keep their minds busy. An unoccupied mind was a dangerous thing indeed.

High N-cog, she'd say. At Theo's blank look she'd translate it from Psych-speak: We have an intense need for cognition.

No kidding, he'd say. Why do you think I have a Ph.D. at twenty-seven?

Like the Holmes boys, Addy would have said if she were here—give me problems, give me work, my mind rebels at stagnation. I abhor the dull routine of existence.

Theo didn't abhor the dull routine of existence, mainly because there was no such thing. If life was a dull routine, he was living it wrong. But he loathed those moments when his mind could find no puzzle to solve, no problem to chew on. It sank its claws into the only thing left and tore itself to pieces.

Whether it was looking for an answer or a question, he was never quite sure.

They cut left at the ground floor and then left again. He hoped the team at home base had done their job thoroughly; there was no way to tell by looking at the cameras if they were on or off. His heart beat faster as they approached the intersection. Here they went.

Dave swung left again, Theo and Maunga sticking to his heels. Halfway down the empty stretch of corridor, Kim spoke again. "Six minutes left."

Straight through the next intersection, right, left, down a short flight, right again. They were close. And then Dave rounded the next corner, and his eyes widened. He faked tripping over his feet and threw out a hand to wave them back from the corner before grabbing at the wall.

Theo pressed himself to the wall, hardly daring to breathe. Someone was right in their way. This could scupper the whole plan.

"Oh good!" Dave hurried forward down the hall, out of their sight. "I was hoping to find someone. Sorry, I was looking for a science lab, but I must have gotten turned around somewhere."

"It's easy enough to do," came the smooth tones of Tracey

Benvenue. "Not to worry, Mr. Richards. Just down this hallway, in fact. Have you lost your brother and his wife, too?"

"No, they've gone already. They had a meeting in town to get to, but I wasn't invited, so I thought I'd have a poke around your science classes while I was here. Now tell me, what's your advanced curriculum like?"

Theo closed his eyes as the footsteps faded. Dave's voice was still clear in his ear as he kept up a series of lively questions. *Thanks, mate.* Dave had studied the maps; of course he knew there was a science lab in the opposite direction, near enough to not be suspicious. But if he couldn't get away from the principal in time . . .

"Two minutes, thirty seconds," Kim said.

Maunga swore under her breath.

"We have to go," he said. "Dave'll catch up if he can."

He had his doubts. Tracey didn't have a class to get back to, as Cynthia had. She'd quite likely escort him around the laboratory and out to the carpark—in which case the presence of their car would give them away.

Keek. Maybe Dave would leave via the front door.

Either way, his chances of dodging the principal's attentions were minimal.

"The car's still in the carpark," he muttered.

The earpiece would transmit it to the key players, namely, Dave. Theo poked his head around the corner, checked that it was clear, and strode forward, mind churning. "Okay. Dave, pay attention if you can; Kim, you'll need to relay this for him later if he's tied up. We deliberately left the car here so that Dave could drop it back at our house this evening. Maunga and I have taken a train into the city for lunch because we're rich and taking a train is the sort of novel thing we enjoy doing, along with setting up scholarships for the underprivileged and dropping handouts at charity bins. Got that?"

"Yes, I understand that," Dave said in his ear. "It sounds like a good system . . ."

"I've got it even if he hasn't," Kim said. "Sixty seconds. Next door on your left."

Theo retrieved one of the blank access cards he'd bought in bulk on his work account, ran a magnetic strip and a bit of infrared buffing cloth over the sensors to fox them, and slid it through the keypad.

The door clicked open.

No time for a sigh of relief. They slipped through and let the door close gently behind them.

"Forty seconds," Kim said.

"We're in," Maunga said at the same time. Theo heard her groping along the wall beside the door, and then the lights came on.

Theo brought up the earpiece control panel on his wrist holo and turned down the volume from Dave's channel. He didn't need to hear an in-depth explanation of the advanced science curriculum, thank you very much. "Kim, I've muted Dave's input through my earpiece. I don't need the distraction. Let me know if he says anything important, yeah?"

"Will do."

"Sorry, Dave," Maunga added with a grin. Even if they couldn't hear him, he could still hear them.

Poor guy. Theo hoped he'd make it. "We'll give him ten minutes. We're not in any great rush now that we've made it out of the camera zone."

"Suits me." Maunga sauntered down the metal steps to poke around the basement floor.

He sat on the top step, elbows on his knees and chin in his cupped hand, heedless of the dirt he was no doubt getting all over his moleskins.

Blast.

Dave wasn't essential to the plan. It wasn't a deal-breaker, not like losing Maunga at this early stage would have been. But it was a blow all the same. Dave knew the maps, he knew every square centimetre of ground from here to the edges of the scavenged blueprints, and more importantly, he knew science, and Breach, and Caroline herself in a way nobody else did. They'd never had the dubious pleasure of working alongside her, for starters.

"Anything interesting down there?" he asked as Maunga disappeared behind a storage rack.

Ten minutes. Dave had ten minutes. More like seven, now. He didn't have the card to get in, but that was why Theo was sitting here, ready to crack the door open at a word from Kim. The cameras would be back on their normal cycle. He winced. That couldn't be helped. Two loops in as many hours would be too suspicious; the camera feeds weren't watched all the time, but if someone glanced over the footage and noticed the glitch, it would raise all sorts of awkward questions about their visit.

"Nothing down here," Maunga said.

The cameras. Keek.

"Kim," he snapped.

"Yeah?"

"The cameras. If they go back through the records and realise that Tracey wasn't in any of them—"

"It's taken care of," Kim said. "Challa's been selectively cycling them to follow the principal's movements. The recordings picked up Dave from the moment he stepped around that corner, but she cut back to the loop before you and Maunga moved from your blind spot. You're covered."

He shoved a hand through his hair, unwilling to admit to it trembling. "Good girl."

"Thanks," said a cheeky voice in his ear.

He jumped. He'd forgotten Challa was listening in on their conversations. She was so keeking silent, he could have sworn she wasn't even there.

Time was ticking. He checked his holo again. If Dave didn't show up in the next four minutes, they'd go on without him. He sat, chin in his hand, one heel bouncing on the step. Maunga joined him, eyes fixed on the glowing digits of his holo, and together they counted off the seconds.

They waited the four minutes.

Dave didn't appear.

CHAPTER FOUR

"Time," Maunga said.

Theo nodded and stood, brushing himself off. "Sorry, Dave. Got to go."

Maunga shouldered her bag and together they stepped down onto the basement floor. If he remembered the blueprints correctly, the door to the sub-level was down the far end, squeezed behind a built-in storage rack.

The alley behind the rack was so narrow he had to slip sideways down it. The door, painted the same industrial grey as the rest of the room, had been set into the wall so well that it was virtually seamless. No wonder Caroline didn't worry about people stumbling on the testing facility accidentally; he wouldn't have found it himself if he hadn't known it was supposed to be there.

But it was there. *Good.* And the door opened on the first try after the trick with the access card. Even better.

Behind the door, a spiral staircase sank down into the darkness. Their footsteps clattered on the tinny metal. The echoes came back dim, muffled by the closeness of the space and the thick stone walls. Theo paused before he'd gone a full turn down. Had the blueprints shown any wiring here? Lights would be welcome. He didn't much fancy descending into utter darkness.

"Do we have lights?" he asked.

"Negative," said Kim through his earpiece. "Or at least there's none shown on the plans."

White light flared behind him and dimmed to a more moderate level. He flinched and swung around, squinting against the glare. It was only Maunga. Theo didn't know what he'd expected, but his jangling nerves were enough to warn him that he wasn't as calm about this as he'd thought.

"The earpieces have lights built in," Maunga said. "Check the control panel on your holo. Should be the second-last option on the menu."

He checked. Sure enough, there was the option for *Light.* He selected *forward* and then *white.* There were secondary options for different shades of white, which he ignored.

Under the flood of light from his earpiece, he examined the twisting staircase. It seemed sound. The walls were dry—no cracks or leaks. His breathing slowly returned to its normal speed. *Better.* At least he could see, now.

"Got it," he said, largely for the benefit of anyone at home base who wasn't watching through the earpiece-embedded holocams. "Thanks."

He carried on down the steep spiral, beam sweeping from side to side, always with an ear on Maunga's movements behind him. The tight turns seemed to stretch forever, unrelenting, left, left, left. There was no sound but the fading echoes of their feet and the rise and fall of their breathing, loud in the silence.

What was the time? Well after eleven o'clock. "Liam awake yet?"

"Not yet," Kim said. "We'd planned to give him until twelve, but we can wake him up if you need him."

The head shake was automatic, beam skittering this way and that before he caught himself and focused on his feet again. "I'd say let him sleep, but it's Challa's call to make, remember."

"I consulted," Challa said. "With my deputy. We're agreed. We'll wake him at twelve."

"And by your deputy—"

"She means me, yeah," Kim said.

"I thought so."

"Why, do you have some objection to that?" Challa asked.

This keeking staircase felt like it would never end. "Not at all. I told you to share the load, didn't I?"

"You did."

"Any sign of Tuku?" Maunga asked from behind him.

"Yeah, she's been popping in and out," Kim said. "She's in a meeting until eleven thirty. I'll get her on the line to say *hi* next time she's passing through."

"Great, thanks. And the twins?"

"They're pinging us every hour on the hour from their current locations. At the last clock-in, Tarata was on a maintenance call-out to reception and Manatu was at the copier near her desk on the forty-fourth floor."

"Te Kaha?"

"Downstairs, keeping his staff in line. His 2IC is in charge of training the new girl, and she's, uh, not doing too well so far."

Theo grinned. "The new girl or the 2IC?"

"Sorry?"

"Which one isn't doing well?"

"From the sound of it, both of them."

"He's only sent Kirsten out the back to calm down once in the last hour," Challa chipped in.

"And we've heard two breakages since we got here," Kim added. "I don't know if she dropped a plate or what, but it was pretty jolly loud. You know those ringing silences when all the conversation stops dead and you can hear a sort of *gloing-oing-oing* noise like a coin spinning and settling? There was one of those after the second smash."

They came around another endless turn of the staircase and Theo's heart leaped. Was that the bottom? It looked like it might be. He sped up. It was! *Finally.* He jumped the last few stairs to the ground. "We're down."

"Roger that," Kim said. "We're watching your visuals. Yell if you need anything."

"Will do."

Maunga stood beside him. They looked ahead in silence. The stone passage, wide enough for five or six people to walk abreast, ran downhill in front of them, edged by shallow gutters. The same featureless stone formed the walls and ceiling. It wasn't a terribly low roof: Theo guessed he had maybe half a metre clear above his head. He inhaled. *Hmm.* Not fresh air, per se, but not stale either. A bit musty, which was only to be expected this far underground.

Well. They were heading into a testing facility. He hadn't expected cow-pats and clover-grass.

Maunga crouched down and set a trijector on the floor. "Activate map." The blue, semi-transparent screen unfolded, and an image of the plans winked into existence.

Theo squatted beside her and studied the view. The red circle at the centre blinked their current location. A tangled spread of corridors and empty rooms covered half a metre on every side—half a kilometre, by the scale. Beyond that, the edges blurred into nothingness.

He traced the quickest path to the boundary with his eyes. Straight down the hall, second left, first right. It seemed too easy, but then, they didn't know what was in any of the rooms. They might run into obstacles and have to backtrack half a dozen times. And, too, they didn't know where Addy was. She could be ten klicks away, far beyond the reach of the map, or she could be in the next room over.

"Straight to the outskirts, do you reckon?" Maunga asked.

He blew out a breath, considering. "I'd rather we explore every room on the map first. The odds of finding her in a half-k radius aren't high, but we've got a better chance of finding her at all if we do this the methodical way."

"My husband, the engineer," she said fondly, and nodded. "Methodical works. Clockwise?"

"It would make sense."

"Or we could do it anti-clockwise, just to be different."

"If you'd like." He didn't mind which way they went as long as they didn't miss anything.

"Nah. Clockwise by klicks is fine." The holo winked out. She tucked the trijector back into her bag, fiddled with the straps, and shrugged it on.

Theo blinked. Somehow the overly-large handbag had turned into a perfectly normal backpack. "How—?"

"Transformative textiles."

"Oh. Right." As if that meant anything to him.

She winked at him and turned away down the passage, flinging back over her shoulder, "Are you coming, husband?"

Ha. He had longer legs; he caught her in three strides. "No, wife, I'm going to stand around and navel-gaze while you find my sister for me. That way I get out of doing any work, see?"

"Hmm. That's a point. You and *work* in the same sentence ... nope. Sorry. Doesn't compute."

"I didn't think it would."

"Slacker."

"That's me." He heaved a mournful sigh. "Is this a bad time to admit that I plagiarised my thesis?"

"You didn't plagiarise. You just paid someone else to write it for you."

"Someone being you, of course."

"Someone being me, yes. Because you can't even spell 'necessarily' right."

That one was actually true. He always got the number of c's and s's mixed up. "And you can. Why else do you think I keep you around?"

She came to a halt outside the first door and cast him a laughing glance. "Oh, I can think of one or two reasons."

"Only one or two?" Theo stepped closer, invading her space, and lowered his voice. "I can think of a few more than that."

He was interrupted by a melodramatic whimper in his earpiece.

"Please," Challa muttered, "please don't tell me Addy's big brother is talking about sex where I can hear him."

Theo barked a laugh. "It's a fact of life, Challa. Get used to it."

"I don't object to sex. Just listening to you talk about it. Or inferring that you—ugh—*do it.* I've known you long enough that you're practically family, y'know, and it's like listening to my brother."

"All the more reason for you to not be embarrassed."

"All the more reason for you to *not talk about it,*" she retorted. "*Please.*"

"Alright," he said, still grinning. "Just teasing. Sorry." He resisted the urge to slip in one last dig. "We're at the first door now."

"We know," Kim said.

Challa's voice came through garbled and distant, like it was being picked up secondhand through Kim's earpiece. Theo waited, but home base had fallen silent. They must have muted their mics on that end.

Maunga shrugged. "She doesn't think we've survived five years of marriage on tea and biscuits, does she?"

"Well, she doesn't now." Theo stepped back and eyed the door. "Ready?"

"Always."

He put a hand on the door handle, gut clenching in a sudden wave of nerves. His head knew that the chance of finding Addy behind the very first door was so small as to be infinitesimal, but that didn't stop his heart from hoping. And in case something went wrong . . .

He bent and kissed Maunga. "Love you," he whispered. And then he was through the door and stepping sideways to press his back against the wall, dropping into a crouch, taking the room in with a sweeping glance.

How anticlimactic.

"Nothing," he said as he stood up.

Maunga appeared in the doorway. She leaned against the frame, arms folded, eyebrows raised. "Oh. It's really nothing. I thought you meant nothing important. But no, you meant *nothing* nothing."

The room was bare. The fine layer of dust raised by his entry slowly settled back to the stone floor. Filthy metal plates covered the walls and ceiling; the room clearly hadn't been touched in years.

Maunga eyed the swirling dust motes in disgust. "I think," she said, "I might get changed before we go any further. If the whole place is going to be as dirty as this room, I'd rather not ruin my favourite dress."

"You brought a change of clothes?"

"What, you didn't?"

That explained the bomb site she'd made of her wardrobe two nights ago. He grunted, stepped back out into the relative cleanliness of the corridor, and pulled his jersey off, followed by his good silk shirt. It felt warm enough for just his green t-shirt at the moment—it was merino, and he tended to run hot in any case.

He'd laid a ratty old hoodie on the mound of things-to-take-in-Maunga's-bag yesterday in case the temperature dropped. He hadn't bothered with a change of trousers or boots, and with the layer of dust already clinging to his shoes and lying in the creases of his moleskins, there would have been no point in changing anyway.

"Here," he said, folding up the jersey and the shirt and thrusting them at Maunga. "Put them in your bag, will you?"

"As you wish."

He watched, bemused, as she put a hand to her ear and withdrew her earpiece.

"Hold this, please."

The bag came off her back. She unzipped it and delved a hand inside.

"And turn your head," she added. "Or cover the earpieces, at least. I reckon Challa wants to see me getting changed about as much as she wants to hear you talk about sex."

He made sure that both his and Maunga's earpieces were covered. Maunga was hardly squeamish about nudity herself, but she had a lurking respect for the sensibilities of other people.

In a few minutes, she'd swapped out her dress and tights for comfy trousers and a warm shirt. She had already been wearing solid boots, of course. Her leather jacket went back over the top to complete the ensemble.

"Nice," he said.

She shouldered the pack again. "Certainly more suited to exploring an abandoned underground base."

"It's not abandoned." Caroline had only moved Addy here four weeks ago. Surely she wouldn't have moved her again so soon?

"This part is," Maunga said. Her voice softened. "Just this part, Theo. That's all I meant."

"I know." He marked off the empty room on the map and watched it turn red. Nothing. "Come on. We've barely started exploring this tier."

The next room was just as empty as the first. Two doors on the far side led to storage closets that hadn't been on the map. They were empty. A third door opened into a narrow hallway. It was empty too, if slightly less dusty than the closed-up rooms had been. There must be more airflow out here.

He marked the rooms off on the map, adding storage closets and alcoves to the database as they came across them. Empty room followed empty room with disappointing monotony. When they found themselves out in the main passage again, he called a break. They sat on the floor, leaning back against the wall, legs poking out into the passage.

"Here." Maunga passed him a nutrient bar.

"Thanks." He ripped it open, waited for the usual puff of steam to escape, and bit into it. *Mmm.* Gooey raspberry and hot chocolate.

"We'll have to take Caroline out of the picture, you know," she said.

Theo accepted the non sequitur without blinking. "I know. Otherwise she'll come after Addy—"

"—if Addy doesn't run straight back to her out of some perverse sense of honour—"

"—and there'll be nothing stopping her from infecting the whole city with Vox Pox again."

"Or something worse."

He nodded. "Don't suppose you've got the trijector handy?"

Maunga tossed it to him.

It was the work of moments to bring the map up. His holo synced with the blueprint, rooms turning from white to red one after another. Their location beacon blinked into life, and he grimaced.

Keek.

They were a bare two hundred metres down the hall from the stairwell. In total, they'd covered just over half the area between the stairs and the edge of the map.

Ah, well. He'd never thought it would be a quick in-and-out retrieval, not when they didn't know what they were facing. "What are you thinking?" he asked, biting off another corner of nutrient bar.

"We've only been going for a few hours," Maunga said. "It's a bit much to expect we would've found her already. Even finding her in the first twenty-four hours would be too much to expect."

Theo hummed in agreement. "The longer we're here, the greater the chance that Caroline will know about us."

"We knew that, though. We knew we were in it for the long haul. We're not leaving without Addy."

"No," he said with a grim smile. "We're not."

"You?"

"Much the same. This place could wind up a dead end ten metres past the edge of the map, or it could be a hundred kilometres to the first sign of life. We've got no way of knowing. But as you say, we came prepared: we've got food, clothing, medkits, energy packs, you name it." He reached for her hand and squeezed it. "We've got supplies for an easy month or a hard three months. As for how long it's going to take to find her . . . that's one of the biggest variables, right behind 'what the keek is in this place'."

Someone cleared their throat over the comm channel. "Actually," they said, and stopped.

Maunga sat upright. "Dave?"

"Yeah, mate. Sorry it's taken me this long to get in touch. My earpiece met with a, uh, mishap in the science lab. Impressive setup they've got there, by the way, there's all sorts of—"

"Oi," Theo interrupted. "Focus. Please."

"Right, sorry."

"Dead keen to hear all about it, of course. Just not now."

"You were asking what's in that place? I know a guy who works in Archives at the Council. He dug up some old drain-laying docs of the East Cape for me. I can't speak for anything west of you, but eastward you've only got a couple of kilometres. Part of an old sewer network runs through there. No way is that facility going to reach past the pipes."

Theo frowned. "They're only pipes. They're not that hard to bypass."

"These ones are," Dave said. "They're massive. I'm talking absurdly spacious here, like you could march an army through them—at least, if you didn't mind the army catching any number of diseases along the way."

"*Gross,*" whispered Kim in the distance.

"So, when you were working at Breach . . ." Maunga said.

"Yeah?"

"You never used these things, you may have heard of them, called PHFs? That's—"

"Personal Hazmat Field," Dave finished, sounding as if he was rolling his eyes. "I know. I used them frequently."

"So the army of diseases thing—"

"Artistic license."

"Right," Maunga said, grinning. "Artistic license. Of course."

Dave muttered something unintelligible under his breath. He continued aloud, "So you won't be able to go very far east. I can't give you any help in the other directions, I'm afraid. Looks like the pipe network bends to the north a couple of blocks over, but that's the extent of what I can see. The docs are keeking old."

"Thanks for the info," Theo said. "And we're sorry you couldn't make it down here with us in person. Sounds like you had a good time with the principal, though. Yell if you need us."

He muted the channel, laid his head back against the passage wall, and laughed.

"Knew it wouldn't be a mistake," Maunga said.

"What's that?"

"Bringing Dave on board."

Theo shook his head. "Definitely not a mistake." He stood and offered Maunga a hand up. "Break's over. Back to work."

She accepted the hand and passed him the backpack. "Your turn to take that, I think."

"You might be right."

"I'm always right."

"Except when you're not."

She grinned and stepped past him to the next door. "No comment."

"You realise that saying 'no comment' is itself a comment, yeah?"

"No comment," she said again and vanished into the next room.

His heart leaped into his throat. Despite himself, despite the cool voice of logic in the back of his mind, he found himself lunging forward. "Maunga—!"

She reappeared, a faint frown on her face, her hands spread. "What? I'm right here."

"Nothing." His heart settled back into its proper place. "Just—don't disappear on me. Please." With home base hanging onto his every word, it was the closest he would come to admitting the stab of fear that had gone through him.

Maunga's face softened. Of course she understood. "My turn to take point," was all she said. But she waited until he was beside her before stepping back into the room.

It was as empty and filthy as the last lot of rooms had been. This whole area felt disused; not even as if it had been used a long time ago but as if nobody had stepped foot in it since it had first been built. Like the only purpose of the rooms was to convince any wanderers that there was nothing important down here.

Sometimes an abandoned building was just an abandoned building.

But not this one.

Another hour and a half brought them back out to the main hallway, smeared with grime and trailing dust. The map showed red space after red space. They'd made significant progress: only a handful of rooms remained before they crossed the edge of the blueprint. In some cases, they'd already hit the wall. A solid line edged three-quarters of the map, jagged as it followed the uneven outline of the rooms. There was no way into the testing facility through those rooms.

Theo took point again and veered left into the first of the few unexplored rooms. Empty. That was par for the course. He thought the dust lay a little lighter here than in other rooms, though. Maybe there had been traffic through here in recent years?

The next two rooms were empty, but the far side of the second room held a surprise. Two doors were set into the wall. The first led to a short hallway that was as disused as the rest of the area. The second door was another matter entirely.

"It's locked," Theo said, trying to wrench the door open and receiving a jarred shoulder for his pains. "And I can't see a—"

"Here." Maunga pointed to the slim slot set in the side of the doorframe. "Just the right size for an access card, wouldn't you say?"

"So it is."

"We'll come back to it," she said. "There's only a few rooms left to check. This one isn't going anywhere."

It might rankle, but it was only common sense. He marked the map with a green question mark and glanced over the door again. It was the way through. It had to be.

But they couldn't afford to leave the last couple of rooms unexplored. There might be another way through, a back door or an escape route that could come in handy. Part of him wanted to forget about the rest of the rooms and barge through the locked door. A much larger part of him advised caution. He'd never forgive himself if they left these starting stones unturned and found out later that Addy was under one of them.

No. Lay the groundwork now, do the hard yards, the research and the context checks. Then they could analyse the best way forward, and *then* they could move. There was no point writing a thesis before covering existing literature on the subject; no point building a working prototype if there were already three products like it on the market.

They made it to the very last room before finding anything. Another door appeared where the map said there should only be a blank wall, and for a second he thought this was it, this was the back door. But the door opened without the slightest resistance, and he found himself looking into a storage cupboard.

Well. So much for that idea.

He checked the final room off on the map and watched it turn red. The entire map showed red, now, except for where he'd marked the locked door in green. The only gap in the solid boundary line was at that door, too. It was clearly the way forward.

They turned and headed back to the locked door.

"We should take a break when we get there," Maunga said.

What?

"A break? When we're this close to finding the testing facility?"

"Yeah. Because we've got no idea what's on the other side. At least here we know there's level ground and a distinct lack of disturbances. May as well grab some rest while we can."

Alright, she had a point. "Sounds like a plan."

They rested as comfortably as they could on the hard ground, sitting shoulder-to-shoulder against the wall and passing a water bottle back and forth. Tuku popped up on the comm channel to say *hi*, which led to the rest of the team saying hi as well, including Te Kaha, who was on his lunch break, and Liam, who had woken of his own accord forty minutes ago.

"I told Challa to wake me at eleven," he groused.

"You needed the sleep," Challa said. "And I'm your team leader. I'm allowed to pull rank."

Theo grinned. *Thattagirl.* He'd had a feeling she'd take to leadership like a duck to water; all some people needed was a bit of responsibility and a chance to shine.

"Thanks," Liam said dryly. "I mean, uh, all hail our glorious leader and all that, but do you often feel the need to ignore the direct requests of your subordinates?"

He could hear the smile in Challa's voice. "I consulted with my deputy. You were overruled by the majority."

"Course I was." Now Liam sounded resigned, but there was a hint of amusement in his tone. "Well, with all due respect, I'd better take—I mean, I *volunteer* to take—night shift. I'll be awake anyway, since you let me sleep for the best part of six hours in the middle of the day."

"No argument here," Kim said.

"I'll put the paperwork through to the committee," Challa said. She paused for a second and then continued, "Request accepted. They didn't see a problem with it, and I've used up my quota of ignoring direct requests for today. You can take night shift starting at ten."

"Lovely. Thank you."

"Welcome."

Theo left them talking. He offered the water bottle to Maunga again, stowing it in the bag when she shook her head. The door was still locked; he would've been surprised if it wasn't. The trick with the magnetic strip and the infrared buffering cloth worked like a charm. He waited for Maunga to shoulder the pack before opening the door.

"Ladies first," he said, waving her through.

He stepped through the doorway on her heels and let the door go.

It clicked shut. There was a *whoosh* of firing pistons as it locked behind them—and an alarm went off.

INTERLUDE

THE VOICELESS WE HAVE HEARD.

CHAPTER FIVE

The sound was so loud it wiped his mind of all thought for a long, frozen moment. He couldn't move. Couldn't think. There was nothing but the screaming noise, so loud he thought his eardrums might burst from the sheer volume of it.

His hands rose of their own accord to block his ears. The right hand jarred his earpiece and the noise fluctuated, growing louder and then softer again as he lifted his hand away. The rest was pure animal instinct, born of the pressing need to *make it stop make it stop make it stop:* he yanked the earpiece out and sent it skittering across the floor.

A ringing silence fell, as absolute as the blaring alarm had been only a second ago.

"*Keek,*" Maunga snarled. Her earpiece joined his on the far side of the hall.

Theo focused on catching his breath. Maunga's voice had sounded dim and distant, even though she was standing right beside him. He hoped there was no permanent damage to their hearing. "That," he gasped, "was sodding loud."

Maunga lifted a hand to rub at her ear. "What?" She looked like she was shouting, but her voice sounded only a little louder than before.

"*Sodding loud.*"

"You can say that again," she said. "But don't."

"You alright?"

She looked at him blankly and shook her head.

He raised his voice again. "Are you alright?"

"Yeah." She was still shouting, judging from the way her throat was straining. He heard the words at something approaching normal volume. “Hearing’s coming back. Slowly.”

“So’s mine!”

“Keep talking. I think *it’s getting better.*”

Theo winced. “Okay, I’m back. You don’t need to shout.”

“*Is that* better?”

“Still a bit overkill. But better.”

“Okay.” Maunga paused for a moment, swallowed, and tried again. “How’s that?”

“Pretty near normal.”

“Nearly back to normal on this end, too.” She blew out a breath and swiped a hand across her forehead. “That was not pleasant.”

“Understatement,” he murmured. “And I suspect . . . ” He padded across the tiled floor to where their earpieces lay.

“You suspect . . . ?”

He bent and picked them up. “Suspect they might be dead.” He tried syncing his earpiece to his holo. Nothing. He tried syncing Maunga’s earpiece. There was the weakest of signals but even as he watched, the connection flickered and died.

Great.

Running a diagnostic turned up precisely *nothing*. They were dead. Without a connection, he couldn’t even finish the diagnostic to see if there was any way of patching them up.

“Dead?” Maunga asked.

“Dead,” he said in disgust.

“That would figure.” Theo would have thrown the useless earpieces back in the bag, but Maunga caught his wrist. “We might as well still wear them. Just because they’re dead on this end doesn’t mean they’re dead to home base. Even if it’s only a locator signal getting through, that’s better than nothing.”

“They’re *dead*,” he said again. “They can’t send or receive anything.”

“Theo.” She was giving him a *look*.

He relented. “Fine.”

"Sorry?"

"Yes. We'll keep wearing them. Sorry," he added, more gently. "It makes sense, I know. It's just—" He waved a hand, not finding the words.

"An enforced change of plans."

"Yeah."

He might have backup plans for centuries, but he wasn't half as quick to switch from one to another as Maunga was. He'd put too much thought into them to turn on a dime. They were there to be used, he knew that, but the knowledge didn't help him process the change any faster.

"Alright," he sighed. "Plan . . . what are we at . . . B." Plan A had counted on the presence of all three of the field team. Plan B lost Dave. C would have lost Maunga. And now they'd lost contact not only with Dave but with the whole rest of the team. *Keeking wonderful.*

At least he still had Maunga.

"Iteration 60." Not that the numbers mattered. They were arbitrary enough—simply a way of cataloguing the many, *many* possibilities, which of course multiplied exponentially the further along they went. In another hour there would be hundreds of sub-iterations of this one plan.

"Plan We've-Lost-Dave," said Maunga. "Iteration And-We've-Lost-Contact-With-Home-Base-Too."

"That's the one." He summoned the ghost of a peeved smile. "Not how I'd hoped to start the day."

She snorted. "It's nearly five o'clock. Hardly the *start* of the day."

He could feel it, too. They'd only just stumbled into the testing facility itself, and he was already fighting weariness. He shoved it aside. They had a mission to focus on. Get Addy, and get out. That was it. He didn't have energy to spare for being tired.

For the first time since they'd stepped through the locked door, he examined their surroundings. He'd been aware of the space before but only peripherally: it was difficult to analyse one's environment while undergoing severe aural agony.

"We should move," Maunga said. "That alarm might be bringing us company."

He waved acknowledgement. "Just getting my bearings."

They were in a wide hallway, all sterile white tiling and ambient blue-washed lighting. The floor was level, he could tell that much after the constant slope of the main passage in the abandoned rooms. He couldn't see any open doorways or even any obvious doors, but that didn't mean they weren't there. They could be hidden in the panelling. The hallway continued straight on ahead of them without a corner. Even straining his eyes, he couldn't see where it ended. At least they'd see anyone coming.

It was oddly anticlimactic. He'd been expecting something bigger. More dramatic. But no, it was just a hallway that would have been at home in any science lab or hospital up on the surface.

He tried syncing his holo with the earpiece again. *Nothing.*

"Coming?" Maunga asked, already ten metres down the hall.

"Mm-hmm." He jogged to catch up to her and fell into step beside her. At least the corridor was wide enough to let them walk side by side. "Any ideas?"

"Nope," she said. "I'm trying not to let preconceptions bias my judgement."

"You used that in your master's thesis, didn't you?" The wording was far too down-pat to be spur of the moment.

"Maybe."

"How many keywords did it hit?"

"Three."

"Not bad."

"Thank you." She looked at him sideways. "You've read my thesis."

"Yes. But I don't remember it. Or at least I don't remember the specifics. I can remember the general gist, but I couldn't quote it word-for-word."

It had been an analysis of psychological recovery in the wake of the Vox Pox cures, with a case study focused on the ten people who had undergone the extended trial at Breach—or rather, the nine people she'd been able to contact. Fascinating stuff, of course, but it was years ago now. He'd pushed it out of his memory in favour of more pressing matters, like his own doctorate thesis.

He sniffed and grimaced. "Can you smell that?"

"The polite thing to say is *pardon.*"

"I'm serious. Something stinks. And it wasn't me."

She inhaled, tilted her head, and shrugged. "Maybe a bit. Could be the ventilation system. We're pretty far down."

"Maybe." They walked in silence for a few minutes. "How long do you reckon this hallway is?"

"Long enough."

"If you had to guess, though. In metres."

She shrugged. "Five hundred? Ten? Maybe more? Can't see the end of it yet, but that's no guarantee. Place like this, we could run smack-bang into the end of it without thinking it looked any different from the side walls. It's all very . . . homogenous." Her nose wrinkled.

"You don't like it?"

"Eh. I prefer a bit of diversity in my environment—by which I mean I like to see some sort of difference between floor and walls beyond mere angle. It's reminding me of that gravity flip room in Addy's psychotic mansion."

Sometimes he forgot that she'd read Addy's flow-state-written account of the three years before she went away. But then, sometimes he forgot that he'd read it himself. The knowledge was simply *there,* like quadratic formulae and weight-bearing calculations. Where the knowledge had come from wasn't important. "The gravity room had a lot of staircases, didn't it?"

"It's more the fact that the surfaces are all the same," she said. "At least if the floor's different from the ceiling, you can tell which way is up—or which way *was* up before the place went topsy-turvy.

All these surfaces are identical, which means we've got no way of telling."

Hmm. Theo wasn't particularly concerned about it, himself; but Maunga clearly was, and she wasn't one to jump at shadows.

His pocketknife hung where he'd stowed it this morning, on the chain around his neck. He levered out the laser cutter attachment and activated it.

Maunga sidestepped away to the far wall, not breaking stride. "What are you doing?"

"Marking the floor." He pointed the laser downward and let it run for thirty metres before switching the cutter off. Still in step with Maunga, he retrieved a match from the little compartment on the side of the knife, struck it on the scratch pad, and flicked it away behind him.

Whoomph.

The freshly carved score down the floor ignited in a line of fire that burnt blue for a second before settling to the usual orange-red.

"There," he said. "That's the floor. No worries."

Maunga let out a short laugh and shook her head. "You just burned the floor. For me."

"I'd do a lot more than that for you." He kept the words light, but when he looked at her, his eyes were deadly serious.

"That's destruction of property."

"Caroline's property. Who cares?"

"*I* will if it sets off a smoke alarm. Or brings an army down on us."

That gave him a moment's pause. He hadn't considered that—at least not seriously. He shrugged. Surely it wasn't anywhere near enough smoke to set off an alarm? And the army would have been here long before now if it had been coming at all. "This place seems pretty abandoned. I doubt she's hidden an army here. We'd find Caroline a bit sooner than we'd planned, that's all."

"We're finding Addy first."

"Course we are. But if we happen to cross Caro's tracks as well . . ." He left the sentence hanging.

She hummed and stepped back across the hallway to walk beside him again. "Warn me next time."

They came to the end of the hallway a couple of minutes later. The walls drew back until they were in a space three times as wide as the hallway had been. Two doors greeted them in the end wall: the one on the left was black with the ubiquitous male silhouette painted on it in white, while the one on the right was identical save for featuring a female silhouette.

"Bathrooms?" Theo asked. "What on earth?"

"I guess we go through," Maunga said.

"Guess so."

He'd thought they might come across a science lab or an office, but bathrooms? Really? "Do you want to follow the guidelines, or are we running counter to stir things up?"

Maunga grinned. "I'd hate to get in the way of your ablutions. Let's follow the guidelines. For now."

"As you wish." He stepped across to the men's door, kissing her on the way past. "Love you. See you on the other side."

"See you there."

He stepped through the door and let it swing shut behind him, eyes up and alert, automatically taking stock. But it was just a bathroom. Tiles in an off-putting shade of pale puke-green lined the floor. The walls were an off-white, not dark enough to be true cream and with just enough tint to look brown at the right angle. At least the surfaces were all fairly plain—there were subtle textures and patterns there, but they'd stuck to the core colours of green for the floor and cream for the walls.

And the smell wasn't half so bad in here. He hardly noticed it.

It wasn't a very large bathroom. To the left lay a row of three sinks flanked by heated dehumidifiers; beyond them were the urinals and to the right were four, no, five stalls.

He stepped into the far stall and reflexively locked the door behind him. The walls here had been painted a darker brownish-white. A peeling poster tacked to the back of the door advised him to *Shop at the Bay Mall and Receive a 10% Discount When You Flash;* the bottom corner had been ripped off, but he suspected the last words might have been something like *Your Employee Card at the Counter.*

This was a working bathroom, then?

It was. The loo flushed without a problem; a full pump-bottle of disinfectant sat beside each sink, and the dehumidifiers dried his hands in less than a full second.

Interesting.

Why were there functioning bathrooms here? Surely Caroline didn't keep employees lurking around? It was a testing facility designed solely for Addy; they'd seen no sign of anyone entering or exiting in the weeks they'd been aware of this location. Even Caroline herself didn't visit. Possibly she had her own secret entrance, but they'd figured it was more likely that she controlled the whole thing from her office at Breach.

He doubted the testing required her constant presence or even hands-on supervision. She'd had years to set this place up. It probably ran itself by now.

There was no door at the far end of the bathroom. *See you on the other side,* he'd said. It had been an unconscious assumption. The hall ended in two doors, and presumably there would be two more doors on the other side. But there weren't. This bathroom, at least, was a dead end.

Frowning, he opened the door that led back out to the hallway—and stopped.

The hallway wasn't there. Instead there was a small room, maybe four by four metres and three high. Matte surfaces, blinding white on all six sides. Ambient lights again, the same blue-white wash as the hall. And another door, set opposite him in the far wall.

Think it through, Theo. The door behind him was the same door he'd used to enter the bathroom, he was sure of that. The space beyond it had changed, that was all. He'd only been gone a few minutes, but somehow the hallways had vanished to be replaced by this stark white room. It looked like a detention cubby at his old high school.

Non-Euclidean geometry, perhaps. Or something of the sort. Like the shifting spaces of Addy's mansion, distances that made no rational sense and doors that led to a different place every time they were opened. Easy enough to comprehend in theory. Rather more befuddling in practice.

He took a breath. There was logic, there was lack of logic, and then there was . . . this. It went right through a plain absence-of and out the other side. Anti-logic? It was as good a word for it as any.

Whatever it was, it hurt his brain.

At least the smell had gone.

Time was ticking. He had to find Maunga. Acceptance would take too long. Avoidance was the faster course of action. Not necessarily the *best* course of action, mind you, but the right one for now, given the time constraints. He strode across the room and reached for the door handle.

It didn't turn.

"Oh, come on," he growled, giving it another wrench. Nothing. It was locked. He still had the access card in his pocket but, on examining the door, he couldn't see a slot to slip it into.

Maybe he was supposed to go back through the first door? No doubt it would lead somewhere that was no longer a bathroom.

But that door had closed behind him, and it was locked, too. He wrenched the handle, kicked it, shoulder-barged it—and got nothing more than a flash of pain up his hip for his troubles.

Keek.

He turned back to examine the room again. There was nothing to examine. White walls, white floor, white ceiling, all the same horribly identical, metre-square panelling that had made Maunga so twitchy earlier on. He tried the door again. Nothing. Strode across the room to the other door. Still nothing.

Keek and blast and blast and keek. His gut clenched, not in panic, not yet, but the anxiety was an easy first step to panic.

Stop. He ran his hands over his face. *Think. Is there any way out?*

The only way out was through the doors, and they were both locked.

Therefore, there was no way out. Not yet. Not unless the doors were unlocked.

Was there any way to unlock the doors?

No access slot. No keyhole. No hinges on this side.

No way to unlock the doors.

No way out.

Conclusion?

Wait. He was sure they'd unlock eventually, if only to spit him out into that ghastly bathroom again.

"Theo."

He jerked his head up. "Maunga?" The room was empty. Where was she?

"Theo, where are you?"

"I'm here." And because everybody was *here* in their own mind and the directive was utterly unhelpful, he added, "A little white room just off the men's loos. The doors are locked. I can't get out."

Silence.

"Maunga?"

"Theo."

Her voice came from everywhere and nowhere. He felt a trickle of sweat at the back of his neck. Where was she? Was it even Maunga? Perfect voice replicators had long since been released on the public market. There was no guarantee that it was Maunga after all.

"Hello?" he called. "Anyone there?"

"I wanted kids, you know." The words were soft.

What?

His reflex was to deny the words. She hadn't wanted kids. They'd been over this, over and over it, long before his physical exam last year. He shook his head, eyes blindly searching the room for her. She was nowhere to be found. "No, you didn't."

"I did." Keek, she sounded close to tears. He could count the times he'd seen her cry on . . . one hand? No, two hands. And a thumb. She wasn't ashamed to cry, she just didn't tear up easily. "I wanted kids, Theo."

"You didn't," he said again, refuting the lie with solid fact. Somehow the words still sounded hollow. "And neither did I."

"I told you what you wanted to hear."

That was ridiculous. Maunga wouldn't lie to him if the world was burning down around their ears and it was their only chance of a fire extinguisher. It wasn't so much the lie itself; it was the fact that she would be betraying herself, her own ideals. She wouldn't do that. It was unthinkable.

He shook his head again, but the words burrowed into his head, *what if, what if, what if.* What if she'd lied? What if she had just taken his own thoughts and echoed them?

"I asked you about it first, remember?" she said. "And you didn't want kids. So I didn't either."

Preposterous. Maunga as a mouthpiece for his opinions. The idea was absurd.

But he couldn't stop the sickening turn of his stomach.

"We've talked about this," he said through numb lips. "Neither of us even *like* children; why would we want any of our own? You've got enough brothers to carry on the family line. I don't care about it on my side. The world's got enough Te Ngawais as it is. My parents haven't talked to me about kids or sex since I was fourteen, and yours know that you're old enough to make your own decisions."

"I like kids," she said.

"You freak out at the first sign of baby drool!"

"Easy enough to fake."

"Why?" Why was she so clearly lying to him? A niggle of doubt touched him. Was it really Maunga after all? *No. It couldn't be.*

"You see what you want to, Theo. I had to agree with you, didn't I? So I let you see what you wanted to see. Which was me, not liking kids. Because I didn't want kids, did I, according to you."

Bile rose in his throat. He knew it was false, but her words fell heavy and solemn nonetheless.

"I lied to you," she said.

Now he was bent double, hands braced on his knees, panting for breath. No. She wouldn't. She wouldn't . . . would she?

What if she was showing him what he wanted to see, mimicking his actions, echoing his words? Would she lie to him? Even if it meant betraying herself, being someone she wasn't, going counter to everything she'd ever said about honesty and authenticity?

"Why?" He forced the word out.

Her voice caught on a sob, and he closed his eyes against the stab that went through him, feeling like the lowest of the low. "Because I love you," she said. "I didn't want you to think—I mean, you like me. Love me, even. *Me.*"

Theo brought a shaking hand to his mouth.

"And it's one of those big things, you know? Kids. Marriage. If I hadn't . . . You love me. And you might have stopped."

He turned his head and threw up the little that was in his stomach. It wasn't real, he knew that somewhere deep down. It wasn't real. But it felt real. She was saying things the real Maunga would never say, and still it felt real.

"Never," he said. "I couldn't. Can't. It's like breathing, Maunga, I can't just stop doing it."

"You say that." Her voice sank, and a chill went through him. "But I know what you'd choose."

"What do you mean, choose? Choose what?"

"Between me and her."

He didn't understand.

"Me and Addy," she said. "Your wife or your sister, Theo. Who's it going to be?"

He sniffed, ran a hand under his nose, felt it come away damp. "I don't—that's not—"

"Not what? Not fair? Life's not fair."

"Not a question," he managed. "That's not a question I can answer."

"Try." The word was steely.

Addy or Maunga? That was no choice. Even the idea of it was unthinkable. He shied away from the thought. "No."

"Tell me."

"No." His head pounded, his breath came in fits and starts, but he knew this much: it was an unanswerable question.

"It's very important."

"I don't care. I can't answer that question." A lump rose in his throat. "I can't, Maunga. I can't choose. Don't make me."

"You're not getting out of here until you choose, Theo."

He shoved a hand through his hair, quelling a sudden rush of anger. "I told you, I can't."

"Then you won't get out of here. Ever."

"What's the point?" he shouted. "Why do you want to know?"

"Do you love me?"

"Yes!"

"More than her?"

"What sort of a question is that? What—" He spluttered into silence, shaking.

Enough. Enough of this. He was done. It wasn't Maunga, it wasn't real, and he keeking well wasn't answering that question. He strode across to the door and pounded on it with closed fists. "Let me out."

"Answer the question."

"No." He drummed on the door again, ignoring the pain, ignoring his scratches and scrapes. The surface wasn't as smooth as it had looked. "Let me out."

"No. Answer the question."

It was pointless, the whole keeking scenario. "Will you let me out if I do?"

"Yes."

"Are you lying to me when you say that?" Even having to check made his heart wrench in his chest.

"No. I'll let you out if you answer the question. Who would you choose: Addy or me?"

The answer came in a flash of clarity. "Both," he snapped. "If you think I'm sacrificing one of you for the other, you've keeking lost your mind. There, I've answered your stupid little question. Now let me out."

There was a short, displeased silence. The door unlocked with a hiss of pistons. He shoved the door open and stumbled through, thoughts a blur, hardly aware of what he was doing.

"Theo!"

Please, no. No.

He couldn't handle any more. He stood, swaying, as Maunga appeared in front of him and dashed forward.

"Are you alright?" Her eyes flicked over him, assessing, cataloguing.

He nearly laughed. "*Am I alright?*" And then, as she came closer, he found himself stepping back, breath hitching in his lungs. "Don't."

She halted, looking uncertain. "Theo?"

"I—" He stopped, confused. Maybe it was really her? "Look, would you say something that only you could say? Please."

She blinked. "It scares me when you disappear off into your mind and I can't go with you."

"Keep going." It was a good start.

"I hate peanut butter and jam sandwiches. I can't think why anyone would want to put those two spreads together, they taste foul. The ladies' was a dead end, but when I tried to leave the door spat me out in this creepy room, and I'm guessing it did that to you too because you look like you've just had the flu for a month straight. How can I help?"

She stepped forward again and he shied backward. His back hit a wall; he slid down it to sit on the floor, knees drawn up, hands dangling loose at the wrist and shaking as if they'd never stop.

"Don't," he rasped. "Please. I can't—"

The anger was still there, sitting just below the surface. It scared him more than he wanted to admit, how close he felt to losing control. "I don't trust myself yet."

"Alright," she said slowly. She raised her hands and took a deliberate step back, and then another step. "Better?"

He nodded, fighting back tears, and lifted a hand to grip his hair, using the pain to ground him in the here and now. He needed to calm down, he needed to think, to find some mental distance and *think,* but fear and anger clouded everything.

"Are you with me?" Maunga lowered herself to sit cross-legged opposite him, her eyes fixed on his.

He stared back at her, anchoring himself in her gaze. "What happened in your room?"

Her face closed over. "I'd rather not talk about it."

Whatever it had been, she seemed to have handled it better than he'd handled his room. Maybe she'd psychoanalysed it to death? She didn't want to talk about her experience; on the contrary, he felt like he'd burst if he didn't get the words out—if he didn't somehow purge the poison from his system.

"You were there," he blurted. "You were there, in my room. Your voice—it—it was everywhere, and you were s-saying . . ."

He couldn't tell her. The words wouldn't come. "You were saying the most—the most *horrific* things."

"It wasn't me," she said.

He let the words wash over him, low and level and steady as a heartbeat.

"I wasn't there, Theo. I was locked in my own little white mental torture cell. Whatever it was, whatever it said, it wasn't me. I didn't say it." A spark of professional interest lit her face, tempered by very personal worry. "Out of curiosity, what did it say?"

He shook his head mutely. He couldn't. The words were locked down somewhere far inside him, and they wouldn't come out until he'd found the distance and the space to analyse them. Space, he needed space. Mental space, physical space. It hurt, being this close to Maunga and still so far away, but he'd be useless until he could fight his way back to some sort of balance again.

"Could you just—give me some space," he said. "Don't talk, don't—move, don't anything. Sorry, I just need . . ." He couldn't even articulate it. He set his teeth, frustration welling, and tugged on his hair again, fighting the pull of his own mind. "Just for a bit."

He could see that Maunga didn't understand. But she nodded anyway. "I'm here," she said. "Not going anywhere."

"Thank you." What had he done to deserve her? She was a godsend.

And then the words of the other Maunga rose, dark and ugly, and he shuddered.

It wasn't real. *Get out.* It wasn't Maunga.

He didn't know how long he sat there, head bowed to his knees, battling with himself. It might have been minutes. Might have been hours. It felt like a long, long time.

He finally surfaced, drained as he'd never been in all his life, and found Maunga watching him. "Okay." The words ripped from his dry throat, rasping painfully. "Sorry. I'm back."

She was across the floor in two paces, flinging herself into his arms. He wrapped his arms around her, breathing in the scent of lime and weariness and pure Maunga, and then he bent and kissed her. "I'm here," he whispered. "Not going anywhere."

"Good," she said. "Because I'd hate to have to waste energy coming after you and dragging you back."

He let out a watery laugh. The question spilled from his lips without conscious thought: "Did you want kids?"

"What?" She sounded incredulous, but she didn't press. "No,

you daft muppet. We've been over this a hundred times. I don't want kids."

He drank in her answer, the baffled light in her eyes, the bemused twist of her lips, and kissed her again. "Just checking."

She drew back, grimacing.

"What?"

"You taste like vomit."

Come to think of it, he could still taste the acid in the back of his mouth. "I slipped some mints into your bag if you want to dig them out. End pocket."

She passed him the water bottle as well. He rinsed and spat, took a mint capsule, and then rinsed and spat again before chugging a few mouthfuls. That was better.

His nose was still running a bit; he scrubbed his hands over his face, feeling the damp smears where he'd dashed tears away. *Ugh.* He was a mess. "Got a cloth of some sort in there?"

"Here." She passed it over. Her eyes lingered on his face with an intensity he only saw in their most intimate moments; after a minute, she leaned forward and took the cloth from him. "You missed a spot."

Theo sat still, content to let her finish up. She obviously needed to be doing something, and the contact was welcome. It had shaken them, whatever was in those rooms. Curiosity nudged him, murmuring an enquiry about Maunga's room. He shushed it. Time enough for that later. Much later. She didn't want to talk about it, and he wasn't sure he wanted to know.

"Are you sure?" he asked.

"Yes." She held the cloth up in his line of sight. "I'm quite sure I have a cloth in the bag."

"About kids, I mean." If he had wanted proof that he was more rattled than he'd thought, that was it. He shook himself. "Sorry, I shouldn't have—don't worry, don't answer that, I'm just being—"

"Theo."

He stopped. "Yeah?"

Maunga opened her mouth and paused, changing what she'd been about to say. "Are you having second thoughts?"

"No. Are you?"

"No."

"But—" He broke off in exasperation. Irrationally, tears welled in his eyes. *Sod it.* They'd never been anything less than honest with each other. "You're not just saying that?" he asked, the words tumbling over one another in their haste. "You're not just—agreeing with me because it'll make me feel better, or—or something?"

It was illogical. He knew it, and from the look on her face, Maunga knew it too. "No," she said again. "Theo. No. I wouldn't. I *couldn't.*"

"Why not?"

"Because I love you."

The words caught at his heartstrings, a painful repetition of what Maunga—the other Maunga, the not-Maunga—had said.

But she continued, "And that's not love."

He didn't understand.

"I can't agree with you just for the sake of agreeing with you. It wouldn't be honest; it wouldn't be *me.* And giving you anything less than me, the *real* me, sarcasm and bitterness and all—" She shook her head. "I can't do that. Love is equal. That's not equal, that's—that's tipping the balance, removing the counterweight."

"You agreed to wash the dishes the other night."

"Dishes." She snorted. "That's irrelevant. I wasn't agreeing with you just to agree with you. I was agreeing with you because marriage is a life-long series of compromises and, let's face it, it's hardly an important issue, is it? Dishes, really? No. But this—Theo, look at me."

The fire in her eyes took his breath away.

"Love is equal," she said again. "Letting myself be subsumed by your opinions and wishes isn't love. Letting *you* be subsumed by *my* opinions and wishes isn't love. We're individuals. We have our own views on everything, and mindlessly mimicking the other person gets us nowhere. If you think I'd let myself become nothing more than a—a mouthpiece for what you think, that room has messed you up even more than I thought. You love me, yes?"

"Doubt truth to be a liar."

Maunga smiled. "You love *me.* Not some empty shell of me who's slowly turning into a clone of you. And," she added, "vice versa. I love *you,* not a Theo lookalike who parrots every word I say. That would very swiftly become intolerable."

She had a point there. "That much sarcasm in one room?" he mused. "Keek, no."

"If I was you, you wouldn't love me. Because I wouldn't be me anymore. So please." She lifted a hand to his temple. "Please stop obsessing about this, okay? Know it here." She moved her hand to his chest. "And know it here. I honestly do not want kids, and I'm not just echoing your views on the subject. That wouldn't be honest, it wouldn't be me, and—" she gave a theatrical shudder "—I can't stand not being me. It would be so boring."

Relief washed over him. "Thank you."

"Welcome. Now sit still and I'll fix your hands."

They were a bit scratched up, he noticed. "I can do it."

"I know you can, but I want to."

"So do I. Is it that important to you?"

"No. Is it that important to *you*?"

"No."

"So is it worth arguing about—"

"No," they said in unison.

"But," Theo added, "I would still like to."

She grumbled under her breath and turned away to the pack, shooting him a mirthful look over her shoulder. "Fine, you can do it. Don't come crying to me if you make a mess of the job."

"Wouldn't dream of it."

They were easy enough to tend to. A little EasyHeal cream, some sticking plaster over the worst of the scrapes, and he was done.

"I don't know about you," Maunga said, digging around in the pack again, "but I'm starving."

"I could eat. Probably should, actually, considering there's not much left in my stomach."

"We've got sandwiches. D'you want cheese and marmite? Or . . ." She tilted her head to get a better view into the pack, "raspberry jam?"

"Whichever. Doesn't worry me."

She tossed him the raspberry jam and took the cheese and marmite for herself. They sat against the wall and ate in comfortable silence. Theo polished off his first sandwich before asking, "You don't like peanut butter and jam together, but you do like cheese and marmite?"

"Mmm-hmm." Maunga chewed and swallowed. "Jam's soggy. Peanut butter's sticky. Together they're a really bad mix. Cheese and marmite, on the other hand, is a *classic*."

"Practically traditional," he agreed.

"Exactly."

"And we both know you have such great respect for tradition."

"Married you, didn't I?"

He blinked. "What's that supposed to mean?"

"You are a *bit* of a traditionalist."

"You're . . . uh . . . not." He tore off a crust with his teeth. "My wife, the reformer."

"That's me. What's the point of life if you can't challenge the status quo?"

Theo groaned. "We're not having this conversation. Not again. It was bad enough last time . . ." Silence closed in. Abruptly he realised how loudly he'd been talking, how peacefully they sat here as if nothing could touch them. He shot a glance down the hall, shoulders relaxing when it proved empty as ever. "Eat up. And then we should get moving."

CHAPTER SIX

They stowed their food wrappers and Theo took the pack again. Eerily, the doors at their backs were identical to the bathroom doors, and the corridor they found themselves in was a twin to the white-tiled tunnel from earlier.

Maybe it wasn't even a twin. Maybe it was the same hallway. Maunga was glad Theo had carved that thirty-metre line of Everburn along the floor. They should find out in a matter of minutes if it was the same corridor or not.

They didn't find out.

The hallway took a sharp turn to the right a hundred metres along.

"So," she said thoughtfully, "either it's a different hallway altogether, or they've closed off one side of the intersection, so to speak, and opened up another."

"It would be easy enough to do with these panels." Theo rapped a hand on the wall. The sound came back tinny; evidently the space behind it wasn't as solid as Caroline would have them believe.

"Feel like getting that laser cutter out again?"

"Reckon that's a good idea." He fished it out and carved an X on the floor in the middle of the hall. After a moment's thought, he extended one line by five metres back the way they'd come and another line out the way they were heading, and then added a couple of arrows pointing ahead. The fire burnt green before settling to orange. "Alright?"

"Alright."

They marked each corner as they went. Thirteen corners later, they hadn't come across their trail markers even once.

"Big place," Maunga said.

"Or very small and very sneaky."

"Because our marker could be just on the other side of that panel"–she nodded to the wall beside her— "and we wouldn't have a clue?"

"That's the one."

When they'd been walking the hallways for three hours and the timestamp on her holo was edging toward nine o'clock, Maunga called for a break. It was more of the same: backs to the wall, water bottles and nutrient bars at hand.

Theo set the trijector up and tried updating the map, but only a chaotic tangle of overlapping spaces resulted. Even switching from a 2-D view to 3-D did nothing. They needed a way of representing two different things in the same area of space, but there was no way of doing it with the current tech.

"Use different layers," Maunga suggested through a mouthful of apple-and-cinnamon crumbs. "Might not be accurate at all, but it's bound to be better than that mess."

It was. That wasn't to say it made much sense, but they got an idea of how many times they must have crossed back over their own tracks.

"Keek." She glared at the zigs and zags and loops of their trail.

"Agreed." Theo crumpled his empty wrapper and shoved it into the bag. "Ever get the feeling we're being toyed with?"

"Do I what. We're like rats in a maze." The words caught at her memory, and she frowned. Where had she heard that before . . . ?

Theo whistled a few bleak bars.

She shivered. "Simon and Garfunkel, right? It's not exactly cheerful."

"No, it's not." The corner of his mouth lifted. "What would you prefer? The Beatles? Or maybe The Lads?"

Maunga groaned and rose to her feet. "How about we keep moving before you come up with any more terrible music from the 1900s?"

"But they're *classics*," he protested. "Like cheese and marmite in a sandwich. You like cheese and marmite."

"They're classics that are more than a century old. Would you want a cheese and marmite sandwich that was more than a hundred years old? No? Didn't think so." She grabbed the pack and started off down the hall.

"You can't compare The Beatles to a hundred-year-old cheese and marmite sandwich!" He fell into step beside her. "That's ridiculous."

"You're ridiculous."

"Married you, didn't I?"

"Case in point," she said, not quite under her breath, and grinned at the expression on his face.

Maybe this place was starting to get sick of them. Before long they were railroaded into a sharp right corner, then a left, then another right, at which point there was a startling change.

The passage ran for maybe two hundred metres without a corner to be seen. The panelled walls rose on either side until they faded into darkness high above. Maunga tipped her head back, squinting, but saw nothing. The ceiling was lost to darkness.

Theo blew out a breath. "That's different."

"Creepy," she said. "I don't trust it."

"I don't think we have a choice."

"No, we don't." She walked forward. The skin on the back of her neck prickled. No, she didn't trust it at all. Anything could drop out of the darkness above them, and they wouldn't see it coming.

"Look," Theo said from a few paces behind her.

She turned, but he wasn't looking up at the darkness. A thin line crossed the floor from wall to wall between them, burning with orange flame. "That's—"

"Everburn." He stepped over the gouge. "We've crossed that bit of floor before. Presumably it's just the walls shifting, then, not the space as a whole."

"Thought you said it was non-Euclidean?"

"Could be. Could be not, too."

"Hmm." A few metres further on, she found another line crossing the space. And then another. "Talk about railroading," she muttered, and heard an answering snort from Theo.

As she stepped over the next gouge, she heard a whisper behind her.

"Sorry, what? Didn't catch that."

"Wasn't me," Theo said.

"Great. Now the walls are talking. Or else I imagined it." She didn't think she'd imagined it, but she could be wrong; they were both suffering a decent amount of strain, after all. It wouldn't surprise her.

The whisper came again and her stomach dropped.

"Hey, dumbo," it hissed. "They'd never believe you."

Maunga swallowed. She knew the words; she'd said them to Addy in the days after she stole her voice, a good ten years ago now. But the voice was new. It wasn't her own voice, or Theo's, or Addy's, or even Caroline's. She couldn't place it at all. It sounded inhuman. The cadence was off, the stresses lay in the wrong places, and the pitch was strangely genderless—not high enough to be distinctly female nor low enough to be distinctly male.

Had Theo heard? She threw a glance over her shoulder at him, but he raised his eyebrows and shook his head again. He hadn't heard it. Maybe she was hallucinating.

And then his head swung around, eyes darting this way and that, and she saw the same flicker of emotion across his face that she had felt: guilt, shame, sorrow. He'd heard something. But whatever it was, it was different from what she'd heard.

"Whatever it's saying," Maunga said, not surprised to hear her voice shake, "don't listen to it."

He faced forward again, eyes still focused somewhere in the middle distance. "Easier said than done."

She strode on down the hall. The whispers grew, coming at her from one direction and then another, soft and loud and soft again, always with that same rhythm and tone that stopped just short of sounding human. Some of the things the voice said were simply petty, others mean, still others downright vicious. Every word stirred memories of the time she'd said it: some more than a decade old, some only weeks ago.

Maunga set her teeth and kept walking. It wasn't a *nice* experience by any stretch of the imagination, but she'd long since realised that she wasn't a particularly nice person. She was a work in progress, the same as anyone else on the planet; she just had further to go than most to be halfway decent, that was all. So she bowed her head against the storm and trudged on, buffeted from every side but unbroken.

The walk seemed endless. Hopping over yet another line of Everburn, she peered ahead and saw double doors blocking the passage. *Finally.*

A glance over her shoulder showed Theo a dozen paces behind. His face was pale, jaw tight, eyes blazing; he walked as if each step cost him a huge amount of effort, but still, he advanced. She faced forward again, braced herself, and kept walking.

One step. Another step. One step. Another step.

She did her best to ignore the whispers. It proved next to impossible; the softer the words were, the more her ears strained to understand them, and the loud ones were sometimes so sudden that she startled at them despite herself.

The whispers faded the nearer she came to the doors. At twenty metres they were a churning mass, incoherent but still quite loud, as if a hundred voices were all talking at once. She found her pace speeding up, giving lie to her belief that she had hardly any energy left. At ten metres they were no more than a faint susurration, like the sighing of the wind just at the edge of her hearing.

At five metres they fell blessedly silent.

She reached the doors and turned back to see how Theo was doing. He lagged ten or twelve metres behind, still walking as though every step took a mammoth effort. His stride lengthened as he neared the doors, shoulders lifting, back straightening. The whispers would be dying down. He didn't stop when he stepped into the five-metre buffer zone. Five long strides brought him to Maunga, and his arms wrapped around her as she stepped into his embrace, natural as breathing.

"I'm here," he said in answer to her unspoken question. "Don't worry. Just a bit . . . shaken."

"It's mutual," she muttered, burrowing closer to his chest.

They stood there for a long time, not speaking.

"Okay?" Maunga disengaged from the hug and stepped back.

Theo nodded. "Yeah." He didn't look happy, exactly, but the flat look had gone from his eyes. He strode past her to the doors and pulled them open.

Darkness met her gaze. She watched as Theo poked a foot into the room, feeling cautiously with his toes before putting any weight on it. His other foot followed. At the third step forward, a line of footlights blinked on, forming a clear lane two metres wide that vanished into the night ahead of them.

"Well, at least there's a floor." He turned his head, his expression half hidden by the shadows, and held out a hand. "Just in case."

Maunga grasped his hand and followed him into the black.

Predictably, the doors slid shut of their own accord before they'd made it a dozen paces inside. Maunga blinked, trying to see something—anything—in the murk. But there were only the white, palm-sized domes at their feet, leading on into infinity. She squeezed Theo's hand and felt his grip tighten in answer. He was still here. *Good.*

She hadn't really expected him to somehow disappear in the three metres since they'd left the hall. But you never knew.

This place was a mess of mind games and trippy physics.

But that was exactly why they'd come themselves instead of delegating the job to someone else. The general gist of what they would be facing had been clear from Addy's book. Theo might not be a physicist, but as an engineer he could do a lot more than most with metal and electronics. The trijectors, for instance, and the earpieces.

And then there were the mind games. Well. Maunga was a trauma psychologist, wasn't she? She knew how to fix people's head-spaces; how to get them through the worst of the storm until they could fix themselves. Sometimes it felt like sticking a band-aid on a slit artery, but every little bit helped.

Of course, they'd been counting on having Dave here, too. He was the perfect fit to round out the field team: as a cognitive neuroscientist, he straddled the line between mental and material, psychology and hard science. And as a former Breach employee, he would've been far more familiar than they were with anything they could expect to face.

But he wasn't here, and they'd lost contact not only with him but with everyone else at home base, too. She'd be lying if she said it wasn't a blow.

Away in the darkness to her left, a shaft of light appeared, highlighting a familiar form.

Autumn glared at her across the chasm, one hand curled around her protruding baby bump. Her voice echoed in the distance. "She said I looked like a whale. Again. It's not the first time she's done it, but I thought she might have learned from last time. I asked her to stop." She shrugged. "Guess she wasn't listening."

Perversely, Maunga felt herself relax. It was only a projection of Autumn. She was talking to someone else, not to Maunga. Talking to Simon? Probably. But had she said that in real life, or was it clever speculation based on Maunga's own memories? There was no way to tell. It didn't matter.

More mind games. That was alright. She could handle mind games. They'd come prepared.

Theo's hand squeezed tight. Maunga wasn't the only one seeing faces and hearing voices. She hadn't expected to be.

Time for some noise, then, to distract them and keep them on track. She opened her mouth to start singing—

Or tried to. Her mouth wouldn't open.

Hmm. If she couldn't sing, could she hum?

No luck there, either. She couldn't make a sound. This was clearly a test of silence, among other things. Alright. That was alright. They could do this. She gave Theo's hand an answering squeeze and rubbed a thumb along the line of his fingers. There was nothing to do but endure and advance.

The room stretched on. Maunga put one foot after another, not letting go of Theo's hand for a second. There was no telling what would happen if she did. She might never find him again. Faces and voices appeared and disappeared out of the darkness, some startlingly familiar, others she hardly recognised.

And then she saw Theo, and a hollow ache formed in the pit of her stomach.

Of course he'd be here. He loved her. They'd been married five years. He would be acutely aware of her flaws, as she was aware of his. They knew each other intimately, the physical and the emotional, the good and the bad.

He paced, eyes red-rimmed, hands fluttering at his sides or rising to scrub through his disheveled hair. "I know," he said. "I know I love her. I think—no, I know she loves me. But—"

He broke off, striding restlessly back and forth, back and forth, his body for once an accurate reflection of the churning turmoil of thought that lay beneath. "I don't know." The words trailed off into a whistling sigh. "I love her. I want to marry her. But it's her fault, Ads."

Maunga's breath caught painfully in her throat. This was before they'd married, then; most likely shortly after he'd proposed. Maybe it was even the same night. She'd told him everything that night.

Everything.

It had been a lot to take in. He hadn't reneged on the marriage proposal, but he had said he needed time.

He hadn't said how much time.

She hadn't asked. She'd told him to keep the ring until he knew for certain one way or the other, and she'd watched him leave, watched him walk away without once looking back, and she'd honestly thought she'd lost him.

And here he was, talking to Addy. Or to the memory of Addy.

Of course he was talking to her. Addy might not be dead—keek, Addy had better not be dead, or there would be a reckoning indeed—but Theo had lost her as surely as if she'd died. Of course there would be a grieving process. He'd have a tangle of thoughts and emotions to work through, and talking to the deceased was an age-old way of doing that.

"It's her fault." His words were stark. "She stole your voice. She condemned you to three, nearly four years of school with no voice, no writing, no anything. It could have been decades; it could have been the rest of your life. Might still be. She got you involved in that VPS programme. She took you to Caroline, and she was going to sell you out."

His eyes rose, dark and wild, staring across the void to meet Maunga's gaze. "She was going to sell you out. And I know the final decision was yours, Ads, but it was her fault you were even in that situation in the first place. It was her fault." He swallowed. His eyes dropped. His last words were almost a whisper, as if he was unwilling to speak them even to himself. "I don't know if I can forgive her for that."

But he had. He had forgiven her. He'd married her, hadn't he? She'd heard nothing from him for a full week after he proposed, and then he'd shown up at her flat and silently proffered the ring box again.

Surely you didn't marry someone if you couldn't forgive them for something that huge.

But she wasn't sure. Theo faded away into the darkness, and Maunga gripped his hand tighter. She wasn't sure, and that was why she hated these stupid mind games: because they sowed seeds of fear and doubt where there was no cause for it. She hated not being sure, and she hated being given cause, however slight, to doubt Theo. *Doubt truth to be a liar,* he'd said, leaving it to her to fill in the next line: *but never doubt I love.*

What if there was reason to?

It was an easy enough fix. She'd just have to ask him when they got out of this everlasting night.

If they got out of this everlasting night.

They would, wouldn't they?

Yes. Of course they would. They *would.*

She squeezed Theo's hand so hard she could almost hear the bones grinding and kept walking.

The lights sloped down before them. A moment later the floor followed suit. It was a long slope, but as they descended the air lightened, going from black to jet to onyx to charcoal, and on and on until she could see Theo easily in the dim grey light. He looked as shattered as she felt. He turned his head and gave her a weary grin as they came to another pair of doors.

This test was over. It was about keeking time.

The next room was long and low, shrouded in pale, golden-white light. The floor and ceiling were the same white tiling that seemed to be everywhere, but the walls were different. Deep alcoves of white stone lined the space, framed by squat pillars. The waist-high ledges bore an eerie resemblance to ancient tomb slabs.

Was this where Caroline laid the dead to rest?

But there were no dead here, not in a literal sense. They hadn't come across the faintest hint of life once since they'd been here, and they'd never seen anyone entering or leaving this place from the outside.

It occurred to Maunga, not for the first time, that it could take a very, *very* long time to find Addy. But that was alright. They had time, and determination, and brains, and supplies, and courage. They'd find her—or die of old age in the attempt.

She grinned a little at that.

"What is it?" Theo asked.

"Just imagining you with that beard turned white and so long that you're tripping over it." At his baffled expression, she waved a hand in dismissal. "Don't worry. It's not important."

He shrugged. "Righto. I won't."

She considered asking him if he still blamed her for what happened to Addy and, more importantly, if he'd forgiven her. But no—he might be looking more settled with every passing second out of the dark, but he wasn't *that* settled.

Not yet.

Better to give him time. He didn't bounce back as fast as she did, and he would be working through his own doubts and fears.

It had waited five years; it would wait another few hours.

Maunga led the way down the middle of the room, counting the alcoves as they went. Ten, twenty, and another five to the end wall made twenty-five down each side. Fifty in total. She'd thought there would be another set of double doors at the far end, but there was just a plain white wall featuring a rather worn carving of the Breach logo.

She was turning to Theo to ask what he thought about this place when he drew a sharp breath. That couldn't be good. She twisted, half-crouching, ready for action.

He stared with wide eyes at an alcove near the end wall.

"What?" she asked.

Theo swallowed and didn't reply. He took a heavy, jerking step toward the alcove, and then another. The movements looked strangely disconnected. A few more steps brought him to the edge of the alcove. He looked down at it in stunned silence.

"What is it?" Maunga asked again, worry threading through the words. It wasn't like Theo to ignore a direct question, not when he was this firmly embedded in the real world.

But he just shook his head. His mouth opened, gaped for a minute, and closed again.

What on earth was he looking at? The alcove he stood in front of looked the same as every other alcove from here. She strode across the floor to his side, curiosity tugging at one hand and concern at the other.

Oh, keek. Keek, keek, keek, keeking keek. That was what he was looking at. The pillar had blocked it from where she'd been standing. *Keek.*

Far back in the recesses of the alcove were signs of occupation. A couple of flattened, commercial-sized cardboard boxes, stamped with the ubiquitous Breach logo, made for a poor mattress. A navy blue blanket, loosely woven, was folded neatly at one end. At the other end lay a makeshift pillow: a small sack of rough hemp, stamped all over with *Breach Laboratories Finest Dark Roast Espresso Beans,* stuffed with what looked like crumpled paper balls.

Maunga shivered. It wasn't much; not even enough to know if it was the only pad here or just one of several. But someone had slept here, that much was obvious. *Addy?* Her heart leaped. Who else would it be?

Theo's hand fluttered at his side, like he'd been about to lift it but had changed his mind. He sniffed and nodded to the back of the alcove. "Look," he rasped.

She leaned forward, peering into the shadows. What was he talking about?

Oh. There.

It was half hidden by the curve of the alcove's ceiling and the dim light but, now that she'd made it out, it was obvious: the original of the picture Addy had taken with her when she left six years ago. Addy and Challa laughed up at her from the page, looking unbearably young and innocent. The paper was worn smooth and discoloured, the edges curling, faded crease marks speaking of careful folding and just-as-careful unfolding.

Her breath sounded loud in her ears. This was it. This was where Addy had slept, maybe where she still slept even now.

They'd found it. Found *her.*

Beside her, Theo lifted a shaking hand to his mouth. His eyes went from the picture to the blanket to the sack and back again, darting over everything as if he couldn't take it all in.

A noise escaped him, sounding something like a breathless sob cut short. The hand at his mouth scrubbed across his face. His mouth gaped, lips trembling, eyes wet with tears. He looked devastated. His other hand rose, shaking uncontrollably, and came to rest on the cardboard mattress.

Maunga knew he was thinking of their fluffed pillows at home, the feather duvet, the thick mattress.

He reached out and ran a finger along the edge of the navy blanket, smoothing a corner that was already as crisp as any linen on a hospital bed.

And then he closed his eyes, dropped to his knees, and buried his face in his hands.

Oh, Theo. Maunga rubbed his back, up and down, up and down and around. She felt close to tears herself.

Six years, it had been. Six years since they'd last seen Addy. Since Addy had seen them. From the look of it, six years since she'd slept in a bed or even had a proper pillow to lay her head on.

Theo's shoulders shook. Maunga stood silent guard beside him, one hand on his back, the other on the blue blanket, and waited for the storm to pass.

CHAPTER SEVEN

A whisper of movement caught Maunga's ear. Her head snapped around even as her fingers dug into Theo's shoulder in silent warning.

Away down the room, one of the ceiling tiles rattled.

Theo's head jerked up. They watched together as the tile popped out of place. It dropped a few centimetres before jerking to a halt. A shadow of a hand, lean and small and caked with dirt, slipped through the gap to grasp the edge of the tile. There was a complex twist-and-pull motion; the tile came away cleanly, and the hand pulled it up through the cavity at a diagonal.

Then there was nothing. No noise. No movement.

Maunga waited, hardly daring to breathe in case the newcomer heard her. Theo's shoulder was stiff beneath her hand, the muscles tense; his expression spoke of mingled dread and hope, agony and anticipation. She knew how he felt.

Movement came again, a soft shuffling sound. A pair of filthy bare feet appeared through the hole. Ankles followed and then bony calves, bare to the shins and as dirty as the rest. The whole lower half of the figure dropped down, facing away from them. The hips and legs from the waist down were covered in trousers that might have once been a violent turquoise but were now so faded and stained with dirt that they were mottled a dull grey; they were rough canvas polyester, such as might be found in any prison yard or tradesman's wardrobe, and the legs had been hacked off unevenly below the knee.

Maunga had a faint glimpse of a darker material around the

hips and waist as it swayed with the motion of the person, but she couldn't have said what it was.

The figure rested there a moment and then swung down to dangle by its hands. Ah, that's what the material had been. The newcomer was almost definitely Addy. She must have found a twin to the navy blanket that lay in the alcove, and she'd cut armholes and fashioned it into a sort of oversized, hooded vest. It wasn't as filthy as the rest of the ensemble. Maybe she'd found it recently, or she'd had a way of keeping it cleaner. A long-sleeved shirt showed under the blanket-vest, grey with dirt like the trousers.

The figure wore the hood of the vest up over her head. It almost slipped off as she let go of the rim and dropped into a crouch on the floor. She straightened it and turned to face the alcove where Theo and Maunga were.

And stopped.

Maunga watched the person—her? Yes, the form was certainly female—watched *her* cautiously. She had frozen, head tipped to the side. Her face was shadowed under the hood. A deeper shadow over the lower half of the face suggested a scarf drawn across the mouth and nose.

"It's okay," Maunga said quietly, breaking the silence.

The figure took a halting step forward. The movement was so much like Theo's had been only minutes ago that Maunga caught her breath.

It was Addy. It *was.* It had to be.

The lean form lifted a hand to the shadow where her mouth would be, forefinger extended. The message was clear. *Don't talk.*

She crossed the floor in swift strides and stood before them.

It was Addy. There was no mistaking those brown eyes, even exhausted as they were, bloodshot and looking decades older than their twenty-two years. They gleamed dully beneath the hood as they flickered between Maunga and Theo and came to rest on Theo.

Maunga followed her gaze. Theo still knelt on the floor, his body twisted to look back over his shoulder and up at Addy. His eyes were bright, every inch of him still and alert, every particle of his being bent on devouring the first sight and sound and smell of his little sister in more than six years. He looked like he couldn't have spoken even if he'd wanted to. There was a glossy sheen to his eyes. His nostrils were flared, but he was beyond tears. His mouth moved to frame a single, soundless word: *Addy.*

Addy bent and pressed her finger to his lips. *Quiet.*

He caught her hand as it fell, folding it between his larger hands with infinite care, like it might break if he made a wrong move. His eyes closed; he lifted her hand to his chest and held it there, head bowed. Maunga could hear his breath stuttering from his lungs, but his hands were rock-steady. He traced the lines of her calloused palms with the pad of his forefinger, followed the veins out to the grimy fingertips, rubbed a thumb over her bruised and scraped knuckles.

Addy. His lips moved. *Addy.* And again and again. *Addy. Addy. Addy.*

She slipped her hand from his grasp and ran it over his head, down his temple, along his bearded chin.

Theo raised his eyes to meet her curious gaze.

Her fingers tugged at a bristling strand.

The sides of his mouth lifted.

Her eyes crinkled a little. She dropped her hand and jerked her head toward the back of the alcove.

Once they were curled safely in the shadows at the rear of the recess, Addy retrieved a metal plate not much bigger than a dollar coin from her pocket and placed it near the entrance. A matching plate went on the opposite side, and a precise tap-tap-swipe activated the familiar shimmer of a noise-blocking field.

"There," Addy said, and swept her hood back from her face. "Now we can talk."

Her voice had matured noticeably in the last six years, Maunga noted. And she *could* talk: that was one question answered. They'd worried that she might still have Vox Pox, but it seemed Caroline had discarded that in favour of other research.

She wasn't any taller than she'd been at sixteen, which was only to be expected. Her face was gaunt, eyes sunken above the black breath mask that swathed her from collarbone to the bridge of her nose.

She'd cut her hair at some point—or had it cut for her. The last time Maunga had seen her, her hair had been long, falling in soft waves to below her shoulders. Now it was short and rough, a thatch of dark, messy hair that stood out from her head in jagged clumps.

Theo drew a breath and lunged, heedless of the dirt, wrapping Addy in a tight hug that was all white knuckles and jutting elbows. Addy made a noise somewhere between a laugh and a sob before returning it fiercely, burrowing her head into his chest and closing her eyes.

Maunga blinked back tears. Six years was a long time to go without seeing someone. Even longer when that someone was your only sibling. They looked more alike than they ever had, with their short hair and lean features.

The breath mask niggled at the back of her mind. Addy hadn't taken it off even here, in her own territory, where she was safe. Did it serve a function beyond the obvious? Had her lungs been damaged to the point where she needed to wear it all the time? Was it hiding something, a terrible scar or a gaping wound?

Peace, she told herself. It would wait. They'd need to know eventually, of course, and likely sooner than that, but there was no need to interrupt the first hug she'd had from Theo in six years.

Addy was the first to draw back, wiping a hand across her eyes and leaving smears of dirt in its wake. "Glad you could make it."

It was such a typical Te Ngawai understatement that Maunga barked a laugh. "We're glad we could make it, too." She clasped a hand to Addy's shoulder and remembered the last time she'd done it, the morning before Addy went off to her supposed extended trial. "You wouldn't believe the trouble we had getting an invite to this place."

Addy's lips quirked. "Oh, I think I would."

"Are we safe here?"

"Safer than most places. I only moved here the other day. It usually takes them a good week or so to find me again. Caro and her minions," she added in reply to Theo's questioning look.

Her voice was hoarse, but it wasn't a fraction as rough as Maunga had thought it might be after a decade of being unable to talk. "Your voice is back?"

"Has been for four years," Addy said. "As near as I can remember, anyway. Caro decided she'd had enough of testing while I suffered Vox Pox and thought she'd test while I suffered the aftermath instead." Her eyes glittered. "I made sure the aftermath was as much like the event as possible. Hence the sound net. I only talk when she can't hear me—and I make keeking sure I don't talk when she *can* hear me. It's going to screw with her results something awful."

"Good girl," Maunga said. Addy might have signed up for this of her own free will, but it was good to see she hadn't just rolled over and passively taken everything Caroline dished out.

Theo slipped an arm around Addy's shoulders and made a move to tuck her in against his side. She resisted the pull. *Interesting.* Theo needing the physical grounding was nothing new; of course he'd take every opportunity to reassure himself that Addy was alive and well. But she would have expected Addy to soak up all the contact he offered.

That clearly wasn't the case.

Then again, after six years without human contact, she'd be a tad wary of all this touching.

"Are you hurt?" Theo asked.

Addy snorted. "Yes."

He bolted upright and reached for the pack. "Where? How

bad? We've got a medkit; it's nothing fancy, but it's got more than just the basics—"

"Theo."

His focus swung from the bag back to Addy. "I'm here."

Something had distracted her. Addy's hand rose to tangle in his green t-shirt. Her eyes went flat and distant for a long moment; there was movement under the mask, and Maunga heard her swallow.

"Theo," she whispered again, blinking back tears. "I thought—" She closed her eyes, her breath ragged, and dropped her face to his shoulder.

Theo ran a hand through her short hair, eyes bleak as he met Maunga's gaze over Addy's bent head. Maunga covered his hand for a moment in silent reassurance. They'd need to know about the mask eventually, but now wasn't the time.

"I thought I'd never see you again." Addy's words emerged muffled. "Thought I'd never say your name—not to your face, not ever."

Theo dropped a kiss on her dark head. "It's okay. I know. I'm here. I'm here, Ads."

She jerked a nod. Drew a shuddering breath. "Yeah." Another pause, and then she disengaged. "Um. I'm not hurt—physically. Or, uh, not too badly."

"We'll be the judges of that," Maunga said. "If you don't mind."

"It's mostly just dirt," Addy said. "Haven't had a wash in . . . I don't know. A long time."

Maunga could do something about that, at least. If not the dirt, then at least the smell. A quick dig through the pack turned up the spray can she was looking for. She gave it a quick shake and passed it to Addy.

Addy blinked at it tiredly. "What is it?"

"Can't you read?" Maunga retorted.

She could tell her, of course, but she'd rather find out just how far below par Addy's brain was running. Exhaustion would account for some of the slowness and chronic undernutrition for some more, but they needed to know if there were any major gaps in her processing, so to speak.

"Course I can read."

"Go on, then."

There was a long silence. Addy frowned down at the can, lashes drooping over shadowed eyes. Maunga was starting to wonder if she'd overestimated her when the frown cleared.

"Ah," Addy said.

"Ah, what?" Theo asked.

Addy's gaze flickered over the text-heavy label. When she lifted her eyes to Maunga, they gleamed in amusement. "That bad, eh?"

"Pretty bad," Maunga agreed.

"Sit back, then."

Theo shuffled back one way and Maunga shuffled the other, leaving enough room for Addy to spray herself. When the mist cleared, she looked significantly cleaner—not fresh-out-of-a-bath clean but vastly cleaner than a minute ago. The smell was greatly improved, too. Maunga was glad she'd thought to get the scent neutraliser added.

"Better?" Addy asked.

"Much," Maunga said. "Now answer the question. Where are you hurt? Is it your jaw? Mouth? Lungs?"

Addy looked flummoxed, or as flummoxed as a person can look with only the top half of their face showing. "Why . . . ? Oh, the breathing mask." She waved a dismissive hand. "No, that's just habit. Nothing wrong there."

"So where?"

She laid her head back against the wall and scrunched up her face in thought. "Low-grade aches: everywhere. Corresponding cuts and bruises: also everywhere. Chronic fatigue, insomnia, nightmares, sporadic hallucinations, headaches, general weakness. Nothing broken that I know of. Twisted my ankle again a couple of months back, or it might have been a year. Not sure. I lose track of time. Um. Ribs were a bit tender for a while—"

Maunga had had a lot of practice decoding Theo's understatements. If Addy's lack of willingness to admit pain was anything like his, 'a bit tender' probably translated to 'teeth-grinding agony.'

"But they've mostly healed up now. A bit of hearing loss, maybe. It's been so long since I've heard another voice, I've forgotten what *normal* sounds like."

"Can you hear us alright?"

"Nah, yeah, fine. No trouble."

"Good. Anything else? What's your mental state like? Anger, fear, despair?"

Addy gazed at her blankly.

"Maunga's a psychologist," Theo put in. "Trauma psychology, specifically."

"Oh." Understanding dawned. "I forget, sometimes. That the world just . . . goes on. Outside. Without me." She took a deep breath. "Right. Um. Euphoria at the moment; that's probably self-explanatory. There was a bit of denial at the start. Overwhelming depression for the first three years. Mostly anger for the year after that. Still a lot of anger, to be honest."

Hmm. "Any bargaining?"

"No." Addy's answer was immediate. "No bargaining. No compromises. Not for Caro."

She hated the woman, that much was clear. Curious that she used the familiar shortening of the name, though. Test subject and overseer, they were hardly intimates. "Have you self-harmed at all?"

"No."

"Anything to numb yourself or to make you feel alive? Overuse of stimulants or depressants? Caffeine, alcohol, medication, anything like that?"

"Because I have so much booze stashed here," Addy muttered, gesturing to the empty walls of the alcove. "No, nothing like that."

It had to be asked. "Suicidal thoughts or attempts?"

Theo's eyes flew to hers, panicked. She quelled him with a glance.

A pause, and then: "No."

Hmm. A pause didn't automatically mean a lie; it could have been surprise at the unexpected, or processing time, or exhaustion kicking in, or simply thinking it through and making sure her answer was truthful. But it was something to note. "Okay. Thank you."

"That's it?"

Maunga eyed her. "I'm sure I can fit in a full counselling session later, if you're comfortable with me taking it myself, but now's hardly the time, kiddo. If you're *not* comfortable—and let's face it, your predominant memories of me won't be the most pleasant—then I can get one of my colleagues to take it. I'd much rather counsel you myself, but—"

"No, I—"

"If you'd rather talk to someone else, that's fine, too. Sorry, you were saying something?"

"Yeah." Addy's eyebrows drew down in thought. "Addy," she said after a moment.

"What?"

"My name's Addy," she said. "Or Adelaide, if you can't handle the short form. I'm not a kid anymore. You don't need to call me *kiddo*."

Maunga nodded slowly. Of course Addy wasn't a child anymore. She was very aware of that. "Alright. Addy." Grim amusement reared its head. "No promises."

"Why not?"

"Because I call you *kiddo* in much the same way that I call Theo, ah, other things."

"I've called him every name under the sun," Addy said. "Don't worry."

Theo's expression was suddenly very fixed.

Maunga bit back a laugh. "Mmm, not quite the same thing,

I don't think." She scratched her nose, making sure to use her left hand, where her wedding rings sat.

Keek. Addy still didn't get it. Oh, well, time to be blunt. "It's affection, Addy, not irritation."

"Oh." Addy blinked and then nodded. "Okay then. You've definitely affected me, so I guess that's fair."

Silence.

"That was a joke," she added.

"I know," Maunga said. She just hadn't expected Addy to be cracking jokes within an hour of seeing them for the first time in six years.

"You looked a bit . . ." Addy trailed off and circled a hand around her face. "And you, too," she said to Theo.

"A bit what?" Theo asked.

"Flat. Uncertain. Surprised. Something like that. Admittedly it's been a while since I've had to interpret facial expressions, so I might've gotten it wrong."

He worried at his lower lip, eyes flickering past Addy's shoulder to Maunga before returning to his sister. "No, that sounds about right."

"I'm allowed to make jokes." Addy's shoulders hunched.

"Course you are," he said. "But we weren't expecting—"

"What?"

He stopped. Blew out a breath. Started again. "It's been more than six years, Ads."

"I know," she said, one eyebrow tilting above the rim of the mask.

"And you're here, a . . . a little worse for wear, sure, but overall you're fine, you're not injured, you've got all your faculties and limbs and everything—"

The other eyebrow rose.

"And you're cracking jokes like you've only been gone a few days."

"Sorry." There was a definite bite to the word. "I can go away and come back again when I've sustained some actual brain damage, if you'd prefer. Or maybe some physical damage? Would you like me to lose a whole hand, or would a couple of fingers do? What if I ask Caro to give me Vox Pox again? Would that validate your rescue mission?"

"*Addy.*" Theo closed his eyes, looking like he was about to throw up. "Stop. Please. It's not—I didn't mean it like that."

"Then how did you mean it?"

"He meant—" Maunga started.

"Stay out of it," Addy snapped. Her eyes flashed above the rim of the mask before softening. "Please. I asked Theo, not you."

Maunga lifted her hands in silent surrender.

"I meant," Theo said, rubbing a hand over his beard, "that we had no idea what to expect. Do you know how many years I've dreamed of this? And when I say dreamed, I mean . . ." He looked away. "I mean I didn't want to sleep—couldn't sleep—for imagining what you were going through. I know you were joking, but brain damage was a distinct possibility. Missing fingers was one of the most minor of my worries. I thought of—of—oh, of every possibility under the sun. If we got here and didn't find you, or found you just before you died, and how much worse it would be if you were alive but—but not *you.* If you didn't know me, if you didn't know *yourself,* if there was nothing left of you but an empty shell—"

His voice cracked. He covered his face with shaking hands. After a moment he went on, his voice muffled. "It wasn't a criticism, Addy. It was anything but. I'm—I'm pleased you're alright, I'm glad, I'm *overwhelmed* that you're in one piece, physically and mentally. And I'm stumped as to how you managed it. Six years without human contact, six years of, I don't even know, of whatever you've been going through. You don't just come out the other end unscathed. Nobody could. But you're here, you're alive, you're talking and thinking and *joking* . . . it's more than I ever could have hoped for. More than I'd *dared* to hope for, even in my wildest moments."

"Ye-e-ah," Addy said, drawing the word out, "but you've never been the most optimistic of chaps, have you."

It wasn't a question. Theo gave a hoarse laugh and dropped his hands, wiping them across his face as he did so. "No," he admitted. "No, I'm ever the realist. Had to face the facts. And them's the facts."

She mimed vomiting.

"What?"

"Your grammar," she said with a disgusted look. "It sickens me."

Theo snorted. "It's an accepted colloquialism. Pedant."

"Lazybones."

"That explains the Ph.D., I suppose."

"Do you?" Her eyes lit up.

"Do I have a Ph.D.? I do. I finished my bachelor's, did another year to get first class honours, took two years off to work while Maunga did her master's, and then she worked while I went back to do my doctorate. Graduated not long ago."

"What's it in? Can I read your thesis? I bet you didn't use colloquialisms in *that.*"

Maunga didn't bother trying to stifle her laugh as Theo rolled his eyes. "Mechalectrical engineering," he said. "Specialising in holo functions and interfaces. More specifically, I wanted to find new uses for holo tech. We're third-iteration shoulder holo users now. There hadn't been any new innovations in the field in nearly five years. It was long overdue for an overhaul."

"And?"

"Yeah, I found a few." He shifted his weight and dug the trijector out of his pocket. "This, for example."

Addy held out a hand. He passed it over. "What is it?" she asked, tipping it into the palm of one hand to study it.

"Holo trijector. Second-iteration, that one is. It's new enough, but the components are getting smaller all the time; I'll be able to cut the size down by at least a quarter in another year or so. It's essentially an ultra-portable screen for your wrist holo. Useful for sharing information from a distance, and much easier to transport than a desk. It's handy for people who can't see quite as well as they used to or who have limited arm mobility—anyone who might need a bigger screen than the wrist holo can project. Let's face it, those are *tiny.*"

"Agreed."

"There were a few other things, but nothing that I brought with me." He unstrapped his wrist holo and held out the worn leather band. "D'you want to try it?"

She shook her head. "Not ri-i-ight now," she said, breaking off in the middle to yawn.

"Another time, then." He replaced his holo, took the trijector back with gentle movements, and slipped it back into his pocket. "You still haven't answered the question."

"You didn't ask a question."

"It was implied."

"Can it wait? You're here, which means Caro will find me soon, which means we need to be out of here in, at a guess, six hours. And until then I need to sleep. If I can." She gave a small, unhappy shrug. "Haven't had a proper sleep in . . . a while. Longer than I can remember. Need to try, though."

"Of course it can wait," Maunga said. She eyeballed Theo over the top of Addy's head and he gave a grudging nod.

"Sure," he agreed. "No worries. It'll keep."

Maunga tugged the pack closer. In her peripheral vision, she saw Addy start to unfold the single blanket and then pause.

"I. Um." Addy almost looked embarrassed. "I've only got one blanket."

"We've got our own," Maunga said, not looking up from the depths of the bag. "And then some. Are you hungry?"

"Ground state of being. I'll do for a few days yet."

Maunga thrust a stasis-peel banana at her. "See if that'll stay down. Thirsty?"

"Water?"

"Mmm-hmm." Admittedly it was water with a concentrated dosage of electrolytes and minerals, not to mention vitamins and a shot of natural flavour; but it was water nonetheless.

"Please."

She pulled the bottle out of an inner pocket and passed it over. "Theo? You hungry?"

"We've got those drumsticks somewhere, don't we?"

"We do. Right here, in fact."

He took the packet out of her hand and started unwrapping the foil from around the chicken. "Thanks."

They ate quietly, content to rehydrate from a second water bottle and take the edge off their appetites. Addy nibbled at the banana, eyes shifting restlessly between Theo and Maunga and the room outside their alcove. One foot tapped an erratic rhythm on the cardboard under them. She yawned more frequently the nearer she came to finishing the banana, and at her third consecutive yawn Theo leaned over and plucked the empty peel from her hand.

"Lie down," he ordered gently.

"Don't tell me what to do," Addy said. But she wrapped herself in the navy blue blanket and lay down anyway, curled at the rear of the alcove with her back to the curving wall.

Theo settled on his back beside her. His gaze was wistful as he glanced at Addy, and Maunga knew he was fighting an impulse to wrap an arm around her. His hand rose to brush a strand of choppy hair back from her face.

"Sleep well," he whispered.

Addy looked at him through red-rimmed eyes. Profound cynicism flashed across her face and was gone, replaced by all-consuming fatigue. She made a movement that could have been a nod or a shrug and closed her eyes.

Maunga retrieved their own olive green blanket and finished stowing the empties back in the pack. After a moment's thought, she found the hunting knife where she'd slipped it down the side of the compartment. It only took a moment to strap it to her thigh.

Better over-prepared than under; they could be facing anything at all on their way out of here.

Theo tilted his head and threw out an arm in invitation. She did a last check of the room. Not that there was much to see. The room beyond the alcove was as blank and white and empty as ever. Addy's breathing came slow and steady on Theo's far side. It was safe. She nestled in beside him, burrowing her head into the crook of his shoulder.

"Well, husband?" she whispered.

Theo shook his head, gaze thoughtful. "Don't know. It's too early. There's too much to process. Far too much."

"She's alive. And remarkably whole. Focus on that."

He looked down at her, eyes over-bright, and drew a breath through his nose. "Yeah." He ran a hand down her side, over her hip, down her leg—and stopped when he came to the knife. His eyebrows furrowed in silent enquiry.

"A precaution."

"I see."

She kissed him. "Sleep, Theo."

"As you wish." The words were light, but he soon sobered. "I love you."

Even after five years of marriage, the words made her heart swell. What had she done to deserve him? Nothing. But then, love wasn't about being deserving. "Love you too."

She rested a hand on his chest, felt the tight weave of his shirt, the steady rise and fall of his breathing. His hand moved upward to settle on her hip. A thumb swept under the hem of her shirt to touch bare skin, the movement familiar as his name on her lips.

Maunga closed her eyes and slept.

INTERLUDE

THE VOICELESS WE HAVE HEARD, AND ON THIS DAY WE VOW
TO TRACE THE SPECTRAL PULSE OF YOUR WOUNDED HEART—

CHAPTER EIGHT

A wild jolt woke Theo from deep sleep. He stared at the sloping ceiling for a moment, mind scrambling for the usual series of split-second realisations, where and why and how and who. A second jolt shook the ledge. He reacted, one hand reaching behind him for Addy even as the other tightened around Maunga. Was the place falling to pieces around them? An earthquake? Was it Caroline's doing, or natural causes?

Whatever it was, they needed to move.

He shook Maunga awake and would have done the same to Addy if she hadn't chosen that moment to bolt upright, sending his hand flying.

"What's happening?" he asked, sitting up and shoving the blanket aside.

Addy was busy folding her own blanket with neat, mechanical movements. She didn't pause. "Caro's expressing her displeasure. Again. Probably nothing to worry about, aside from the fact that this room won't be here in another ten minutes."

Maunga reached for the pack. "Ten minutes?"

"Mmm. She likes to keep me on my toes, especially since I stopped testing full-time." The picture of Addy and Challa came off the wall; Addy folded it and slipped it between two creases of blanket. The whole bundle slid into the under-stuffed pillowcase and she slung the drawcords over her shoulders, ready to go.

Clearly the cardboard was staying here.

She didn't test anymore? Theo rolled up his blanket and shoved it into the open neck of Maunga's handbag-backpack. "What do you mean, since you stopped testing?"

"Later." She knelt to deactivate the sound plates and slipped them into a pocket. "We have to go. Are you coming or not?"

"Of course we're coming," Maunga said, dropping down out of the alcove to the floor. "Door or ceiling?"

"Ceiling."

Theo shouldered the pack and followed them, his brain struggling to catch up. He hated not having enough time to wake up properly. It made him feel so slow, especially because Maunga had an annoying tendency of springing out of bed and thirty seconds later looking as alert as if she'd never earned that glorious case of bed-head. It wasn't that he took hours to wake up; it was just that he didn't have a superhuman ability to do it in ten seconds flat.

They reached the cavity in the ceiling tiles. For a moment he wondered if Addy would want a hand up; but of course, she must have done this a hundred times before without their help. She leaped, grabbed the lip, and chinned her way up without a sound. Good thing the ceiling was low.

Maunga went next. Theo brought up the tail without too much trouble. It was a tight fit to get through—the opening had been made with Addy's scrawny frame in mind, not his broad shoulders.

The hole in the ceiling was cramped. To either side of them fell empty space, flimsy-looking backsides of tiles, and the skeletons of wires and cross-braces. A beam perhaps a metre wide provided stable footing. At least they wouldn't be walking on tiles that could give way at any second.

Light ghosted up from the hole they'd come through. Theo rolled away from the edge and Addy reached for the ceiling panel to replace it. He peered along the cavity; it was the same thing as far as he could see, wires and beams and cross-braces, on and on into the greying light.

He just hoped Addy knew where they were going—assuming there was any choice. This beam they were on looked rather lacking in options; it was forward, back, or nothing.

By the time Addy had replaced the panel, there was barely enough light to see where to put his feet.

"Surprised you had time for that," he murmured, worming his way past her to where Maunga squatted a few metres down the tunnel.

"Always," Addy said. "It takes Caro time to check the cameras. Anything to delay her and stop her catching up to me."

"That happen often?"

"Not for a while now." A tremor ran through the beam. She waved them on down the tunnel. "Keep going. The ceiling's keeking low, I know. Hands and knees is your best bet, or you can try crouch-walking if you don't mind the strain on your hamstrings. No, Caro's only caught my location three or four times since I left, for which I'm grateful. It's not a nice experience when it happens."

They shuffled along in silence for a few minutes and then she added, "I'm getting better at finding my way out. Last time it only took me five and a half weeks."

Theo wasn't sure he wanted to know. "Out of where?"

"Testing." And that was it. She might as well have flashed a sign that screamed *topic closed, move on.*

"That's an expansive explanation," Maunga drawled from her place in front of him.

The old Addy would have flushed and subsided; this one made a dismissive noise in the back of her throat. "Well, it's all the explanation you're getting for now, so deal with it."

There was no verbal response, but Theo was sure he caught a flash of white teeth in a pleased grin. Maunga liked pushing, and she liked a healthy bit of pushback, too; pushing people and having them fall over and submit to the teasing was no fun at all.

Sometimes he caught himself wondering what she did in counselling sessions when she couldn't push and push and push until she got a reaction. Professionalism would take over, he supposed. She might get away with pushing a little bit for those of her clients who needed it, but for the ones who didn't need it or wouldn't handle it, she'd just have to bite her lip and button up the sarcasm for later.

Ow. His hamstrings burned. He sighed and shifted onto his hands and knees. That was better, even if it was arguably the most undignified method of travel since the bum-shuffle. The strain eased almost immediately from his thighs.

No, strike that—it was even more undignified than the bum-shuffle. At least with a bum-shuffle you could stay mostly upright and not have to crane your neck at a horrific angle to see where you were going.

The tremors grew stronger until they were inching their way along the beam, staying low, clinging to the edges with spread knees and outstretched fingers. More than once Theo thought the bucking might throw him off, through the flimsy panelling and into the disintegrating room—or whatever now lay below them. It was hard to tell how far they'd come. He only gave a passing thought to how far they still had to go.

"Everyone still there?" Maunga called back from the front.

"I'm here," Theo said.

"Here," Addy seconded. "It's okay. It'll stop soon. Probably."

"Probably?"

"It can take Caro hours to destroy a room and reform it, but we're nearly out of the blast zone. Maunga, there should be an intersection coming up. Hang a left when you get there."

"Will do."

"Had much experience with this?" Theo asked, gritting his teeth and hanging on for dear life as another ripple shook the cavity.

Addy prodded him from behind, urging him to keep moving. "A fair bit. Practice makes, uh, better. I'd rather not bump into her minions. It's easier to be up and moving when I know the consequences of *not* doing it are . . . undesirable."

Ha. Undesirable.

If that wasn't the understatement of the century, he didn't

know what was . . . although Maunga's *I don't want kids* probably ran a close second, if he was honest. He shuffled on. Maunga turned left a second before she called back, "Left turn here."

"Good," Addy said.

It was an awkward business, moving through a right-angle turn to another beam that was maybe half as wide as the first. But he managed it. The thought crossed his mind that Addy had been crawling paths like these for years. She'd always been smaller and lighter than him, mostly by dint of being four years younger and female. She'd be, what, maybe half his weight now? And a beam that had easily held her slight frame now had to bear three people, two of whom were, well, *not* suffering the effects of chronic malnutrition.

He hoped it held.

"So what's with the crazy physics around here?" he asked.

"Don't know," Addy said. "I have a couple of theories, though. Either this place rearranges itself around the room you're in—"

That would explain the change of scenery while he'd been in the bathroom.

"—or Caro found a way to weave VPS tech into the walls, and it's all a giant hallucination. It's been different since the last time they moved me," she added, frowning.

"You know you've been moved?"

"Yeah. I've got no idea where I *am,* mind you, but I didn't know where the last place was either, so it's no great loss. I just know they've moved me."

"Who's *they?* You mean Caroline?"

"And her underlings. You know she went rogue from Breach a few years back?"

Theo blinked. "No."

"She said she got sick of their constraints. But since we moved here it's like she's not in charge anymore. The whole place feels different. Maybe she got bored with me and put one of her minions on the case so she could work on something else."

"Minions?"

"You don't want to know."

"Which way now?" Maunga called back, interrupting them. "We've got a left, a right, and a straight ahead."

"Right," Addy said. "Not too far down. I'll tell you when to stop."

It was probably only ten minutes, but it felt like at least an hour. His muscles were on the verge of full-blown cramp when Addy called a halt, slid her head and shoulders over the edge of the beam, and started working away at a panel. He promptly sat down, wriggled around until he could stretch his legs out in front of him, and started massaging his left calf.

"Alright?" Maunga asked. She scooted closer and gave him a hand with the other calf.

"Will be." He set his teeth against a fresh wave of almost-cramp and blew a breath out as it passed. It was his thigh that time; he targeted his brisk rubbing at the problem areas, and by the time Addy had the panel up he felt safe to move again.

"You two can go first," Addy said.

Maunga shot a glance at Theo but dropped down through the hole without demur. Theo followed, bending his knees against the jarring landing, and twisted to keep Addy in his sight. She stayed up in the cavity for a minute or so, hands busy, and then slid through in her usual way: feet, legs to the waist, balance, swing down to hang by her fingertips, and then drop from there. She made as if to walk off down the hall and then stopped.

"Actually," she said, "if you give me a leg up, Theo . . ."

"Yeah?"

"I'll put that panel back."

He laced his fingers and boosted her up without a word. Keek, she was light. He'd thought it wouldn't be much of a test of strength, but this was so easy it would have been laughable if the reasons behind it weren't so sobering. Lifting a twenty-two-year-old woman to ceiling height wasn't supposed to be practically effortless. He tried not to think about it too much, focusing on holding her steady while she pulled the panels back into place, and failed miserably.

What he wanted to do was feed her a triple bacon cheeseburger and large chips, washed down with a chocolate nutrient shake, but that would be a recipe for disaster. Her stomach would be . . . keek. He didn't even want to think about how much it would have shrunk over the last six years.

She found food often enough or in adequate quantities to avoid starving to death, that was clear. But it still left a host of options, each more troubling than the last. *Hunger was a ground state of being,* she'd said, and, *I'll do for a few days yet.*

He wanted to hunt down Caroline and strangle her with his bare hands.

Maunga would never let him, he knew. Partly because she knew exactly the sort of psychological damage taking a life could do and partly because she wanted that privilege for herself. And wasn't that twisted: the psychologist wanting to murder someone in cold blood herself, because she was better prepared to take a life and better prepared to bounce back from the experience. It was incredibly selfless, in some ways. She didn't want blood on his hands, so she'd do it herself. He could understand that. He didn't want blood on her hands, either.

He'd held her through too many sweat-soaked nightmares, when she woke panting with bloodlust, her system surging with adrenaline, that ugly light of violence and deep-seated rage in her eyes. Something inside her wanted it, wanted the thrill and the payback.

He knew what lurked in the darkness of her dreams.

But she didn't have to give in to it. He'd spare her that, if he could. Even if it meant doing it himself.

And he knew it lacked any semblance of logic, he knew it was stupid that they each wanted to kill Caroline to spare the other person having to do it. Stupid didn't even begin to cover it.

But love made you stupid, sometimes. He'd meant it when he said he'd do a lot more than burning Caroline's floor for Maunga. He loved her with every molecule of his being; there was very, *very* little he would balk at to keep her from harm. And killing Caroline would harm her, he had no doubt about it. Medics made the worst patients, and that held true for medics of the mind, too. She couldn't cure herself, and all the theory in the world wouldn't save her from the ugly, retching reality of what it was like to take another life.

She thought she was prepared. Maybe she was.

But he didn't want her to have to find out.

"Hey." There was a hard rap on the top of his head. "You can let me down now."

He shook himself and lowered Addy to the floor. Enough. There was no point worrying about it before it got here.

But that was the only way he knew to steel himself: if he thought out every pitfall ahead, every twist and turn of the path, every way the situation could go wrong and what he could do to stop it.

They found themselves in a wide, featureless hallway. White tiles stretched before them, covering floor, walls, and ceiling without a break. Theo stifled a groan. He was sick of white tiles. They made him feel like he was stuck in a loop of hospital corridors—though thankfully without the ever-present smell of antiseptic.

"I hope you know where we are," he said to Addy. "And where we're going would be even better."

Her eyes crinkled over the rim of her mask. "We're in-between, as much as there's ever an in-between. And we're going *out.*"

"Helpful," Maunga muttered. "In-between where? And what do you mean, *out*?"

"What do you think I mean? Out as in out, obviously."

"You know the way out of the testing facility?"

"Yep."

"So why are you still here?"

"Because I might be able to find the way to the border, but the problem is getting past the exit." She started off down the hall, Theo and Maunga hard on her heels.

"What's at the exit?" Maunga asked.

"You'll find out."

"Or," Theo broke in, sick of Addy's delay tactics, "you could tell us now so that we've got time to prepare for it, instead of being taken by surprise when we get there."

Addy's stride faltered. "I could." One hand slid under the drooping lapel of her blanket-vest to scratch at her collarbone. "Sorry. I forget it's not just me anymore."

"We're right here," Maunga said.

"I know." Her pace picked up again. "You might be here—" she waved a hand around them at the panelled hallway "—but I'm having trouble keeping you *here*." She tapped a finger against her temple. "It's not the first time I've hallucinated people coming to rescue me, and please don't waste breath telling me that you're not hallucinations, because that's what they said too."

Theo reached out and pinched the back of her neck, right where he knew she'd drop her head and hunch her shoulders against the sensation. He'd done it often enough as a shock tactic when they were kids.

She did hunch her shoulders, but she also slapped his hand away. "Please don't."

"Sorry." He dropped his hand. "Still think we're hallucinations?"

"I'm almost certain you're not. Have been since I first saw you. It's just a case of reminding myself of that."

Maunga skipped ahead to fall into step beside Addy. "How can you tell?"

"I'd rather not get into it."

He thought Maunga would press the issue, but to his surprise, she backed off. "Alright. Back to the in-between thing, if you don't mind."

"I don't mind. In-between is, well, that. We're not in a space designated for testing or travelling between tests. It's non-space, if you'd like, and therefore less observed than the testing grounds."

Theo fought an impulse to check around them for holocams. "We're still observed?"

"Indubitably." There was that ironic lilt she'd always injected into the word. "Or at least we would be if Caro wasn't looking elsewhere right now. Which she is. I think."

"You *think*?"

"Mmm. I keep a few distractions set for when I need space to myself." She slid an amused glance at Theo, clearly catching the projected thought that she'd *always* needed space to herself, even when she was coming off the tail end of a week-long reading binge. "I know. But sometimes I need it more than usual. Caro's not very good at respecting that, so I have to guard it with a certain, ah, vehemence."

"For example . . . ?"

"I may have taught myself how to build and set distance-tripped, time-delayed explosives."

He barked a laugh and heard Maunga laugh with him. "Good on you."

"So right now she'll be focused on the room right next to the crypt—"

That must be the room they'd slept in. "Is it actually a crypt?"

"No idea. But it seemed as good a label for it as any."

"Ha. Sorry, carry on."

"When she started disintegrating the crypt, I started the timer on the mine. It was set to half an hour or four hundred metres, whichever came first. I'm never certain of distances around here. I think four hundred metres was about when we took that right-hand turn. Knew where we were headed for, of course; I wanted her to be looking the other way when we dropped out of the ceiling."

"And she is?"

"Reckon so. She's never been as good at keeping an eye on

the in-between spaces, anyway. Seems to think I live my life on the testing track—which I have done but only when I didn't have any other options." The angelic arch of her eyebrows was a stark contrast to the hard glitter of her eyes. "I've got options now. Lots and lots of options. And now that you're here, one of those options is *get the keek out of this place.* Thanks for that, by the way."

"You don't have to thank us for coming to rescue you," Theo said.

"I'm not."

What? That was unexpected. "Oh . . . kay then."

"I didn't need rescuing."

Maunga snorted.

"But I did need help finding a way past the border. And you can help with that."

"So glad we're of *utility* to you," Maunga said, laying a peculiar stress on the word.

Addy stopped walking that time. Maunga stopped too and stared her down, arms folded, feet planted. Theo looked between them, puzzled. What on earth were they on about? Maunga clearly knew something he didn't; she looked peeved, and Addy was losing composure under that steady glare.

Addy's eyes dropped. She heaved a tremulous breath. "Sorry. I shouldn't've . . . I'm sorry. You're not just utilities."

"No," Maunga said. "We're not." Her face softened. She stepped closer to Addy and laid a cautious hand on her arm. "It's okay, Addy. I know it's been a long time, and it'll take even longer to recover. But you can. You can recover, and you will."

"I used to think that, too." Addy kept her eyes averted. "I'm pretty resilient, aren't I?"

"You are."

"But resilience isn't the same thing as recovery."

Maunga's eyes narrowed. Her head tilted. "No. It isn't."

Theo knew the signs of her client-brain rearing its head. Something had struck her as curious or unexpected. She was balancing on that knife-edge she'd mastered so well over the last five years, client-brain analysing while her personal-brain empathised.

"Quite different," she said. "But it's fine. Like I said, Addy, you can recover. We can help."

It took him a moment to interpret the sound coming out of Addy's mouth: a laugh, rusted and mirthless. "Sure you can."

Maunga's lip twisted. She turned to him. "Theo."

"Mmm?" He tore his gaze from Addy's face.

"Those nights you can't sleep . . ."

Even the memory made his stomach drop. "What about them?"

"Tell Addy what I tell you. Please."

He closed his eyes and summoned the memory of the words and the force of emotion behind them. "We'll find her. We'll bring her home. And if she's broken then we'll fix her."

"And I mean it. We both mean it."

Addy looked between them for a long moment before shaking her head. "What if I don't need fixing?"

She turned on her heel and strode down the passage, leaving them staring perplexedly after her.

Theo swore under his breath.

"Steady," Maunga murmured.

"What does she mean, what if she doesn't need fixing? Of course she keeking needs fixing! Didn't we just prove that with the forgetting-we're-here thing? And the rescuing-her thing? And the keeking I-don't-think-I-can-recover thing?"

"I can still hear you," Addy called back.

He grunted and jogged to catch up to her, falling into step on one side of her as Maunga did the same on the other side. "Look," he said, trying to sound reasonable, "you can't just say you don't need fixing, Ads."

"Can," she said. "And did, in fact. Would you like me to say it again?"

"I don't think that's necessary," Maunga put in dryly.

"Looks necessary from where I'm at."

"Why's that?" Theo asked. They turned a corner and he saw Maunga shiver as a gust of cool air blew over them.

Addy huffed a breath. "You're not listening."

"I am."

"No, you're not. You might be hearing me, I don't know, but you're sure as keek not *listening.*"

"So tell me. Talk to me, Ads; talk to *us*. I'm trying, okay? And you sidestepping the real issue isn't helping."

"The real issue?"

"Yeah."

"What—" She broke off, brows contracting in bafflement. "The real issue, what do you—?"

"Theo," Maunga cautioned.

"Where do I start?" Theo grasped for patience and missed by a mile. He ignored the clear warning from Maunga. Addy always had needed a bit of a push to start talking. "The testing. What did it involve, who carried it out, how did you escape? The startling lack of any major trauma, the small miracle that you're not curled up a sobbing wreck on the floor? What have you been *doing* these last six years? And why are you so keeking stubborn and you won't accept our help? Maybe it slipped your mind, Addy, but we broke in here to get you out! The least you can do is answer our questions!"

"The least *you* can do," Addy retorted, "is respect my boundaries! I said I'd tell you later!"

"That game's getting really old, really fast! Why can't you tell me now?"

"Because I'm not ready!"

Her words struck him like a slap to the face. He fell silent, breathing fast and shallow, and was startled to see tears in her eyes.

"I'm not ready," she said again, more quietly. "Can't you—can't you respect that? Please, Theo. I'm trying, too."

Well. Now he felt like the worst brother in the world. He'd made her cry. "Addy," he said bleakly. He groped for the right words, but they wouldn't come. "Addy—don't—please don't cry. I'm sorry. I didn't . . ." He trailed off and scrubbed his hands over his face, feeling very old and tired. Addy had always needed a push, but she wasn't *that* Addy. Not anymore. "I shouldn't have pushed. I'm sorry."

He opened his arms, bracing himself for rejection, and wasn't surprised when she hesitated, eyes wary over the rim of her mask. But she stepped into the embrace willingly enough, wrapping her arms around him and tucking her head under his chin. He stroked her horrid hedgehog haircut and tried not to hear her valiant efforts at stifling tears.

She shouldn't have to stifle them. He shouldn't have caused them in the first place.

But they hadn't been the closest of siblings even before she went away. The four years between them had felt like four decades, sometimes. He'd been puffed up on his intelligence, so convinced that he was light years ahead of her and that she'd never catch up.

He'd held up his work ethic as an example: she'd be in bed at ten while he was still up and studying at one in the morning, but he'd ignored the fact that she was up at six most mornings while he didn't wake up until ten or eleven unless he was dragging himself to an eight o'clock class.

She'd been younger and shorter and quieter, more immature and less capable of holding what he deemed an intelligent conversation, and he'd used that, all of it, as justification for not even trying to get along with her.

But how often had he tried to have an intelligent conversation with her before she lost her voice? Or before *he* lost his voice, even, for those hellish four weeks?

Not often. Not nearly often enough.

Life as a whole was one big learning process. Twenty-seven felt like a lifetime too late to start learning how to relate to his little sister. Twenty-two probably felt too late to her, as well, especially after the isolation and abandonment of the last six, nearly seven, years. But it was better they learned late than never learning at all, wasn't it?

Even if she was adamant that she didn't need fixing, she still needed support. She might not think she needed counselling, but he knew she did. She sure as keek didn't need fights, and that he could agree with.

And she could do with a hug, couldn't she?

Yeah, he thought as she snuggled closer. She could definitely do with a hug. She'd missed so many of them over the years.

Time to start making up for it.

But she disengaged after far too short a time, stepping back and pivoting on her heel to continue on down the hall. He was growing used to it. He could have stayed wrapped around her for hours, content to just feel her breathe, but her tolerance for prolonged physical contact was clearly at an all-time low. She had good reason for that, he knew. He was happy to accept what little physical affection she would give.

Any was better than none—and more than he'd expected when they planned this expedition, if he was honest.

"Alright?" he asked Maunga, seeing her shiver again. They turned another corner in the everlasting in-between. He was unsurprised to see yet another white passage stretch before them. But he supposed, if this place was the back of everywhere, there was no need for any variation in lighting or colour or floor level. It wasn't like Caroline was expecting anyone to use it.

And speaking of Caroline . . . He darted a look over his shoulder. Nothing. Strained his ears. He could hear their breathing and the faint ever-present humming of the facility, but nothing else. Safe, then. For now.

"It's keeking *cold*," Maunga said, wrapping the loose folds of her leather jacket around herself and tucking her hands back into her pockets. "Aren't you freezing?"

It was a bit cool but not enough to make him unpack his hoodie. "It's not that bad." He'd always run hot.

She groaned under her breath and called ahead to the slight form away down the hall. "Oi! Hold up a second!"

Addy turned and started back toward them. Maunga dropped the pack to the ground and rummaged through it. "Cold?" she tossed over her shoulder at Addy. "I can find you some gear if you want."

If she was looking for validation, she was disappointed. Addy shook her head. "Is it cold? Hadn't noticed. I'm used to it."

Used to doing without, anyway. Theo tamped down on the reflexive surge of rage that came with the thought.

He watched with no little amount of amusement as Maunga shrugged out of her black jacket, pulled a thick jersey on over her warm shirt, and put the jacket back on. She wound a wool scarf around her neck, tucking the ends down and through in a movement he didn't quite catch. The end result looked something like a very stylish pretzel. After a moment's thought, she retrieved a knitted hat and stowed it in her pocket for later.

"Right." She shouldered the pack. "Let's go. Before Caroline catches us."

CHAPTER NINE

Three corners later, Theo had to admit that the temperature was dropping. Maunga had pulled her scarf up over her nose and mouth, shaking her head at him as she did so. He grinned back at her. He was still warm enough in just his merino shirt. He might dig out his hoodie in a while if it kept getting colder, but he was fine for the moment.

They needed to keep moving if the expression on Addy's face—or what little he could see of her face between the black breath mask and the raised hood of her navy blanket-vest—was anything to go by. But a short stop to drag their winter kit out wouldn't hurt. Better a minute or two of delay now than suffering frostbite or hypothermia later.

Keek, would this in-between space never end? On they walked, and on, and still there was nothing but gleaming white tiles to be seen on every side. He caught himself suppressing a shiver and nodded to himself. About time.

"Maunga," he said. "Hoodie?"

She shot him a knowing glance. Rather than lowering the pack, she simply turned her back so he could open the flap. "On the top. Gloves are there too, if you need them."

He frowned. "I didn't pack winter gloves."

"They're your engineering gloves. Of the thin, warm, very insulated variety."

"Oh, those ones."

"Mmm. Those ones."

"Thanks." He pulled out his ratty old hoodie and shrugged it on. "But not now. Maybe later."

"Alright."

"I can take the pack if you want."

She shook her head. "I'm fine."

They caught up with Addy, who had stopped at the next intersection to wait for them.

"Warm enough now?" she asked Theo.

"Yes. Are you sure you're not too cold? We brought extras for you."

"Told you, I'm fine."

He wasn't fool enough to say he didn't believe her. "Okay. Let me know if that changes."

Addy grunted, but whether it was an affirmative grunt or a dismissive one, he couldn't tell. "We should keep moving. We're getting near the border."

Already? He'd expected at least one overnight stop before they reached the edge. It couldn't be that easy, could it?

But Addy had said it was that easy to get to the exit. Getting *through* the exit, on the other hand . . . that might take a bit more work.

That was alright. Work was fine. What was life without a challenge? If they could just walk out of here . . . well, for one thing, Addy would have done it years ago, and for another, he'd be looking over his shoulder for the rest of his life wondering why Caroline had let them go.

Now *that* would be a dastardly plan to instil a boatload of paranoia in them. Somehow he didn't think it was her end game, though. She was more the immoral-neuroscience-testing-for-moral-neuroscience-advances type.

Or at least she had been six years ago, from what he'd gathered reading Addy's book. Who knew? She could've changed since then. Keek, he'd changed, and Maunga had changed, and Addy had definitely changed. It wasn't much of a stretch to suppose that Caroline might have changed, too.

A flicker of a headache jabbed him behind the eyes. *Ugh.* How long had it been since he'd had a drink? He dropped back a couple of strides to keep pace with Maunga and slipped the water bottle off its strap. It was still more than half full, and icy cold as it hit the back of his throat.

Mmm. That was better. Maunga held out a hand as he was about to fasten it to the strap again, and he passed it over.

"Careful," he said. "It's cold."

"Better than being hot," she murmured and forestalled his next comment with a quick flick of the eyes.

Ha. Was he really that predictable? "Didn't say anything."

"You were thinking it."

"Was I?"

"Yes. You were."

He smiled, and then the headache made itself known again, stabbing deep at the back of his eyes, and the smile slid into an involuntary grimace.

Maunga frowned. "What's wrong?"

"Nothing. A bit of a headache, that's all. It'll pass."

She thrust the water bottle into his hands. "Drink."

"I just did." He drank anyway, relishing the first few gulps of cold water. When the third sip turned sour in his mouth, he pulled away in shock, spluttering, water splashing down his hoodie and onto the floor.

"Careful!" Maunga grabbed for the bottle. "I said *drink*, not drown yourself."

"That was—ugh." He worked saliva into his mouth and spat, trying to get the bitter taste out of his mouth. "Yuck."

"What?"

"It's *rank.*" He took a cautious sip, ready to spit it onto the floor to prove his point, and blinked. Swished. Swallowed. "That . . . what? That one was . . ."

"Aaaanytime now."

"What?"

"You," she said. "Speaking English. In full sentences."

"Speak for yourself."

A trace of a grin appeared on her face.

"It was sour," he said. "That mouthful, when I pulled away. It tasted foul, like it'd been dredged from the bottom of a sewer pond or something. But now it tastes fine."

"Problem?" said a voice behind them. Theo turned to see Addy drumming her fingers against her leg.

He frowned and took another wary sip of water. It was fine: cold, clean, not even the faintest hint of sewer sludge to it. "No problem," he muttered. "Must have been my imagination."

"Hmph." She beckoned them forward with an over-elaborate flourish. "If you wouldn't mind keeping up . . . ?"

He proffered the water bottle. "I'd rather we didn't fall foul of dehydration."

Addy rolled her eyes but took the bottle, drank two of the measliest sips he'd ever seen, and passed it back. "Happy? Can we go now?"

They went on down the hall in a cluster of three. Theo could see sporadic puffs of steam in the air when he exhaled, and he wouldn't have been surprised if the white glitter of tiles was hiding ice crystals in their corners. Good thing they'd thought to bring winter gear, even though it was barely mid-autumn up in the city.

They rounded the next corner and Addy faltered, causing Theo to bump into her. He caught at her shoulder to steady them both. "What is it?"

"Unexpected," she said, a puzzled twist to her mouth. "Is what it is."

Before them, the endless white came to an abrupt end. A smooth wall rose in a horribly familiar shade of puke green to block the end of the passage. The monotony of smooth plaster and unrelenting colour was broken by a gaping hole at the base. Theo took a step forward, squinting.

Ah. No, it wasn't a hole; it was a doorway. The door itself was no more than a sliver of shadow on the other side of the wall, and he could see the dim gleam of metal steps starting up from the floor beyond it.

"This isn't the exit, then?" Maunga asked.

Addy shook her head. "This is where the exit has been every other time I've made it this far. It was here just yesterday."

"And now it's not," Theo said. *Ominous.* "Caroline must have known Maunga and I were here. We weren't exactly being quiet on our way through."

"You did set fire to her floor," Maunga said. "Multiple times."

"She deserved it."

"Yeah, but it wasn't the most stealthy thing to do, was it?"

He shifted from foot to foot. "Perhaps not."

"And now she's moved the exit," Addy said.

"Can she do that? Move it, just like that?"

She flashed an empty smile. "She can do a lot more than that." She blew out a breath. Her right hand dived under the collar of her shirt to scratch at her collarbone. "I don't like it."

"I'll second that," Maunga muttered.

"Thirded," Theo said. "But can we risk going back? Or do we have to go on?"

"No such thing as binary," Addy said.

"Sorry?"

"Binary. There's no such thing, not here."

He didn't get it.

She sighed. "You're still thinking in pairs. Binary. Zeroes and ones, back or forward, do or do not. It's not that simple. There's never only two options. Never."

"So, what, you want to head up through the ceiling again?" He hoped not. His hamstrings throbbed at just the thought of it.

"Or we could take a couple of panels off the wall and see what's on the other side—I'll give you a hint, it's probably a testing chamber—or go down through the floor, or . . ." She trailed off, lifting an eloquent hand. "You see? Options."

"Options, right," Maunga said. "That's all well and good. But we still have to make a decision."

"Obviously we're going that way." Addy nodded at the open doorway.

"Obviously? Why's it obvious?"

Addy's eyes crinkled at the corners, the ever-present weariness and cynicism lifting for a fleeting moment as that age-old light of mischief and adventure gleamed in their depths. "Because it's new." Her voice thrummed with a tone Theo hadn't heard in more than ten years: amusement, bone-deep assurance, the infinite thirst for knowledge and the deep joy of discovery.

"Alright then." Maunga rubbed her hands together and met Addy grin-for-grin—or rather, smiling eyes for smiling eyes, since she still had her scarf wrapped around her nose and mouth. "Let's do this."

"Hang on," Theo said. "We're just going to wander on in there? When we know that Caroline knows we're here, and that in all likelihood she knows that we know she knows? She moved the exit specifically because she knew we were coming! She could have put anything on the other side of that door."

Addy considered this. "Yeah, but we're not going to find out what's on the other side by standing here, are we?"

"It could be dangerous."

"Most likely."

"And you still want to go?"

"Dangerous is old hat. It's nothing. But new territory . . . that's exciting." She bounced on the balls of her bare feet. "I thought there was nothing here, Theo. Apart from the exit, I mean. But now there's *something*. Don't you want to find out what it is?"

"Not really."

"Tough," Maunga said. "Because we're going. So unless you want to be left behind . . ." She shot him a look that said, *I sympathise with you but this is not a fight you're going to win, so just go along with Addy for now, please?*

He nodded grudgingly, hiding a wince as the headache throbbed double-time in his temples. "Fine."

"Thank you."

"Just . . . proceed with caution, yeah? There's no telling what she's hidden in there."

Addy snorted. "Thanks for the advice."

Theo dropped back as they approached the doorway, letting Addy take the lead and Maunga go next. The headache was building steadily. With any luck, it wouldn't cross the threshold from discomfort to true pain, but he didn't like his chances. Of all the times to get one! Maybe the close air in here had brought it on. He'd suffered a few in that way while writing his thesis in the cramped storage cupboard of an office the faculty had given him.

Behind the wall lay a square bit of floor, maybe twenty metres by twenty metres. The walls angled outward as they rose, fading from light grey through charcoal to black. But . . . huh. That was strange.

He took a quick step back to the door, then another step so that he was out on the white tiles, and cast an assessing look straight up. No, he'd been right. The wall on this side was perpendicular to the floor. That was definitely a right angle—as right an angle as he'd ever seen in ten years of engineering.

But from the other side . . . he stepped forward again and through the door. Another look up. It made his head spin. He lowered his gaze quickly. The same wall sloped outward from the top of the doorframe, its angle matched by the angle of the other three walls.

Non-space. Or dual-space. Right. That was fine; he just had to not think about it.

In the middle of the room stood a metal staircase that zigzagged its way upward in the dim light. It wouldn't have won any design awards: it was bare-bones industrial, red metal grillwork below and orange metal handrails to each side. Landings jutted out high above, balconies and catwalks springing off from the main staircase and disappearing into the gloom.

Well. It was better than climbing into the crawlspace under the ceiling again, and not too much worse than the Grosvenor Block at uni, which past generations had affectionately dubbed the Fire Tower.

"Going up?" he asked.

Addy nodded. "Going up."

Again, he let the women take the lead. He hated to admit it, but his head was still spinning from that deliberate look at the impossibly sloping walls. No doubt it would settle as he climbed. He took a deep breath in through his nose, held it, and let it out through his mouth.

One foot after another. He could do this. The metal of the handrail was cool under his palm. He wrapped his hand around it, welcoming the grounding. Time to climb.

He counted the steps automatically. Sixteen up the first flight to the turnaround. Sixteen again up the second flight to another turnaround, lungs burning in his chest. The third flight was easier. His breathing eased as he stepped off the last rise and onto the landing. Maybe it wouldn't be so bad. The landing wrapped around the staircase, catwalks lancing out from two sides, a wide platform jutting from a third. No safety rails there, he noted. Caroline wouldn't be the sort to worry about Health and Safety compliance, not way down here.

Addy and Maunga were already halfway up the next flight. He started after them. Just focus on the next step. And the next step. That's it.

The headache grew, pressing at his temples from the inside. The handrail was sweaty under his hand. Strange. He hadn't seen Addy hold the handrail at all, and it was far too cold for Maunga to be sweating. The rail felt slick the whole way up to the turnaround, and even past it. He blinked, eyelids heavy. Keek, he was tired. And cold. Or was he hot?

It was him sweating, he realised. That was why the rail was slick. He was sweating and feeling his own sweat. That explained it.

Why were the others so far ahead? They'd reached the next landing and were starting up the next flight. He'd barely cleared the last turnaround. Above him, a dark head appeared over the side and called something to him. The words filtered down, muffled and distant. He shook his head at them, raising his free hand to shrug. The head paused and then turned to its twin for a quick conference before yelling something else. He caught parts of it that time.

"We . . . wait for . . . next . . . okay?"

He shot the dark head a thumbs-up and vaguely hoped they weren't from a culture where it meant something offensive. His feet were so heavy. One step. Another step. One step. Another step. And again. Keep trudging. Thattaboy. Man. Human . . . thing.

His mouth was dry. Because he was breathing through it, that was why. He closed it and tried to breathe through his nose, but that became suffocating after two or three breaths, so he went back to suffering the icy sting of cold air on the roof of his mouth. It might be cold, but at least he was getting enough oxygen that way.

He reached the landing, turned, and kept climbing. Only a single flight from here to the next landing, thankfully. He could see the two dark heads waiting for him. Maunga.

The fog retreated, the pounding in his head lessening for a brief, blessed moment. Maunga. Maunga was up there, and—and someone else. Addy? Why had she crossed his mind? He hadn't seen her in years, not since she decided to be all self-sacrificing and went traipsing off to test with Caroline for the rest of her life. But she stuck in his mind anyway, a slim, dark burr that he couldn't for the life of him shake off. Fine. Let her stick, then. Maunga was there, and Addy, for some insane reason, was there, and—

And he was in trouble.

His hand shook where it clung to the rail, white knuckles

stark against grey-brown skin. He wasn't thinking straight—and the effort it took to summon that thought, to grasp the individual words and cudgel them into line, made him realise just how much he wasn't alright. His head was clouded. His temples ached. His heart pounded, ribs tight, eyes hot and gritty. His hands sweated; he knew that because the rail was slippery from it, but still his fingers shook as if from cold . . .

He was in trouble.

Keek. Was he what.

The half a flight remaining stretched into infinity. Had Caroline done something to it? It looked endless. He could climb those stairs forever and never reach Maunga.

His heart clenched at the thought.

No. No, that couldn't happen. He had to see Maunga. Had to—had to—something. Tell her something. Ask her? No, tell her. He licked his lips, the movement clumsy and slow, and felt a drop of moisture fall. Sweat? Saliva? He didn't know. It didn't matter.

"Maunga," he said. It emerged as a rasp, dry and croaking. He could barely hear himself; there was no way she would have heard it, not kilometres away up those stairs. He tried again. "Maunga." Better, but not by much.

He wiped a trembling hand over his mouth. His hip hit the rail.

What? Oh.

He'd taken his hand off the rail and his body had overcompensated for the lack of balance. And now there were two rails there, blurring into and through one another. Dual-space again? Two things inhabiting the same space had always seemed impossible. This place delighted in making the impossible exist. He grasped for one rail, missed, flailed, reached for the other one, and found it. He wrapped his hand around it and found that the shaking in his hand had spread to the whole rail.

Keek.

He brought his left hand up to steady his right. Pressed down hard on it. The shaking petered out. *Whew.* He'd thought the place was going to shake itself to pieces around him, and all because his stupid hand wouldn't stop trembling.

"Theo?"

He jumped. There was someone right in front of him. "Sorry," he muttered through dry lips. He was blocking the staircase. Of course they wanted to get past. He pressed up against the rail, redoubling his grip, not daring to look over the side.

"Theo."

Whoever it was sounded concerned. He raised his eyes to peer at them and felt his eyelid spasm. Maunga. It was Maunga. "Um," he said. There was something he was going to tell her. Something important. "I'm—not feeling good."

"You think?" A warm arm slipped around his back. "Come on, lean on me. We'll just get to the next landing, Theo. Ten steps, maybe fifteen, that's all it is. You can do it."

"I—yes. I think." They were moving. He tried to grip the rail and found himself gripping Maunga's shoulder instead. That was alright. It was a nice shoulder. Very warm, and, and comfortable . . . "I think," he repeated, more firmly that time. That was right. He *did* think. It was one of the things he did best, thinking.

"Good to hear. Addy!"

"Yeah?"

"He's in trouble."

The air turned blue ahead of them. It couldn't be Addy up there, then. Not his Addy. His Addy didn't swear like a sailor. It must be a different Addy. She was even using words that he didn't recognise, and that was an achievement in itself.

"If you're quite finished?" Maunga sounded as if she was walking a fine line between amused and stressed.

The swearing stopped. "Right. Done. Yes. Sorry. How bad is it? What're his symptoms?"

"He said he had a headache earlier. We thought it was just a spot of dehydration. His taste buds went weird, too; the water was fine, but he swore one mouthful had tasted sour or—or bitter or something. But he tasted it again and it was fine, and I tasted it and it was fine, and you didn't notice anything off about it, did you?"

"Can't say I did." Addy's voice sounded close now.

"Here we go. One last step, that's it."

They'd reached the landing. His eyes had fallen shut at some point, Theo realised; he opened them and frowned. It was dim and shadowy up here, and everything looked strangely blurred. "Who t-turnnededdd . . ." Oh, that wasn't good. He stopped, gathered his scattered cotton-wool thoughts, and tried again. "Who turned . . . the lights . . . out?"

Addy swore again, short and sharp.

"Hey," he said. "Lang . . . lannnggg . . . guage."

"Sorry." A shadow crouched in front of him and a cool hand touched his forehead. *Mmm. That's nice.* "Theo." Her voice was tight. "Can you focus for me? I need to know your symptoms."

"Symptoms?" He'd managed a whole question that time. That was something to be proud of, surely.

"Symptoms. What's wrong? Does anything hurt? Can you breathe properly? How's the headache?"

Ugh. Too many questions. He squinted against the shadows and muttered, "Achy."

"Yeah, I know." Addy drew a breath. "Please, Theo. Think. Symptoms."

His flailing hand caught her wrist and, despite the shaking, he managed to wrap two fingers around it to touch the pulse point. That was better. She might not be *his* Addy, but she was *an* Addy. He could do anything if Addy was alive in front of him.

Even summon enough coherent thought to relay his symptoms.

"Headache," he said.

"Good. Anything else?"

"Hands are . . . shaking. Might be cold. Feel hot. And cold."

"Okay. Your forehead feels hot; you're likely running a fever."

"Eyes are itchy. Heavy. 'm really . . . really tired." The headache took him again, stabbing white-hot pressure into the backs of his eyeballs. He tightened his grip on Addy's hand and rode it out, gasping.

It passed, sweeping away the fog with it. He took advantage of the brief clarity. "Head," he panted. Tears prickled at his eyelids; he blinked them away and sniffed. "Hurts. A lot. S-sweaty. Shaking. Hot and cold. Balance is . . . completely off. Memory's fuzzy. Can't breathe properly through my nose—"

The pain came again, suffocating any conscious thought. He held his anchor and gritted his teeth against it. It would pass . . . it would pass . . . would it pass? . . . please let it pass . . . please.

It drew down, tighter, tighter, stifling the air in his lungs . . . let it pass . . . and it passed, lifting away like morning fog before the warmth of dawn. He breathed, grateful as he had never been before for cold air in his lungs.

"Here," a voice said. A hand cupped his mouth. He flinched away. "It's okay, Theo, they'll help." Strong fingers prised his jaw open. Slipped the capsules in. Held his mouth shut while he fought the hold, blinded by the ebb of the pain, and then a fingertip stroked down the middle of his throat and he swallowed convulsively. "They're down," the voice said, and the hands let him go.

He couldn't move. When had he sat on the floor? He didn't know. "Please," he said, hearing his voice shake, hearing the tears in it and not caring, "please."

"What do you need, Theo?"

He knew that voice. It washed over him, soothing, warming him from the inside. "Maunga."

"I'm here. Not going anywhere." Her voice held an echo of his pain. "What do you need?"

He shook his head, all coherent thought flown before the onset of the storm. "I—I don't . . . " It hurt. It hurt so much, not just physically but mentally, and he couldn't think, he couldn't move, there was nothing but pain. He had to tell her. Had to—had to tell . . .

If he managed nothing else, let him manage this. He lifted a hand, grasping. "Maunga."

She caught his hand. He'd know those fingers anywhere. That smooth skin. That heat. "I'm here," she said again. The words were light, a flimsy veil of nonchalance over the bottomless well of her worry. She was hiding her concern. Making this easier. For him.

Godsend. That's what she was.

"Can you stand up?" Addy asked. It took him a long, long moment to realise she was talking to him. "We need to move, Theo. We can't stay here. We're too exposed. If we can make it across one of those catwalks, there might be some place we can shelter. But we can't stay here."

The words flowed around him. He was dimly aware of them. He even understood them, the way a stone understands the river that washes over it without leaving a mark. "Maunga," he said again, and heard Addy draw a shaking breath. The sound rang a dusty bell in his memory. She was important. Even if she wasn't his Addy, she was still *an* Addy, and Addy was important. She should know that. "Addy," he said.

"We're here," Addy said, taking his other hand. Her fingers were so small. So thin.

He worked saliva into his mouth, overdid it, felt some dribble over his lips. Took a gasping breath. His ribs screamed. "Love you."

The pain came down again and darkness took him.

CHAPTER TEN

Maunga caught Theo's head and got an arm around his shoulders before he could hit the ground.

Keek.

Pulse, there was a pulse fluttering in his throat. Good. His colour was terrible, and the air rasping in and out of his open mouth sounded like someone had shot a whoopee cushion with a splinter gun, but at least he was still breathing.

"We need to move him," Addy said from where she crouched on the other side of Theo.

Maunga nodded, trying to pummel her thoughts into some sort of coherence. "Yeah. Can't leave him out here." She lifted a shaking hand to tuck a loose strand of hair behind her ear. "Do you know what's wrong with him?"

Addy's eyes darkened. She didn't answer the question. "If you want to take his shoulders, I can take his legs."

Grip. Brace. *Lift.* "Oof, he's heavy."

"Yep." She jerked her head toward the nearest catwalk. "Down there. There might be a room we can put him in."

There was. The catwalk took them through the sloping wall to a narrow corridor lined with doors. They left Theo slumped against the wall and went to investigate.

"Office," said Addy after peering into the first room.

"Same here," said Maunga from the other side. The door was thin plywood. Dark grey carpet lined the floor. The walls were the same pale green she'd seen throughout the complex. Caroline must have bought the paint wholesale. Clearly she had no sense of aesthetics whatsoever; it looked like someone had downed an entire bag of frozen mint peas and then upchucked in a hospital waiting room. *Ugh.*

They went down the long hallway to the first corner, checking each room, and found only office after office. Had a team worked here once? Or was it just more scene-setting, like the bathrooms yesterday? The rooms were furnished sparsely: desk, chair, empty bookshelf, filing cabinet. Nothing in the desk drawers. Nothing in the filing cabinets, either. Had they been used and then abandoned? Had they even been used at all?

Who knew?

"In here." Maunga backtracked to the second office on the right and pushed the door open.

"Why that one?" Addy asked.

"Why not? It's clean—"

"They're all clean."

"And empty—"

"They're all empty."

"And the first door on either side is too obvious."

"Which makes them a better place to put him."

Maunga frowned. "Double bluff?"

"Exactly."

"Somehow I doubt it really matters."

"You don't say." Addy bent to take Theo's legs again. "Second office it is. She'll find him anyway if she really wants to."

And wasn't that a cheerful thought?

They made Theo as comfortable as they could in the corner, sitting him on the floor with his back propped against the wall, legs outstretched. Maunga pulled the olive blanket out of the pack and wrapped it around him. Addy made sure that his head was tipped well to the side so that he could breathe, and then she knelt down and started fiddling with the straps of her breathing mask.

"What are you doing?" Maunga knew Addy had said there was nothing wrong with her, but she couldn't stop the lurking concern that there was an underlying condition, whether diagnosed or not. The last thing she wanted was for Addy to collapse from a damaged lung. At the same time, she was insatiably curious about what lay beneath.

As it turned out, what lay beneath the mask was Addy's face. Admittedly it was rather cleaner than the rest of her, and even a smidgen paler, although that could have been due to the lack of compacted dirt. But it was definitely her face. That was a relief. And her breathing was fine even without the mask—another relief.

"Tip his head forward a bit, will you?" Addy asked.

Maunga did so carefully, acutely aware of the sweat-slicked skin, the clamminess, the uneasy movement of his eyes under the closed lids. Addy slid the breath mask around the back of his head, fitting it over his nose and mouth before strapping it closed and sealing the rims with deft fingers.

"There," she said. "That'll help. I don't think it'll do anything for the poison already in his system, but it should help his breathing, and it'll stop him ingesting anything more."

"Poison?"

It shouldn't have been so surprising. They'd had a remarkably smooth trip so far, even counting the mental mind-trip of the hallways with the voices. But it was surprising. Shocking, even. Maybe she was so used to the psychological that she'd been discounting the merely physical.

But it wasn't *merely*, not when Theo lay here passed out from the pain. He'd been in such agony that he could barely think. Couldn't even string a coherent sentence together. No, it wasn't *merely*. Not by a long shot.

"Poison, yeah. It's not life-threatening, don't worry. It won't even leave him with permanent damage if we can get to the antidote in time."

"What?" Panic swelled, ugly and suffocating. "Permanent damage. What do you mean, *permanent damage*?"

"Calm down—"

"Don't tell me to calm down, not when my husband is lying there unconscious!"

Addy eyed her over Theo's slumped form. "He's my brother. I know what it feels like, okay?"

"Sorry." Since when was Addy the rational one? Maunga forced the fear down. Panicking wouldn't do anyone any good.

Addy muttered something under her breath.

"Sorry?" Maunga said again. "Didn't catch that."

"I said," Addy repeated, "this is exactly why I didn't want anyone doing the stupid thing and charging in to rescue me."

"It's not stupid."

"Looks it from where I'm standing."

Maunga took a deep breath and broke eye contact. "Why didn't you want anyone coming to get you out, then?"

"I didn't say I didn't want people getting me out of this place. Would've done anything to get out of here the first few years. But I don't like having other people in here with me."

"Why not?" Maybe if she repeated the question often enough, Addy would actually answer it.

"Because it's just one more person to get hurt. Or two more, in your case. And when one of them is Theo . . ." Her mouth thinned. "I can't afford that."

"I don't want him getting hurt either."

"When it's just me, it's fine," Addy went on, as if Maunga had never spoken. "I can handle it. I get hurt, sure, but it's only me. I don't have to pretend not to care when it's just me. But Theo's different, he always has been, and you're here too, and it's a vulnerability I can't afford right now. Not when I'm this close to finally getting out of here."

That was some twisted logic, Maunga thought, but on some levels it made sense. "We might be a vulnerable spot for you. I know Theo is, anyway."

She wasn't too sure how Addy felt about her, Maunga, with the contrast of a) stealing her voice way-back-when and b) marrying her brother, and now wasn't the time for a heart-to-heart chat on the subject. "But it doesn't make us something you can just write off. We're here to get you out, Addy, not drag you down."

"You'll get hurt." Addy's eyes were fixed on the wall.

"Then we get hurt," Maunga said. "We knew the risks when we started planning this jaunt years ago. We knew that you'd likely be hurt yourself, and we knew that we could be hurt, and we decided it was worth it. One or all of us could die and it—well. I was going to say it would still be worth it, but it might not, to be honest. Depends."

"Depends on what?"

"On who dies. And who lives. And who's doing the weighing up about whether it's worth it or not. If Theo dies and you live, he'd probably say it was worth it. Don't know that I would."

Addy's eyes flicked across to meet her gaze for a split second before darting away again. "Got it."

Keek. "Whatever you got from that—it's not what I meant."

"You're not willing to trade his life for mine. I get it. It's fine. I'd probably say the same to you."

But she wouldn't. Maunga could tell she was lying, or at least flubbing the truth. She wouldn't look Maunga in the eye and say, *If you die and Theo lives, it's worth it*, not even after the hell of the last six years. She wasn't that sort of person.

She'd trade herself for either of their lives, no questions asked; had done, in fact, on the day of the VPR session. She'd sacrificed herself for the well-being of Theo and Maunga and five hundred others. But it was like she said—it was *different* when it was just her.

Talk about a hero complex.

If it was Addy's life and only her life on the line, she was content to make the trade. But if it was a choice between the lives of two friends, or a family member and a friend, or a family member and an enemy-turned-cautious-ally-turned-sister-in-law . . . nah. She couldn't make the call, not then.

All lives were equal . . . except her own. Addy thought her own life was worth *less* than anyone else's.

Again with the twisted logic, and wasn't that a whacked-up inversion of the way it usually went. Most people's self-survival instinct was so strong they'd trample children in a crowd trying to get away from perceived danger; Addy's would probably have her racing *toward* it.

Oh, it wasn't unheard of. Far from it. Dozens of historical greats had suffered from an overwhelming sense of selflessness, or rather enjoyed it. But it didn't make it any easier to understand, this casual upside-downing of hedonic motivational theory.

Maunga could comprehend it in a small way. Take her and Theo, for example. They'd been distant acquaintances, and then a friendship had been born out of mutual emotional hardship. Deep friendship had grown from there, and love, commitment, marriage, and the rest. Divorce rates were catastrophically high for the first few years of marriage. They'd survived five, and their love had only deepened over time, despite the fights and the petty frustrations of everyday life. She would die for him. Or kill for him. Or give up the rest of her life, as Addy had done, so that he could be free and whole and well again.

And he would do the same for her, she knew.

Which was essentially what Addy felt: that she would give up—had given up—the rest of her life so that Theo could be well. But she hadn't just done it for Theo; she'd done it for everyone with Vox Pox, all five hundred of them. And if Maunga was right, if Addy's sense of self was so eroded that she saw herself as worth less than any other individual on the planet . . . she probably would have done the same for just one of them.

Munted, that's what it was. Abso-keeking-lutely munted.

Of course, the six years of isolation wouldn't have helped her self-esteem. No doubt her self-worth was at an all-time low. Keek, if Maunga asked Addy to run off and die so that somehow she and Theo could escape this place, Addy would probably do it.

But Theo would never forgive her. Truthfully, she wouldn't forgive herself, either. She might have further to go than the next person to get to some level of basic human decency—no, actually, it was about twice that far, considering the next person was Addy—but even she wasn't callous enough to send a traumatised young woman off to die. She had been once; there was still a twinge of guilt when she thought about taking Addy to that confrontation with Caroline like a lamb to the slaughter. But not now.

She wasn't nineteen anymore.

"Got a spare scarf?" Addy asked.

Maunga shook herself. The poison. Right. "I can do better than that." This could have all been avoided, if only they'd *known*—

But they hadn't.

She reached for the pack and undid the flap. It took a few minutes of rummaging—she hadn't expected to have to use them so soon—but she found the black strips of cloth and pulled them out.

"Here," she said. Despite her frustration, her worry, the all-devouring fear raging against her breastbone, her voice sounded nothing but tired. "Breath masks."

She held one out to Addy, who took it without breaking eye contact. "You had two in your pack? All this time?"

"No." Again, as much as she would have loved to inject some sarcasm into the word, there was only weariness. "There were four in the pack. One for me, one for Theo, one for Dave, and one for you. I told you: we came prepared. If we'd known—" But they hadn't, and it would be unfair to push the blame onto Addy.

She stopped. Ripped her scarf off and focused on fitting the mask to the lower half of her face instead. That was better. Her scarf went back around her neck in loose folds; she didn't need it for warmth quite so much in this small room, but no doubt she'd be grateful enough for it once they were moving again . . . if they were moving again. "You said there was an antidote?"

Addy nodded. She strapped her mask closed, tugged her hood up, and was once again little more than huge eyes and gaunt cheekbones in a dirty sliver of face. "There's always an antidote."

"And there could be permanent damage?"

"Crippling pain and hallucinations in the short term, followed by complete incoherence, partial paralysis, and a general inability to remember who he is, where he is, or who *we* are." The recitation was clinical, detached. "If we don't get the antidote to him in time, the paralysis spreads. I—" The detachment broke; her eyes dropped to Theo's still form. "I don't know what happens after that, if it spreads to the lungs and heart, if he could d . . ."

Die, Maunga thought. A creeping coldness stole over her. "He won't. We won't let him." She didn't need the reason behind Addy's sudden ignorance explained. The lines around her eyes were tight with remembered pain and fear.

How many times had Caroline infected her with this before she'd learned to keep the breath mask on? Even then, she couldn't keep it on all the time; she had to eat and drink. And Caroline wouldn't have had the antidote delivered in a nice, hand-wrapped package, either. She could see it now: Addy testing, whatever that involved, with the slowly spreading poison as a stick and the antidote the very effective carrot. She would have had to earn it. But there were bound to be days when she couldn't, when the poison spread too fast, when she'd ingested too much of it, and once the paralysis took hold . . .

Well. Not much she could do then but hope that Caroline wasn't quite finished with her.

"He won't die," Maunga said again. The icy hand gripping her heart loosened at the words. "Where's the antidote?"

"Back the way we came." Addy turned toward the door. "You can stay here with him, I'll go—"

Maunga took two strides and caught her shoulder, spinning her around. "Not on your life."

"You don't know where it is, you can't go."

"Nobody said one of us had to go it alone, you idiot. We're both going."

Addy's gaze darted over Maunga's shoulder. "But Theo—"

"We'll be fast. He won't even know we're gone." She doubted he was aware of anything but the pain.

"I'd rather go by myself," Addy muttered.

"Last time you went off alone anywhere near Caroline you ended up volunteering for a lifetime of unpaid labour. I'm not letting that happen again."

"Please don't pretend you care about me."

Maunga blinked. Was she that blind? "Of course I care about you."

"Why?"

That was the question, wasn't it. *Because I still feel guilty about stealing your voice* was only part of the truth. *Because you're Theo's sister* was another part. "Because I respect you," she said finally. "And I respect very few people, believe you me."

Dark eyebrows contracted over hollowed eyes. "Why?"

"Why do I not respect many people?"

"No, why do you respect *me*? I'm no one important."

Talk about the fundamental misunderstanding of the century. "But you are, don't you see? You found a cure for Vox Pox."

"Finding the cures wasn't hard. You took me straight to her."

"But to get them out of that office, to negotiate for citywide distribution, and in such a short period of time—that was incredibly important."

"Anyone could've done it. You could have, if you'd wanted to. Anyway, that's only what I did, it's not *me*. It doesn't make me important."

"It does." She didn't understand, Maunga could see. "It's not just what you did, it's the way you did it. I went into that room fully prepared to sell you out, I admit it. I would have used you as a bargaining chip, traded you for Seth's release, for freedom. I wanted out from under Caroline's thumb and I didn't care what it took to get that. And *you*—" She shook her head. "You could have pre-empted me. Used me as a bargaining chip the same way I was going to use you. But you didn't. I . . . I still don't really understand why. I would have deserved it after everything I'd put you through. But you didn't. You did what I would have done, you used *you.*"

"So what?"

She really didn't get it, did she? "You *did what I would have done.* You used my own tactics against me, but you twisted it so that somehow, incredibly, you were only hurting yourself." Maunga rubbed a hand over her face. "How do I explain this . . . do you know the concept of a worldview? A paradigm shift?"

"More or less, yeah."

"What you did that day, Addy . . . it flipped my world upside down. I mean, okay, Theo's your brother. So what? I wouldn't subject myself to eternal slavery for *my* brother. Theo was, what, twenty? An adult. Well capable of taking care of himself. He didn't need you to rescue him. But you did it anyway."

"You need to widen your social circle. Or expand your leisure reading. Because, seriously, it's in a lot of books."

"I didn't say I still believe that *now.* Just that I didn't believe it *then.* Six years is a long time. A lot of things change."

"You're telling me." Addy's eyes lingered on Maunga's left hand, where her wedding rings gleamed.

Maybe it was time for that chat. "Does it bother you?"

"We need to get moving," she said abruptly.

Or maybe not time for that chat after all. "Okay."

"If you've got anything in there—" she jerked her head to the pack at Maunga's feet "—that'll help with the pain, I suggest you give it to him. And make it a double dose of whatever amount you were considering. He'll need it."

Maunga nodded. She wouldn't do a double, not with the risk of heart failure at those concentrations, but stronger-than-usual, that she could work with.

She found the vial of somno-analgesic and fitted a dosage-

and-a-half to the injection gun before crouching at Theo's side. His eyes curled tight with pain as she watched; cheeks mottled a ghastly grey-brown, he groaned and stilled. The familiar tousled curls fell over his forehead, damp with sweat. She brushed them away. His breathing hadn't improved since they'd laid him here. Hopefully the pain reliever would help with that, taking him through this agonising half-sleep into true unconsciousness.

Reaching for a travel towel, she wiped away the worst of the moisture from his forehead and temples. It was a pointless effort. As soon as she took the towel away, more droplets sprang up. But she had to do something.

Hmm. She couldn't get at the usual injection site with the breath mask in the way, and she wasn't willing to risk moving the mask, not even for something as small and quick as a jab with a vapo-needle. The secondary site would have to do. It was equally as effective in terms of potency. Just a little more, well, embarrassing for the patient.

But Theo was unconscious, and it was nothing she hadn't seen before, and with the way Addy was positioned, she wouldn't see a thing. She'd have to be peering around Maunga's shoulders to see the site.

Maunga tugged the sterile cap off with her teeth, yanked the waistband at the back of Theo's trousers down while lifting with a knee under his thigh, and slid the needle home. There. In. And out. Done. She dropped her knee to the floor, pulled the trousers back into place, and recapped the needle. Pain relief administered in two seconds, and with the patient's dignity—and that of his immediate family—intact, no less. Her emergency first-aid instructor would be proud.

"What was that?" Addy asked, stepping over Theo's legs to squat at her side.

"Something for the pain. Combined sleeping agent and pain reliever. Somno-analgesic, if you want to be technical about it."

"Double dose?"

"A double could kill him. I gave him strength and a half."

"Alright, then." Addy stood and took a step toward the door. "If you're ready to go now?"

"Ready when you are." She changed the needle out for a clean one, threw the injector gun back in the medkit, and tucked it out of sight under Theo's blanket. She wanted it within easy reach in case he woke up while they were gone. As an afterthought, she slid a pack of emergency food rations under there as well. And a water bottle. You never knew.

Cold-weather gear in place: check. Breath mask in place: check. Pack on her back: check. Addy's makeshift sack on *her* back: check. Good to go. She waved Addy onward out the door and stepped out after her, pulling the door half-closed as she went.

Time to move.

~

Footsteps faded away down the hall outside the little office. The echo of quiet voices lingered and then dissipated. The memory of strong emotion stayed longer: wide splashes of red anger, swirls of brown-black pain, tight coils of worry in dark blue shadowed by purple guilt and sneaking deep green blame. Two colours underpinned it all. Fear loomed, suffocating in dark grey; and love spread everywhere in blinding white, brighter and louder where it shone through the fear.

Silence drew down, hovering near the ceiling at first and then spreading with more confidence. Along the ceiling to the corners of the walls. Down the corners. Out across the floor. Before long it clung to every centimetre of pale green wall and soaked into every strand of the thick carpet.

But it didn't touch the burly figure in the corner.

Every time it tried, there came another gasping breath. The sound tore from deep inside him, ripped from some unfathomable place that still clung to life. It emerged small and fragile to reverberate in his small corner of the office, reaching less than a metre into the silence before dying away.

The battle continued. Silence ... and sound. And silence ... and sound.

Now he thrashed his head weakly from side to side. A thin moan trailed from dry lips. Eyes flickered behind heavy eyelids. He didn't wake.

Silence.

And sound. Another shallow breath.

Silence.

Silence.

Sound.

His breathing deepened, grew steady and slow. His eyes ceased their uneasy movement. His head slumped against the wall and stilled.

The silence drew as near as it could, watching. Waiting.

A noise disturbed it. A quiet *click*, so soft it would hardly have been heard by human ears.

It retreated in a small flurry.

A hairline crack appeared in the wall not far from his head. Grew until the outline of a square could be seen. The top of the panel swung out and down as if on a hinge. It halted when it reached just past the horizontal, a perfect square plate of shiny white metal, startling in this dull room of green and grey and brown.

If he were awake, he would have seen two thin, raised edges on the plate, like train tracks or guide rails.

If he were awake, he would have seen a vial of viscous blue liquid roll down the rails and bounce to a neat stop against the rim.

It was within easy reach. If he were awake, he would have lifted his hand and taken it.

And he would have read the label: *ANTIDOTE.*

INTERLUDE

The voiceless we have heard, and on this day we vow
To trace the spectral pulse of your wounded heart—
It matters not the time, it matters not the price—

CHAPTER ELEVEN

They set off down the hall at a loping run, heading for the stairs. Maunga's pack bumped up and down on her back. She reached for the hip straps to stabilise it and then remembered that this model didn't have any. *Blast.* She gritted her teeth and tightened the shoulder straps. It helped a bit. Not much, but a bit.

Her boots clattered on the grillwork as they emerged from the carpeted hall to the metal of the catwalk. Addy was as quiet as ever, padding along on the balls of those calloused, bare feet.

It had felt a long way along here when they were carrying Theo's inert form; it was much shorter heading back, and not just because they weren't lugging an unconscious, fully-grown man. She drew back a little as they came to the landing, letting Addy take the stairs down a step ahead of her. She didn't know where they were going. Addy did. Letting her lead could save them precious seconds.

Where they were going, it turned out, was right back down to the ground floor. By the time they got there Maunga's lungs were burning. She breathed through the pain, clamped an arm to the cramp in her side, and kept running. Jogging a leisurely ten kilometres on the virtual rollerbelt was a tad different from this mad dash down flight after flight of stairs. She was surprised Addy was still ahead of her, to be honest; she'd thought she was fit enough for this jaunt, whereas Addy was about as far from peak physical condition as you could get.

But perhaps the testing relied on a certain level of fitness.

Whatever it was, she was grateful for it. They didn't have time for cramp or pain or delays—not from her, not from Addy. Thighs aching, lungs protesting, she kept running.

As they careened through the open door to the everlasting white tiles, Addy slowed to a loping jog. Maunga slowed with her. This place had changed since they were last here: the tiles stretched forever, straight and wide, in a line that sloped gently upward without kink or corner.

"How long have we got, do you think?" she asked between breaths.

"An hour, maybe." Addy faced forward, eyes darting from floor to walls to ceiling ahead of them, not once coming close to looking at Maunga. "Longer if we're lucky. Less if we're not."

Nothing like a bit of time pressure to get the old heart racing. "How long will it take to reach the antidote? Actually, where *is* the antidote?"

"Knowing Caro? It'll be in the reward stand at the end of one of the hardest test chambers I've never completed."

Wonderful.

"And I don't know how long it'll take to get there. Depends on how this place is feeling. Could be ten minutes, could be ten da—"

The floor gave way beneath their feet. Maunga grabbed the scruff of Addy's vest and yanked her back from the edge almost before conscious thought had had time to form. White tiles fell into darkness as one row collapsed. Heart pounding, fingers still firmly curled into the blanket at the nape of Addy's neck, Maunga watched as a second row followed suit, and then a third.

And that was it. Three rows gone. Nothing else moved. The walls, ceiling, and remaining floor tiles were as still and solid as they'd ever been. It was just this abrupt chasm at their feet, three tiles wide.

The tiles were, what, a metre square? About that. It would be a three-metre leap to get across, then.

She uncurled her fingers from Addy's vest and let her hand drop, noting the tremors running through it in passing.

"Has that, uh, happened before?" she asked Addy, marvelling at how steady her voice remained.

Addy moved her head slowly to one side and then back, eyes fixed on the vanished floor before them. "Nope."

"Are we going on or around?"

"On."

"Can you jump it?"

By way of answer, Addy stepped back three paces. She took a deep breath. Tucked her chin. Ran forward and *leaped*—

And landed safely clear of the far edge.

"Yep," Addy said. Maunga was sure a cocky grin lurked under that black mask. "Question is, can you?"

Maunga could, and did. "My legs are longer than yours, ratbag," she said from where she'd landed an easy half-metre past Addy. "And I'd lay money they've got more muscle, too, but that'd hardly be fair."

They went on, sticking to a fast walk this time. Maunga found her fingers itching, trying to fasten themselves onto Addy's collar even though the danger had passed. She stilled them with an effort. Addy wouldn't appreciate the mother-hen-ing, and she had better things to be doing than turning overprotective on her twenty-two-year-old sister-in-law, no matter how traumatised the girl was or how vulnerable she appeared to be.

The vulnerability was only an appearance at times, she was certain. Of course, at other times there was no doubt that six years of undernutrition and stress and physical hardship and psychological horror had taken their toll: when she got out of here and the PTSD set in fully, Maunga was going to have one hell of a recovery case on her hands.

But sometimes the dirt and the exhaustion and the leanness was just a veneer over something deeper and stronger than Maunga could even guess at. Sometimes there was an amused gleam in Addy's eye, an adroit lift of an eyebrow in response to something Maunga or Theo had said. It was enough to make Maunga wonder about her dominant and secondary stress reactions and how they might have changed since she went away.

A phrase hovered at the back of her mind and on the tip of her tongue: a single double-barrelled word for what this was. She could describe it in six syllables. But she wasn't sure yet. And she had to be sure. There was no room for error, not here. So she watched, and waited, and felt the guess solidify into near certainty.

Further on down the hall, the floor collapsed again. Even at their ground-eating walk, they had plenty of time to step back from the edge. Maunga watched in silence as one row fell away, and then a second, and a third, and a fourth. The fifth started to fall. She was just starting to feel nervous—five metres was a long way to jump even for her, and Addy was shorter and physically weaker than she was—when the rows stopped plummeting into the black.

Five. Five rows. Alright. They could do this.

She backed up a couple of paces and took a breath, ready to leap the chasm—

And Addy held up a hand to stop her.

"What?"

"Look." Addy pointed to the side of the hole, where white tiled walls plunged down and vanished into bottomless black.

It took Maunga a moment to narrow in on it. The movement was slow, but movement there was. A single row of tiling slid down the wall as if carried on a conveyor belt. As it reached the level where the floor used to be, the angle changed; it flowed around the invisible curve and slotted into place where the first row of tiles had fallen away. She watched, fascinated, as it reached the far wall and stopped, seamlessly filling the gap. The next tile in the row followed suit, and the next, gathering speed now—down the wall, around the curve, across the floor to slot into place without the faintest hint of a gap.

But when the first row was filled and the second started to do likewise, she frowned. Surely there weren't enough tiles? They would have to run out at some stage. But it seemed not. High up where the wall met the ceiling, the tiles cascaded down in a line, white panel after white panel appearing past the join of wall and ceiling and coming on without pause.

Well. This place was huge, she supposed. There were probably kilometres of floor and wall left unused. The tiles could just be requisitioned from the spare room to the guest room, so to speak. Like laying a new carpet. Except it was the floor itself.

Really, she wouldn't be surprised if there was a white panel production factory hidden somewhere down here. There was certainly enough space. It would be cheaper in the long run than buying them in bulk, even at wholesale prices. There had to be millions of the things. Breach had never been short of cash, but several million metal panels at a metre square each would put a dent in anyone's budget.

The second row filled and the third began. The tiles were moving faster now. The fourth row half filled before the third finished, and two seconds later the first tile slammed into place in the last row. She almost stepped forward over the gap—it was only a metre wide now, and that was hardly more than a hop, even for Addy—but caution won out. The tiles might not be set yet. Whatever was causing them to fall away might make these ones fall again. She didn't know, but it would pay to wait until the new tiles were finished before she tried to walk on them.

The final tile slotted into place in the fifth row. The row extending up the wall settled and stilled, and once more the hall was an unbroken stretch of white square panels.

Maunga exhaled a whistling breath. "Let me guess—you've never seen *that* happen before, either?"

"Good guess," Addy said. "That was. Um. Weird."

"Agreed." She rolled her shoulders, trying to ease the stiffness. She hadn't realised how tense she'd been watching the tiles fall away and be replaced. "Reckon it's safe to walk on?"

"Reckon there's only one way to find out."

"That wasn't a yes."

Addy's eyes laughed at her over the rim of the mask. "Yes, I think it's safe. Or as safe as anything can be around here, which isn't saying much. And there really is only one way to find out."

"Alright then." Maunga stepped forward, probing the floor with the toe of her boot before putting any weight on it. She made it a mere four steps and then heard a quiet rush of movement from behind her. Addy sped past. Bare feet smacking against the hard tile, she pushed herself high with each bound until she resembled nothing so much as an upright and very dirty deer. Once she was past the danger zone she slowed, winding down to a trot and then a walk. She bent over to catch her breath, eyes twinkling at Maunga from her position upside down.

Maunga moved more confidently after that. She joined Addy, shaking her head. "It's your lookout, kid."

"It is, isn't it?" Addy agreed, head still hanging down between her knees.

"Yes. That's why I said it. It's all well and good doing things like that and nothing goes wrong, but what would you have done if something had? If you'd been mid-leap, gambolling about like that, and the tiles dropped out from under your landing spot?"

"I would've dealt with it like I've dealt with everything else since I've been here. This place is weird, and I mean seriously weird. You haven't seen the half of it. And I thought that TheraRPG session was bad." She snorted.

"I've got a pretty good idea of how weird it is," Maunga said. "And I know the consequences would've been bad."

Addy lifted a shoulder in an eloquent shrug. "Look, you're not my mum, okay? You can stop worrying about me. I'm fine."

I'm fine. It was such a *normal* thing to say. It fitted fine in the world out there, above them, with jobs and friends and casual passing enquiries about your health; but down here, in this strange environment of endless white tiles and random bathrooms and voices that spoke out of nowhere with your deepest fears . . . down here it stood out like a curse in a cathedral.

Maunga couldn't help herself. She laughed. It emerged

belly-deep and full of mirth, an unexpected explosion of humour in the sterile air. It was a sea breeze on a hot summer's day, a mug of steaming coffee after a crisp autumn walk. Refreshing.

But she felt more than saw Addy take an involuntary step back, hollowed eyes uncertain. The laugh stopped.

"I'm sorry," she said, grinning and shaking her head, "but really—*I'm fine?* Is that the best you can do? It's an outright *lie,* Addy. You're not fine, not in any way, shape, or form, any more than I am or Theo is. You don't have to pretend. I'm not going to judge you for being a bit under the weather after close on seven years of hell."

"Ten," Addy said, shoulders stiff, her eyes averted.

Interesting, that—dating it from the day she lost her voice rather than the day she signed up for the testing. Between thirteen and sixteen, Addy had still had what amounted to a fairly normal life: the routine of classes and assignments, the support of family and friends, the familiar environment of a bustling city.

Going off with Caroline had ripped all of that from her. She'd had nothing down here, no routine, no family or friends, not even a whisper of a connection to the city above. It had just been her and Caroline, for whatever that was worth, and a sterile and increasingly hostile environment.

Maunga couldn't wait to dig deeper into that. Had that first three years been worse than she'd thought? Or maybe it had all rolled into one, the trauma and the horror blurring the lines between past and present, between there and here. Addy was twenty-two now. How much of her life before thirteen could she even remember, before the testing, before Vox Pox?

She was willing to bet it wasn't much.

"Ten," Maunga agreed. Addy had said ten, and so ten it was—according to the self-perception of the client, anyway. She would reserve her own judgement until she'd had time and opportunity to explore that more. Her inner therapist was rubbing her hands already, awaiting the challenge with bated breath. *Bring it on.* Physician, heal thy sister-in-law.

She would—that was, if her sister-in-law hadn't by some miracle healed herself. It was possible. Probable, even, putting the pieces together and adding one thing to another. But there were bound to be bits that didn't click, the odd jigsaw piece that was out of whack. A corner here, a mis-cut hole there. She could help. She *would* help.

Addy would be well.

They walked on in silence. Addy's step was a little less jaunty now. Maunga's stride was longer than it had been, more confident. They kept pace beside each other with ease, and Maunga for one was content just to walk and watch and think.

It wasn't an uncomfortable silence. They'd always spoken more with silence than with words. She couldn't remember a single proper conversation between them in the weeks between their TheraRPG session and Addy leaving; well, apart from the fight, but that was different. After they'd made up, it had been enough just to spend time with someone who had been through what they'd been through. To know that there was someone who really understood. There had been long silences broken by scattered sentences, bits of conversation that blossomed and died.

She didn't mind the silence, and she didn't think Addy did either.

~

The antidote sat motionless on the guide rails. Beside it, Theo's head drooped, forehead propped against the pale green wall, breath coming steady and without the pained rasping effort that had characterised it when Addy and Maunga left. He slept deeply, far from the agony, far from the knowledge of the havoc the poison was wreaking on his system. The room lay silent. There was no clatter of footsteps on the metal catwalk heralding their arrival, no whisper of air conditioning, no hint of the movement of hundreds of panels floors below him as they shifted in their circuitous dances.

And then there was sound: a long, drawn-out blare of sound, featureless aside from sheer volume.

It came from the earpiece that had been thought dead, still tucked in his ear.

"—we in?" said a voice.

"I don't know," said a second. "Are we?"

"I'll try the signal breaker again," said the first.

The long blare of sound came again, loud enough to make flurries in the silence on the far side of the room. Theo didn't stir.

"That should do it. I'm surprised we haven't heard him yet. I thought you said he was asleep, Challa."

"No, he's drugged," said Challa. "You were in the bathroom when it happened. I'm sure I told you."

"Drugged?" The sharp question was at odds with the sound that came next: a gaping yawn, rising and rising again before falling to rest.

"Yeah, Dave," she said. "Drugged. Now shut up, please, I need to talk to Theo, and I can't concentrate with you nattering in my ear. Grab us some coffee from downstairs, will you? Ta." Footsteps faded away. "Okay. Theo, are you there?"

He was, of course. But he wasn't awake.

"Theo? I need you to wake up. I know you're drugged out of your mind, which is a good thing, really, because your mind isn't a pleasant place to be right now, what with the overwhelming pain and all. But I need you to wake up now. Please."

Theo slept on.

"Come on, Theo." Challa's voice rose and fell in careful measures, the cadence steady as a heartbeat. If she was worried, if the matter was urgent, it didn't show in her tone. There was an unhurried note to it, an ebb and flow and an ebb again. She could keep it up for hours. "We need you. Maunga and Addy need you. I need you to wake up now, Theo. The antidote is right in front of you. All you have to do is lift your arm and take it. We've got your visual; we've got Maunga's visual, too, but we can't get through to her.

She's too far down, buried under too many layers of interference. Wake up, Theo, just open your eyes. You're on the right track. This is the way to the exit. The twins did a spot of careful hacking, and the staircase was behind Addy's exit all along. It's at the top of the stairs, Theo. Your exit is at the top of the stairs."

She went on, measured, unhurried, beating back the silence with her words.

Theo's breathing was just as measured, deep and slow, safe within the shelter of blessed unconsciousness. He didn't wake.

CHAPTER TWELVE

"How long's it been, do you think?" Addy asked after a while.

Maunga scrunched her nose, thinking. "Dunno. Forty minutes?"

"I would have guessed fifty."

"Then why did you ask?"

"Because I wanted to laugh at your silly underestimation of time." She looked at Maunga, straight-faced. After a moment her eyes crinkled at the corners. "Because I wanted a second opinion. Obviously."

"It wasn't obvious if I had to ask."

Addy grunted and didn't reply.

They jumped another gap in the floor. Maunga hoisted her pack higher on her back and hummed in thought.

"What?"

"Oh, just wondering what the point of it all is."

"There isn't one," Addy said with all the assurance of having lived here for years. "There's no point to most of what goes on here. It's all supposedly for science, but . . ." She shook her head. "Nah. No point. Well, no point besides 'let's screw with the heads of whoever's in here.' That's about it."

Maunga blinked. "That was gloriously cynical."

"Thanks."

She hadn't meant it as a compliment. Or as an insult, for that matter. Just an observation. "Welcome."

They walked on. And on. And *on.*

"Me, too," Maunga said when she noticed Addy flinch as her foot landed on white tiles and the floor failed to give way. "Who needs a collapsing floor when you can make paranoia do the job just as well?"

"I hate this," Addy said through gritted teeth.

"Join the club." Maunga took a hasty step back, but it was only her imagination. She blew out an irritated breath and kept walking.

Another hundred metres down the hall, the floor really did give way.

"Uh oh." Addy scooted back from the edge, dragging Maunga by way of a hand on her wrist. "That can't be good."

"You don't say?"

It wasn't just one or two rows collapsing this time, or even five or six. The whole floor for a hundred metres or more fell down into bottomless black. The ceiling receded upward, and the walls drew back, too. In less than a minute, a bottomless pit the size of a rugby field lay in front of them.

And then tiles started to slide back into place.

"Keek," said Addy.

"What is it?"

"If I'm right . . ." But she didn't finish her sentence.

They watched in silence.

Tiles rose up along the centre of the pit, forming a narrow, curving bridge that connected the floor at this end to, Maunga assumed, the floor at the other end. There were no handrails, not even a shin-high ledge to demarcate the line between white tile and black space. It would be a single-file job.

But they weren't done yet.

The walls drew back again. Single rows of panels slid outward, six from each side, leaving massive gaps between them. They shot out toward the centre of the pit. She thought they would join the bridge to form a sort of grid, but they stopped short. Was it too far to jump? She squinted, trying to gauge distance. Yeah, that looked way too far.

More panels lanced out from the sides to slot into place beside the existing rows. For a moment it looked like the world's weirdest double-sided bar chart. If she tilted her head, she could almost see the pattern to it . . .

No. It was gone now.

The bars grew thicker by the second. Another minute and they'd all be joined together down the length of the field. But they grew shorter, too, each outward growth stopping closer to the wall than the last. And then the last rows slammed into place, linking the whole thing together, and Maunga saw it.

Oh. Clever.

The pit was an ocean, of course, and the central path was the bridge. Jutting rows of panels formed six narrow peninsulas down each side of the bridge. And each peninsula was joined to the next by a curving bay of tiles, the path from one point narrowing to a single panel along the edge of the wall before it widened again and swept out to the next point.

Clearly they were meant to walk across the bridge and so be exposed from both sides. She wasn't that stupid. Could they go around this space? Pry off a wall panel, sneak around the back? Maybe. It could take a long time, though, and she'd hate to stumble into one of Addy's test chambers.

Hang on. Maunga straightened, peering at the empty gap between the floor she stood on and the nearest end of the linked peninsulas. It didn't look too far. How many seams in the wall beside it? One seam. Two panels. That made it a two-metre jump.

She and Addy could hop that. It would sure beat traipsing down the bridge.

Opposite each peninsula, wall panels slid up and away, leaving two-metre-tall openings at regular intervals down both sides of the pit. Something stirred behind each doorway. She felt Addy tense beside her.

A moment later shadows blocked the doorways. Chinks of lights filtered past at the top corners, but that was all. Whatever the shadows were, they stood nearly two metres tall and almost a metre wide.

And then they stepped forward in unison, the tops of their heads brushing the frames of the open panels, and the light fell on them.

Oh, *keek.*

They looked like a robotic cross between an overgrown human and an octopus. From the waist upward they were more or less humanoid: sleek metal heads, broad shoulders, a curiously hourglass torso. Below the waist, where she would expect to see two stout legs on a human, there were a dozen or more curving, metallic tentacles. They were black and oily, a stark contrast to the smooth silver torso.

At first she thought they edged the bottom of the torso like a long, stiff skirt. But then the creatures started to move and she saw that she'd been wrong.

There were three rings of tentacles. It was the neat overlapping and interlocking that had made them look like a single layer. When the creatures moved, the tentacles undulated, the inner and outer layers moving one way and the middle layer moving counter, keeping them upright as they slithered their way across the floor toward the tips of the peninsulas.

The human half of the creatures had arms that looked like they could knock you unconscious with one blow. But that wasn't what scared her. They carried guns: hefty, two-handed things that looked like assault rifles on steroids, quad-barrelled and solid-stocked with a laser sight jutting out one side. What were they loaded with? Poison darts? Hollow-tipped bullets? Splinter shells that burst into a shower of hot, sharp metal fragments just before they hit their target? Whatever it was, it was unlikely to be pleasant.

The human-octopi hybrids—Humanpi? Octomen? Octomen would do in the absence of any better label, she decided—slithered forward down their allocated peninsulas, and halted in the middle of each metre-square panel that formed the tip.

The rifles came up, metal stocks pressing into metal shoulders, safety catches off, fingers at the ready alongside the trigger guard. The laser sights lit up, forming thin rafters of red light that angled up from both sides and intersected in the air over the bridge. Those alien faces turned, smooth and featureless, to face the end of the bridge a bare five metres in front of Maunga and Addy.

"You have *got* to be kidding me," Maunga said. "She doesn't expect us to waltz down that bridge into their firing line, does she?"

"Hope not." A fey light glowed in Addy's eyes—a challenge extended and accepted. "If she does, she's in for a surprise. You take the left side, I'll take the right."

"We're splitting up?"

"Of course we are. I've dealt with these fellas before; they're not half as tricky as they look. Just keep an eye on me and follow my lead." And before Maunga could say *yes* or *no* or *are you out of your mind, we're not splitting up, Theo would kill me if I lost you,* Addy barked out, "Now!" and sprang away to the right.

Maunga was only a second behind her. She set her teeth and ran left, away from Addy, fully aware that in following those instructions she might never see her again.

But this was Addy's home ground and they were facing an enemy beyond anything she'd ever seen before. It wasn't the time to disobey direct instructions, not from her frustrating sister-in-law, not from anyone. Her ego wouldn't get in the way of her survival—or Addy's survival, for that matter. Once they got out of here, it would be a different matter. But for now, Addy knew best.

Maunga tucked her chin and kept sprinting, expecting any second to hear the dull thud of darts being fired or bullets pinging the ground behind her. But the pit was silent. The octomen ahead of her hadn't moved from their guarded poses. It was a small relief.

Addy must have reached the right-hand gap before her. Maunga leaped across the two-metre drop and saw Addy already out on the first peninsula, following the curve of the bay around to where the guard stood, rifle raised. Maunga mimicked her arc, running onward but slower now, watching to see what happened. No weapons, no tools, nothing but her wits and her hands and the sack bouncing up and down on her back—what on earth could she do?

When Addy was within ten or so metres of her chosen octoman, the guard nearest to Maunga moved. It had seen her. It stared across the chasm with that featureless face. The rifle lowered to track her movements. Maunga drew a sharp breath, waiting for the shooting to start, but Addy had judged it well. The gun was too slow, the movements oddly delayed for something that had crossed the floor with such fluidity only minutes before. Before the gun had lined up, Addy reached the guard on her side and ducked down behind it, using it as a shield.

The sight lowered until it rested with pinpoint accuracy on Addy's guard's chest. Would it shoot one of its own? Addy's hand waved out to the side and retracted before the laser could find it. She did the same on the other side. That time the gun fired, something small and shiny flying through the air to impact on the far wall. She'd pulled her hand back in time, though. Closing in on her own guard, Maunga frowned. What on earth was she doing? Was there a point to that, or was she just playing for time?

The guard started to tilt forward.

What?

Its whole body was angling up, away from the stable ground of the peninsula and forward toward the bottomless black. The guard on Maunga's side started firing, small silver pellets flying over the bridge and smashing into the octoman on the other side, who was blaring in alarm. When the first pellet hit, its head turned, automatically seeking the enemy, and found its twin staring back. The next second bullets flew in both directions.

Maunga pushed herself into a sprint. If she wasn't there to tip her guard over the edge and he kept firing when Addy's shield was gone . . . *Keek.*

"What do I do?" she yelled.

Addy's voice came back hoarse and tinny in the distance, panting with effort. "Lift with your legs! And keep behind cover!"

It was that easy? She nearly laughed. Lift with your legs. It was old advice, so old she could remember her grandfather saying it.

Addy's octoman was too busy shooting its twin to take the time to shift its focus to her. She crouched down behind hers, gripped it by one slimy black tentacle-leg, and lifted, pushing up from the bottom of her feet, using every muscle in her calves and thighs, up through her shoulders and forearms. Keek, that was heavy. But it was smoother than she'd expected, too; she wouldn't get it off the ground in one movement, but she didn't have to. It felt like it was on a hinge. She just had to bear up and up, steady, *steady*, keeping the pressure on until it overbalanced and plummeted forward and down into the darkness.

"Alright?" Addy's voice floated over the vast gulf.

"Yeah!"

"Mine's nearly there! Make it quick!"

Maunga grunted and heaved, lifting it another few centimetres in one go before it settled back to its old, slow tilt. "Doing my best!"

Another pellet thudded into her shield. She flinched and adjusted her grip. She heard answering fire, and then another bullet impacted. Her guard gave a wailing bleat and fell silent.

Was it dead? Could they be killed after all? She'd thought it was bulletproof, judging from how much fire it had taken without going down, but it seemed it had finally died.

Good. Now she didn't have to worry about Addy losing her shield and getting shot.

She just had to worry about losing her own shield and getting shot by Addy's guard. *Wonderful.*

"Mine's away!" Addy shouted. "You're getting close. I can tell from the angle. A bit further!"

Good, she didn't have to worry about Addy's octoman. Pity

she couldn't see it fall; the guard was bulky, and she couldn't spare the energy to peer around it.

Drops of sweat stung her eyes. She blinked them away and gave one last heaving pull. *There* it went, tipping up past the axis and falling forward and over the edge. It screamed as it fell, some morbid programming letting it rail against its demise even after it had died. The tentacles were stiff and motionless, curving upward like so many strands of seaweed as it fell; the gun was still tucked to its chin, face blank.

Addy crouched on the far peninsula, eyes bright between hood and mask. She straightened to watch the second guard fall, then shot Maunga a thumbs-up and turned away from the edge. "Next one," she called back over her shoulder. "Good job. Two down, fourteen to go."

Ugh. Maunga's shoulders were tired after just that first one—not sore, not yet, but weary. Another seven on each side would take effort.

But that was alright. Survival took effort. Love took effort. Life itself took a lot of effort.

Now that she knew what to do, the next guard was easier. She reached the shelter of its bulk at about the same time as Addy ducked behind hers on the opposite side of the bridge. Maybe it would be easier to grab onto two different tentacles and lift from two points rather than just one? She tried it, gained a little ground, and then shook her head and went back to the two-handed grip she'd used on the last one. The tentacles were too greasy; a one-handed grip slipped and slid all over the place. Even with two hands, she had to alternate wiping them on her trousers to dry them off. No wonder Addy's cut-offs were so filthy if this was what she'd had to deal with for the last six years.

"Hands!" Addy called.

Oh, yeah. She waved a hand out one side, feeling like an idiot. It started shooting almost immediately this time. Had the death knells from the first two guards put the others on the alert? She repeated the movement on the other side, pulling her hand back in half a second before the bullets started flying. That was better. Maybe Addy's guard would get a lucky hit in and her octoman would stop shooting sooner than the last one had.

She took her two-handed grasp again and started to lift. Her shoulders twinged, a dull tiredness spreading out from her shoulder blades. She pushed it to the back of her mind. It wasn't true pain—wasn't even on the threshold of pain yet. It might be painful by the time she was halfway down her line of eight octomen, but that would be a while away yet.

What she needed, she thought as the guard slowly tilted up on its axis, was a way to take out the guards so that they couldn't fire at her or Addy anymore. Then they could run straight down the rim and jump the far gap without worrying about being shot at. The octomen's targeting abilities were shoddy, but they were improving the longer she and Addy stayed here. Before long they'd be firing at the slightest hint of movement, and firing with a fair degree of accuracy, too.

They couldn't afford that.

Should've just run straight down the rim without waiting to tip the guards over. They could be home free by now. But her first guard had started targeting Addy when she was still more than ten metres out from the opposite guard. Was it further than that to the side walls? She wasn't sure.

It could be a recipe for disaster: sprinting down the rim, they would be tracked by the laser sights from the guards opposite, and each guard would target them faster and with more accuracy and would start shooting sooner . . .

That could go very, very wrong. Maybe Addy was on to something after all. Take out the guards as they went, using each pair as a shield from the bullets.

What would Addy have done alone?

Maunga shivered, wiped her hands one after the other on her trousers, and focused on tipping her octoman up and over its axis.

It didn't take long. This time she could feel when it gave way. It was like an abrupt tug on a line before the line went slack, and the guard started to fall. Addy's octoman stayed silent. It was safe to move. She ducked out from behind her guard and stepped around so that she was beside it as it overbalanced. She didn't try to touch it, but she made sure she saw what she needed to see: the gun still tucked close to its chin, the finger still touching the trigger. This one took longer than the last to topple; the sightless face turned to gaze blankly at her as it finally tipped over the edge and fell away into darkness.

"Clear!" she shouted.

"Clear!"

They turned away at the same time, heading around the curve of the next bay to the third pair of peninsulas. It was the same again: Duck down behind their respective octomen. Wave a hand out one side and retract. Wave a hand out the other side, flinch as a bullet flew a little too close, and hurriedly retract.

They were getting faster with their shooting, but she and Addy were getting faster with their ducking and waving, too. The tiredness in her back and shoulders was verging on light pain, now. That was fine. If what she had in mind worked, she wouldn't have to finish tipping this one.

Lift and heave and heave and lift, while the bullets smashed into her shield and her shield returned fire. The recoil thrummed deep down into it, sending tremors through the tentacle-legs she was holding. Come on . . . lift . . . this one seemed heavier than the others, or else she was more tired. Well, she *was* more tired, she knew that. But maybe it was heavier as well.

Lift and lift and lift and tilt and *there* it went, a line pulling taut and flying loose. Addy's guard still fired, but there was no time for hesitation. Theo was dying. They'd spent too much time taking out these monsters as it was. Maunga rose in one swift movement and slipped around the side of her shield, trying to make her body as small as she could.

Fumbling fingers reached for the gun. She steadied them with an effort and started to prise that cold metal finger away from the trigger. It resisted. The featureless face turned to stare at her from a centimetre away. It bleated an alarm, loud and piercing, and she jumped. Keek, that hurt her ears. And now it tried to swing the gun around to point at her.

Not on your life, mate.

Addy's guard was shooting, bullets zipping past her far too close for comfort. But it still aimed at the octoman beside her. She ripped its finger from the trigger, grabbed the gun, and yanked hard. It came away with an effort and then too easily, like a plunger pulling up from strong liquid. Maunga stumbled back half a step and caught herself with a heel on the lip of the peninsula.

Her stomach plummeted. *Keek. Too close.*

But she had the gun now. She righted it and ducked back behind the slowly-tipping guard for cover. How did you use this thing? Trigger there, good; safety catch there; power setting there. Easy enough. The dial went from zero to sixteen. She spun it from three to ten, planted her feet, and sent a blast into the back of the octoman's neck from point-blank range.

The bleating alarm shrilled to a wail and then died. Finally. And she wouldn't even have to tip it over the edge. Fantastic. That would save her sore shoulders.

Now to take care of Addy's guard.

It was quick work to lean around the shielding bulk and squeeze off a few blasts. They impacted on the wall metres above the guard's head. *Hmm.* For all its overgrown size the rifle was strangely light. The bullets had flown straight without any sort of drop or trajectory curve to them. She adjusted her aim and fired again. That was better. They struck true that time, smashing into the torso and head of the guard. It ceased its return fire and gave the same wailing alarm before falling silent.

"Clear!" Maunga shouted. "They're down, Addy. Don't bother with the tipping!"

"Got it!" Addy appeared around the bulk of her guard. Maunga couldn't make out her expression from this far away, but she saw the surprised lift of her shoulders. "You have a gun?"

"Thought it would speed up the proceedings!"

Addy nodded. "On to the next lot, then!"

Having the gun made things so much easier. It had a fair range to it—Maunga could take out the guards with two shots from the boundary of their targeting area. Without having to worry about crossing the expanse of white tile and tipping the octomen over the edge, it became a simple matter of run and shoot and shoot, run and shoot and shoot. Addy lagged behind, sticking close to the wall, waiting until Maunga had cleared out the oncoming guards before crossing the tiles.

At one point Maunga saw her stick her hands in her pockets and lean a hip against the wall. She grinned. This had gone from a life-threatening, adrenaline-inducing do-or-die to something that resembled shooting clay birds from the back of a ute on a balmy summer's evening. There was little danger to it anymore. Likewise, there was little fun.

Run and shoot and shoot, run and shoot and shoot.

The last guards fell silent. Nothing but the final gap kept them from stable ground. Maunga slipped the safety on and slung the gun strap over her shoulder, then jogged to the edge and jumped across. Easy. A quick glance showed Addy had made it safely, too. She turned right and darted along the edge of the chasm to meet Addy by the bridge.

"Having fun with that thing?" Addy nodded toward the gun.

"Boatloads," Maunga said, grinning. "Do you want a turn?"

"No, I'm fine without. You're probably more qualified for it."

Maunga tried to hide her smirk, but Addy must have noticed something was off. Her eyes narrowed.

"What is it?"

"You're right," Maunga said. "I am better qualified."

They headed for the exit.

"You might have to explain that. Better qualified, how? D'you have a gun license or something?"

"No 'or something' about it."

"You have a gun license?"

Maunga hefted the assault rifle. "Strictly speaking, it's not for something as big as this. But I have one for most common firearms, yeah."

They stepped through the far doorway and into another ubiquitous white hallway, straight and endless with that slight uphill tilt.

"Theo and I go to a shooting range in the city sometimes. It's a good way to de-stress."

"Wouldn't have thought you get stressed."

"Everybody gets stressed, kid."

Addy huffed a breath. "Call me *kid* one more time and I'll—"

Touchy, touchy. "You'll what?" If it annoyed her that much, Maunga would stop, but she couldn't resist needling her a bit more first.

"I'll start calling you *sister.*"

Maunga whistled. "That's a low blow."

"I mean it."

She bit back a laugh. "Well, with that hanging over my head, how could I refuse? Addy."

"Thank you."

"You're welcome. Addy."

Addy groaned. "I'm going to regret that, aren't I?"

"Not at all . . ."

Addy looked at Maunga.

Maunga looked back, her smile angelic. "What?"

"Nothing," Addy said, scuffing her bare foot on the tiles. "Nothing whatso-keeking-ever."

"Anyway, as I was saying, it's a good way to de-stress . . ."

CHAPTER THIRTEEN

He breathed. In. Out. In. Out. It felt like a sack of bricks was sitting on his chest, weighing him down. Every inhale set his ribs screaming as his lungs expanded; every exhale brought relief, which only made space for the rest of his body to start up a cacophonous protest. And then, of course, he had to inhale again. He couldn't go without oxygen forever, much as he would like to. Inhale, and scream, and exhale, and protest.

Agony. Relief. Agony. Relief. In. Out. In. Out.

Where was he? He didn't know. There had been the hallway, white tiles white tiles white tiles, and then the green wall and the red stairs going up up up. The memories were a bit fuzzy there. He'd made it up the stairs, he thought. Or had he? He dimly remembered sitting on a landing, metal grating digging into his backside, a knobbly railing gouging holes in his spine, and gazing up at the switchbacking stairs that rose above him.

So he hadn't made it up all the stairs. But he thought he'd made it up some of them, at least.

It was important. Was it important? It felt important.

Keek, it hurt to breathe. He didn't even want to *think* about moving.

"Ooooo?"

It was just the wind whistling past. Odd. He hadn't felt a breeze.

"Eeeoooo."

Now it was moaning. Still no breeze. Mmm. A breeze would be nice. A whisper of cool air.

"Theo."

The wind had said his name. A vague urge to laugh floated

through his mind. He stifled it without effort. Thinking about laughing hurt. Everything hurt. He was clearly hallucinating.

Ugh. Poor Addy. No wonder she'd looked at them as if she could hardly believe her eyes when she first saw them. If she'd been hearing voices like that for years . . .

"Theo. Are you awake?"

Oh, it had asked a question? Well. It would be rude of him not to answer, even if it was only an inanimate . . . something . . . asking. Inhale. Scream. He tried to speak on the exhale but the words wouldn't come; there was a dry rasp, no more than a whisper, and that was it. He'd hardly heard it himself.

"Theo?" It sounded female. Why did it sound female? It would be even ruder of him to not answer.

"Es," he managed. Another rasp, a little louder than the last. The wind might have heard him, or it might not. He didn't know. His lips were dry. He licked them and felt material covering his mouth. What? His pulse sped up. Blood pounded in his ears. No wonder he couldn't breathe properly! *Get it off!*

He tried to lift a hand. He managed to lift a finger. Again. It flexed at the wrist that time. He swallowed pooling saliva. *Again.* There. His hand came up. Even in the dark behind his closed eyes, he knew it shook with effort. He fumbled at the cloth, felt for the edges, found them: one over the bridge of his nose extending out to the ears and around, the other draped around his neck like a scarf.

His hand dropped, exhausted. He tried to puzzle out the meaning of it. From the feel of it, material covered his nose and mouth, and wrapped around his head. He could feel the straps digging into his neck when he turned his head. He should recognise it, he thought. He almost did. The conclusion was there, fluttering a tantalising centimetre from his grasping thoughts.

Too much. He let it go, let it rest, felt his thoughts settle. He didn't have the energy to spare. Didn't have energy at all. Ah, the wind was back. Strange how there was still no breeze.

"Theo? Did you say something?"

"Yes," he muttered. He'd managed a whole word that time, and at something approaching normal volume, albeit rather croaky. Progress! Progress was good.

"You're awake!"

Oh, come on. That was too easy. "Obvi . . . ously." He was moving; he was speaking; he was clearly awake. Who'd have thought the wind had a penchant for stating the obvious?

"Can you open your eyes?"

Hmm. Good question. "Dunno. Prob'ly."

A small huff of something like laughter. "Will you open your eyes?"

Oh. *He* was the pedant now, was he? Okay then. "I'll try." He cracked his eyes open. His surroundings blurred and then resolved themselves into shapes.

Ugh. He'd certainly woken to more pleasant sights—did so most mornings, in fact. Puke-green walls and shaggy grey carpet weren't the nicest sights in the world. "That's . . . disgusting," he managed, pausing for breath between words.

"What is? Are you alright? Can you see?"

He put a hand to the floor and struggled to push himself more upright. "Who chose this colour palette?"

"What?"

"The colours . . . in here're . . . appalling."

The wind paused. But was it the wind? It was very localised; it seemed to be directed in his right eardrum. "Um. Probably Caroline," it said after a minute. "I'll, er, make a note of it."

"Good." He was firmly upright now. The mention of Caroline sharpened his thoughts. That was right, she was here somewhere. He'd been . . . been . . . sick. Or something. And Maunga and Addy had gone off to find a way of making him better. At least that's what he thought had happened. The jumble of voices and emotions in his memories weren't very clear on that.

Maybe the wind would know? It seemed to know a lot, for being stuck in his . . . right . . . ear.

Not the wind, after all. Home base.

"Hey," he said.

"Yeah, mate?"

"Uh. What happened?"

"You've been poisoned. Maunga and Addy went off to find an antidote—"

"Retheykay?"

"Sorry?"

"Are—they—okay?"

"We don't know." It came to him then, who the voice belonged to. Challa. "We don't know if they're okay. They're too far down. There's too many layers of interference in the way. And they don't need to find the antidote anymore—haven't had to since about five minutes after they left."

"Why'szat?"

"Do me a favour and look straight in front of you."

He turned his head and blinked. A sort of lap table poked out from the wall. On it sat a vial filled with blue liquid. He squinted. The label swam before his eyes and then, very slowly, came into focus.

"Oh," he said. "Keek."

"Our thoughts exactly. Can you reach it?"

He could try. His arm was better after its rest. Not nearly so shaky. He managed to lift his hand and grab the vial off the tray. Deprived of the small weight, the panel tipped up and slotted back into its place in the wall. "Got it," he murmured, letting his head fall back to rest against the wall. "Now what?"

"Now you'll need to inject it."

He pulled the blanket off him with his free hand. That was why he'd been so hot. It wasn't much better without it, if he was honest; either the air in here was stifling or he was running a fever.

"Theo?"

Challa. Right. He heaved a small, resigned breath. If he'd had his druthers, he wouldn't have picked his little sister's former best friend to be the voice in his ear when he was the sickest he could ever remember being. Ah well. Time to swallow his pride. "You'll need to walk me through it. My head's fuzzy as, and I'm not focusing at all."

"That's the poison. No worries. Tell me when you need to rest."

"Will do."

"You've got the vial?"

He grunted confirmation and waved it in the vague direction of his earpiece's sightline. "Right here."

"Uncap it. It's a screw cap, judging from the visual on this end. Press in on opposite sides and give it a twist anticlockwise."

She took him through it step by step, waiting for his confirmation each time before moving on. At regular intervals she asked if he needed a break; he declined every time but one, and initiated rests twice when his hands grew too shaky and his head too cloudy to function. He'd never had a problem with needles. It slid home with hardly a whisper while he tried to hold it as steady as possible.

"Done," he said once the vial was empty. He retracted the needle, capped it, and let it fall to the carpet with a muffled thud.

"Ka pai," Challa said. "Give that a few minutes to start working, and then we'll get you on your feet and moving."

He really did laugh at that—a rusty chuckle that trailed off into a groan as it jarred his ribs and set every muscle in his body throbbing. Even sitting upright made everything hurt. How on earth was he supposed to stand?

"Theo?"

"'M fine," he panted. "Remind me . . . not to laugh . . . next time you say something ridiculous."

"Hardly ridiculous."

"Yeah? Tell that to my . . . everywhere. It keeking *hurts,* Challa. I can't move."

"You're going to have to." Her voice was steely. "Because Addy and Maunga are going to need all the help they can get, and you're the only one with a hope of opening that door if they don't find the code."

He blinked. It took him a while to process the words. "Code?"

"The exit's locked—"

"Big surprise there."

"And we don't know the code."

He really, *really* wished he could laugh without hurting. "I'm shocked." He paused for breath. In. Agony. Out. Relief. "Really. Shocked."

"Cut the attitude, Theo." Her voice softened. "I know you're hurting. You've been poisoned, for keek's sake. But they're counting on you. *We're* counting on you. That's the only way out and you're the only one near enough to have a hope of finding a way to open it."

Talk about emotional blackmail. *Blast it.* It was working, too. The idea of standing up didn't seem half so ridiculous now that he knew he was near the exit.

"How are you feeling?"

"Sore," he said. "About the same. It's hard to tell." He shifted uncomfortably and felt his leg hit something under the lump of the blanket.

What? Oh. A water bottle. And some food. And a medkit. *Maunga, you angel.*

His hands were steady enough after the prolonged rest; he managed a few gulps of water before unwrapping a nutrient bar and shoving it in his mouth. *Mmm.* Much better. Amazing what some cold water and solid food could do to make you feel more human.

"Can you stand up yet?" Challa asked.

"What's the damage?" he asked by way of a dodge. No, he couldn't stand up. Not yet. But maybe with the help of whatever pain meds were in the kit . . .

There was a distinct silence on the other end of the comm channel. "You don't want to know."

"Try me." He tugged the medkit closer and opened it. Sticking plasters, wipes, a small bottle of disinfectant. He lifted the top tray out and checked the next layer. *Aha.* That was more like it.

"The breath mask stopped you ingesting any more poison, but it can't help with the toxins already in your system."

He dug deeper, pulled out a painkiller vial from the bottom of the neat racks, and raised his eyebrows. That would do. "Hence the antidote."

"Hence the antidote, exactly. But even that—I'm not sure what it *does*. It might stop the progress of the toxins, it might try to reverse the damage, we don't know."

"Guess we'll find out." The vial slid into the injector gun. He caught himself before finding the vein and changed the needle out. There. All set.

"What are you injecting?" she asked, voice sharp.

He held up the vial in the earpiece's line of sight so she could see the label.

"That, uh, that might not be the best idea, not on top of everything already in your system—"

"Don't care." He missed the vein on the first try. And the second. His hand just wouldn't hold still. He finally made it on the sixth try. There'd be some bruises there later, but right now he had more important things to worry about. He pressed the plunger and watched the vial empty. "This is the only way I'm going to be up and walking in the next six hours."

"If you say so."

He just had said so. His hand shook as the needle came out, tearing the tiny hole wider. Blood welled up, dark and wet, overflowing the wound and trickling down the inside of his elbow.

Keek. The pain was nothing, a sharp stab that was there one second and gone the next. He balled a corner of the blanket and pressed it to the crook of his arm. Ow, okay, that hurt once the pressure came on. But he'd rather not leave a trail of blood everywhere he went.

"Alright?" Challa asked.

He didn't bother explaining his pained grunt. She had a visual from his earpiece and he was looking straight at the injury. "Just a scratch."

She snorted but didn't say anything besides, "D'you want to try to stand up?"

"Might as well have a go."

His hands felt more capable of holding some weight now. He sat forward, braced himself on the wall, and started to ease to his feet. *Ow ow ow.*

"Keeeeek," he hissed, getting as far as a crouch and pausing to rest. The sweat poured off him, sticking damp curls to his forehead and dripping down his neck. He leaned left, propping his shoulder against the wall. That was better. His hands shook. His thighs ached from the strain already.

He couldn't hold this position for long. Up or down. He had to move.

He pushed up, one hand on the floor, one on the wall, not trusting his trembling legs to power him that far. A snarling growl tore free from his throat as the pain surged and settled, and then he was standing, swaying, head swimming, black spots dancing in front of his eyes.

He staggered back, felt his shoulder hit the wall again and let it take his weight. That was fine. He was upright, that was all that mattered. The spots cleared. He concentrated on breathing.

In. Agony. Out. Relief. He could do this. The meds had taken the edge off the pain, but all that meant was that he could move without screaming. Barely.

Small blessings. He was grateful.

"Where'm I—going?" he gasped. His pulse thundered in his ears, too fast, too loud. Standing was torture, breathing was agony, moving would be unbearable—but he would have to bear it somehow. For Maunga. For Addy. He fixed their faces in his mind's eye. He could do this. He *had to* do this. For them.

"Left," said Challa in his ear. "Through that door. And then left down the hallway and across the catwalk to the landing, and up the stairs."

Ha. Stairs. He'd forgotten under the onslaught of pain that he would have to make his way not just down a hall but up a flight or two of stairs. His knees wobbled at the thought. He curled his fingers into the wall and stilled them with an effort. There wasn't time for that. They were depending on him.

Maunga. Addy. Maunga. Addy. Theo took a breath. Agony. And exhaled. Relief. "Let's do this."

He turned and staggered for the door.

~

"I'll take you to one." Maunga hopped over the latest metre-wide gap. "Me and Theo usually go to one in the city centre because it's closer, but I reckon you'd like the one out the South End better. It's got a simulated outdoor environment as well as indoor practice rooms. Cross-winds, poor lighting, birds flying through, terrible smells to throw off your concentration . . . you name it, they've got it."

"Yeah?" Addy followed her over the gap. They kept walking up the shallow incline.

"Yeah. You'll see. Just you and me at the range. I'll show you the ropes."

"Ha." Shadow-bruised eyes narrowed. "What for, girl bonding time?" The words were disdainful.

"Nah. Therapy. De-stressing, remember?"

Addy grunted.

"I *am* a psychologist, you know."

"I know. You going to try to get me into counselling?"

Five rows of panels dropped away in front of them. They waited for the walls to flow down and fill the gap before proceeding.

"Going to counsel you myself." Maunga kept the words light

but made sure Addy saw the sober intent behind them. "As long as you've got no objections and the Ethics Board approves it, but I'm fairly certain they will. I have intimate knowledge of your case already."

That garnered a snort.

"Why do you think I went into psychology in the first place?"

"Dunno," Addy said. "So you could try to fix the cesspit that was your life?"

Maunga let the words roll off her. "Part of it. But the postgrad? The trauma specialisation? That was all you, Addy."

"Yeah, right."

"I mean it."

Addy cast a slantwise look at her. "You went into a lifetime career and did, what, five years of training, all for the sake of your husband's little sister who you'd only met three times? We spent a grand total of maybe twelve hours together."

"I was enrolled in a psych degree long before that VPR session, you know. Of course you haven't been my sole focus for the last six years; you haven't been around. But I can't deny that my core motivation for a few years now has been wanting to help you."

"Really."

Oh, the sarcasm. "Yes, really. It's a professional field I love; of course I want to use every skill I have to try and help you. You wouldn't turn down Theo fixing a broken leg for you if he was a medico, would you?"

"That's different." Addy looked away.

"How?"

"He's my brother."

"And I'm your sister-in-law." It was the first time she'd said it seriously.

Addy blinked, a tiny *v* forming between her brows. "You hardly know me."

"You'd be surprised what I've learned about you in five years of being married to Theo."

The frown deepened. "You know I've been gone nearly seven years, right? A lot's changed in that time, and I don't mean just you marrying my brother. A lot changed at this end. With me."

"I know it did," Maunga said patiently. "Which is why I want to *help*, Addy."

Addy was silent. It could have been exasperation, but from what little Maunga could see of her face, it looked more like thoughtfulness. *Good.* Maybe she was finally getting through to her. She'd tell her every day if she had to, or, keek, wake her up every hour on the hour and scream it in her ear. *Earth—to—Addy—I—want—to—help.* Whatever it took to get that message through to her.

It could take years for her to know it and years more for her to understand it, but that was fine. They had time. As long as they both got out of here alive—which was by no means a given, but they'd survived so far, hadn't they?—they had plenty of time to work on such subtleties as *you have PTSD, Addy,* and *you can talk to me any time of the day or night, Addy,* and *yes I do genuinely want to help you, Addy.*

A two-metre gap opened up and after that a four-metre that filled, and then another two. They jumped them or walked over the replacement tiles as needed.

And then it changed.

The hallway opened out ahead, walls flowing outward to frame a wide end wall. A broad set of double doors met them, mirrored and silver, reflecting their haggard faces back at them.

Maunga put a hand to her hair. It was a mess. Loose tendrils hung all around, wisps flying this way and that. A huge streak of dust ran down the sleeve of her leather jacket. That was the problem with black, it showed every speck and spot of dirt. Her boots, of course, were covered in grime. Her trousers were filthy too, but that was only to be expected after the crawlspace they'd been in that morning and the slimy octomen tentacle-legs.

She caught Addy grinning as she tried to tidy herself up. She knew that look, even under the mask. *Ha. Let her smirk.* With any luck her face would end up stuck like that, and she'd be the world's first eternally grinning trauma victim.

She couldn't do anything about her boots. A stiff rub and a vigorous shake-off made her trousers just this side of presentable. The smear on her jacket wiped off easily, and her jersey under it wasn't too bad. She transferred the worst of the dirt from her hands to her scarf before shaking it off and winding it around her neck again. As for her hair, that was easy enough to fix.

Addy cleared her throat. "Shall we?"

"Reckon so." Maunga twitched one last strand of hair into place and rammed a pin home. "Ready when you are."

"Ready or not," Addy said, "here we come."

She opened the doors and they stepped through.

~

Theo was gasping for breath by the time he made it across the catwalk to the landing. He collapsed against the railing, grabbing it with both hands and clinging for his life before his legs could give out on him. In. Agony. Agony. Agony. Out. Relief.

His lungs burned in his chest, every breath searing trails of fire through his breastbone and up into his windpipe. The pinky finger on his right hand dropped off the railing and curled in against his palm, spasming manically. He couldn't spare the energy to still it. Let it spasm. What did it matter?

It grew worse. Okay, that wasn't so good. The tremors spread until his whole hand was shaking where it held the rail. They started to move down through his wrist. He grabbed his right hand with his left and tried to still it. It worked a little.

His gaze fell on his hands. A dull red flush spread from both pinky fingers up the outside of his hands. It made a garish contrast to his white-clenched knuckles.

Keek.

He stretched his fingers out one hand at a time, not daring to let go of the railing. Curled them back up. Stretched them out. Contracted them again. It wasn't enough.

He rested his whole weight on the railing and took both hands off. It felt incredibly unsteady, but he could manage for a short time. He laced his fingers together and stretched them out, arms and all, until the knuckles cracked. That was better. The shaking had lessened now. He shifted his weight, swayed, and grabbed for the railing.

Too close. He couldn't trust his balance; he didn't have any. One hand on the railing at all times, mate. He couldn't trust his legs, either. They felt weak as a kitten and wobbly as a fawn, not that he'd ever seen a newborn fawn in real life. But the holos were enough. Gangly legs and stumbling steps, that was him. And if he wasn't careful, the faceplanting would be him, too.

Just call him Bambi.

"Theo."

He groaned and muttered an ungentlemanlike suggestion at Challa.

"Thanks all the same," she said, "but I think I'll pass. You need to keep moving."

"Scintillating," he rasped. "Insight. Dupin."

"Who?"

Ugh. "Never mind. Just waiting for my legs to maybe have a shot at holding me up. Give me a minute."

He gave the rising staircases a baleful glare. They were doing it on purpose, he swore, being all . . . tall . . . and—and steep like that. He was sure they hadn't been that steep when he'd climbed the lower flights. Had they always been that garish shade of red, with the orange rails? Surely not.

Although, come to think of it, he did have a vague memory of that diamond-patterned grillwork in fire-engine red. Maybe they had always been that colour.

"How are you feeling?" Challa asked.

Theo took a deliberate breath, held it for three careful seconds, and then released it. It hurt so badly he thought he might pass out, but he did it anyway. Better that than biting her head off for something that wasn't her fault. She was only trying to help. "I'm alright," he said, knowing that she knew it was an outright lie. "Ask me again at the turnaround. Now don't talk for a few minutes, please."

There was the sound of muffled movement and a sharp snap of the tongue. She'd mock saluted him, the cheeky beggar. A second later the silence deepened. She must have muted her mic.

Fine by him.

Now to tackle these keeking stairs . . .

He tightened his grip on the handrail and lifted a foot to the first step. His breath left in a pained rush. *Keek.* He set his teeth and dragged the other leg up to join it, leaning on the rail. Breathe. In. Agony-agony-agony. Out. Relief. One step down. Fifteen to go to the turnaround. He could do it.

Couldn't he?

He had to.

Tears sprang to his eyes as he started up the next rise. Lifting his foot was bad enough. He still had to shift his weight onto it and bring the other leg up. Keek keek keek that *hurt*. One foot in place. Okay.

A strangled whimper escaped him. His shin bone was trying to stab upward through his knee, his kneecap was melting into ashy cinders down either side of the joint, and as for his femur—he didn't even want to think about his femur.

And that was only his *right* leg.

Transferring his weight elicited another snarl of pain. Every bone in his foot ground together, splinters of pins and needles jabbing down through the arch and into the nerves under the toe-nails. How did it *do* that?

He didn't think he wanted to know.

He gripped the rail with both hands now, skin grey-brown

in places and flushed with heat in others, the knuckles white, the beds of the nails tinged blueish-purple. Ha. Regular walking circus, he was.

As long as he could *keep* walking, it would be alright.

He shifted the bulk of his weight to his hands and managed to bring his left leg up to join his right. Resting as little weight as possible on his legs made the pain a smidgen more bearable, but his arms were shaking with the strain already. He couldn't manage that trick the whole way up. His limbs would never take it.

But they had to. Somehow, they simply had to. He had to get to the top.

Pale and sweating, jaw set, dark eyes fever-bright, Theo moved his grip on the railing and hauled himself up to the next step. Rested. Next step. Rest. Another step, yelling out in pain when a muted whimper wasn't enough. He didn't care. There was no one here to hear, and he was long past thinking about his dignity. He couldn't think of anything but the pain, ever-present, stabbing and grinding and utterly unbearable, but Addy hung in his mind's eye, and Maunga. They were watching him, *needing* him.

So he kept on.

After a decade he made it to the turnaround. The thought of resting here was tempting beyond belief, but he couldn't. If he stopped now, he'd never start again. He had momentum, however small and fleeting, and he intended to use it.

Alright, he conceded once he made it up the next flight to the landing (approximate time: another decade, plus a few weeks). Maybe he did need a rest. He'd be no use to anyone if he passed out.

"Theo?" Challa sounded nervous. That was right, he'd told her to stop talking for a while. Politely.

"Just resting a bit," he muttered, quelling a slow surge of nausea. The aftertaste floated up to his taste buds, all acidic bile and stale hospital-smelling air. He grimaced. "Everything okay at your end?"

"Mmm." She didn't sound sure. "We're fine for the most part, but Liam wants a—" she broke off to clear her throat "—a word with you."

If it was another whine about how they'd let him sleep for too long and woken him too late so that he couldn't sleep that night, Theo would rather give it a miss. He suppressed a sigh. "Put him on."

"Already here, you sodding great stupid daftie," Liam said. The usual soft-spoken gentleness had given way to something raw and raging.

Theo braced himself against the rail as Liam proceeded to dress him down every which way to Sunday.

Ow. His ears hurt. Or one ear, anyway—the right, where his earpiece was. Keek, was Liam *still* going? He could barely even make out what the man was saying, he was so angry. It was all clipped syllables and sporadic full-blown roaring, vacillating back and forth between a very angry medical professional and an even angrier friend who just so happened to also be an angry medical professional. With one final shout of, "Just what in the name of ever-loving keek did you think you were doing, Te Ngawai?", Liam fell silent.

The silence rang.

"I'm waiting." The rant hadn't taken more than a slight edge off Liam's anger. Theo could feel it radiating all the way down here.

"I thought," Theo said, the rasp not robbing the words of their own edge of bloody-minded determination, "I was finding the quickest way to facilitate standing upright without screaming and passing out from the pain. And it worked."

"For now. What are you going to do when your system realises you've absorbed close to a triple dose of concentrated analgesic on top of an unknown antidote and an unknown quantity of unknown poison, and *that* on top of a serious case of combined dehydration, undernutrition, and sleep deprivation?"

Surely not. "You're exaggerating."

"I'm a paramedic." Ah, he was through shouting anger and out the other side into whispering rage. "I don't exaggerate, not when there are lives on the line, and *especially* not when two of those lives belong to my friends. You should know that."

"I, uh." Theo fought to think through the fog of pain. "I do know that. But I drank a whole lot of water not that long ago. Maybe a couple of hours."

Silence.

"Hello? Liam?"

The reply, when it came, was startling in its softness. "Do you have any idea how long you've been down there?"

He'd thought he had a pretty good idea, but in the face of Liam's question, he felt horribly unsure. *Keek.* Theo closed his eyes against the throb of a weary headache. "Twice as long as I thought?"

"More like three times."

Inhale. Agony. Exhale. Relief. He took the blow with a slumping of the shoulders. "I see."

"Do you? Theo. You've hardly slept, all three of you. You've eaten a bit, but you and Maunga could stand to eat a jolly sight more. Addy I'm not so sure about: I'd rather give her a full examination before prescribing anything more than the basics. Your liquid intake has been, quite frankly, atrocious. The levels in your water bottles have hardly moved in the last eight hours. And as for you personally—you've been poisoned with something, we don't know what with or in what quantities. Addy's obviously struck it before. She knew what your symptoms meant, at least. Maunga dosed you with quantity-and-a-half of a high-concentration somno-analgesic. A single dose should have had you sleeping for twelve hours straight; a double dose could have given you heart failure. And then you woke up before time, which could have been due to the havoc the poison is causing on your insides, and promptly injected yourself with *another* full dose of the strongest analgesic in that kit."

Well. When he put it like that, it did make Theo's actions look . . . not so smart. "I did what I had to do," he rasped.

"And if you die from it?" A river of weariness lay behind the dam of Liam's anger.

Theo swallowed. Forced a smidgen of lightness into his voice. "That's what I've got you for, mate. To make sure I don't."

"*Theo.*" Utter disbelief. "This is serious." His next words were bleak. "You could, you know. Die. You'll probably start seizing within the next hour. There's nobody there to hold your head off the ground; if it hits hard enough, it could mean brain damage. And heart failure's not far behind, not with those drugs you've got rocketing through your system. With the poison on top of everything, the toxins . . . I don't know what they'll do. How long they'll be in effect. What those effects will be."

"It'll be okay," someone murmured in the distance. Kim, maybe.

"Will it?" Liam asked.

What could he say to that? Knowledge of his own mortality loomed, bitter at a mere twenty-seven years but spiked with sweetness too. They'd found Addy. He'd seen her with his own eyes, held her in his arms, even made her cry for the first time since they were children. That was an accomplishment in itself. He just had to get her out. It was all that was left to him. "What do you want me to do?"

A gusting breath blew through the comm channel. Theo could almost swear he felt the wind of it against his eardrum. "Not much we can do, now. The less you move, the slower your system will metabolise everything, but it's no help to anyone, least of all yourself, if you sit there and wait to die."

That earned a snort. *Sit down and wait to die* was at the very bottom of his to-do list, under *procreate with Caroline if she was the last person on earth* and *divorce Maunga.* He couldn't give up on living even if his life depended on it. He was too much of a survivor for that.

"Any other bright suggestions?" he asked. "Jump off this

landing and make it quick, perhaps? Change my will and sign away everything I own to Breach?"

Without waiting for Liam's reply, he turned toward the next flight of stairs. He'd stayed here too long already. They could chat while he walked—or, to be more realistic, Liam could chat while Theo gasped and whimpered and shouted in pain, with a few colourful oaths for variation.

He hoped Liam didn't mind a cluster-bomb of swear words at times. He knew the man had views about that sort of thing, even if Liam himself occasionally let his control slip.

In. Out. Right leg up. Shift his weight. Try not to scream as his kneecap ground against his femur and his ribs drew tight, constricting his breathing. The nerves at the back of his neck flared. His pelvis felt like a shattered mess of bone shards and trailing sinew. It was a good thing Maunga didn't want kids; he'd never be able to do his part of *that* job again. He hauled his other leg up, found black spots in front of his eyes, and let out his breath in an explosive huff. In. Agony. Out. Relief.

"Not much, no," Liam said finally. "We can get at the exit from this side. I'll have the ambos waiting for you—"

And before Theo could snark a comment about Liam not meeting them personally to force something putrid down his throat—

"And I'll be waiting there myself with a litre of diuretic, which you will drink without argument and pass without delay, is that clear?"

Theo winced, but only an idiot would argue with the team medic. Keek, he'd appointed the man himself. "Yes, Liam."

"What are you going to do?"

One foot. Shift weight. Other foot. "I'm going to unlock the exit—" gasp, one foot "—and drink the stuff that makes me pee–" shift weight, brace ribs "—and pee as soon as possible."

Whimper, other foot, wipe sweat. And repeat ad infinitum, ad literal nauseam. "I guess that's the fastest way to get rid of the toxins from the poison?"

"Your guess would be right," Liam said, grimly cheerful. "Unless you want an emetic? Swift-acting nausea inducer?"

Theo groaned and started up the next rise.

"Yeah, vomiting your guts up isn't really your style. Didn't think so."

"You—didn't think—correctly."

Liam chuckled in his ear. "Funny boy."

"You're one—" gasp, fight for breath, bite back nausea "—to talk. Now shut up and let me suffer in peace."

"If you insist." The friendly mockery faded; Liam's voice was soft and intent once more. "Call me if you need me."

"Can do, will do."

"Chatham out."

Ah, blessed silence. Theo sucked a sharp breath through his nose, let it out, drew it in again. He pressed the back of a hand to his mouth, but his lips wobbled treacherously all the same. Too much. It was too much.

The pain, the friendly voices—so close, so keeking close, but still so far—the worry and the concern and the *caring* . . . it was too much. They'd hear him, of course; their microphones might be muted, but his wasn't. He wasn't even half tempted to switch it off. They needed to stay in contact. If that meant them hearing him bawl his eyes out, so be it.

They'd find he was human after all.

It hurt. Everything hurt—his body and his mind and his heart, not knowing where Maunga was, or Addy, not even knowing if they were *alive*, let alone uninjured.

He hauled himself up another step, gave a yell as the pain surged and spiked, and let the tears fall.

CHAPTER FOURTEEN

An army could have marched down the room without brushing elbows. Maunga raised a cynical eyebrow at the vaulted ceiling, the lines of marble pillars down each side, the walls inlaid with some sort of textured white panelling. It stretched for days, the far end lost to the haze of sheer distance.

And there was no way out.

Or rather, she corrected herself as they padded forward, no way to tell. It was just a hunch. The passage had been taking them *somewhere*. She rather thought this might just be the somewhere. As for what they would find here . . .

She'd have to wait and see. It might be the antidote. She hoped against hope that it was, that they could retrieve it and race it back up to Theo.

If he's still alive, said that treacherous whisper in the back of her mind.

She shoved it away. Of course he was alive. He'd been breathing fine when they left. It wasn't that long ago—an hour, maybe two. He was alive. She'd know if he wasn't.

Oh, she wouldn't feel it, at least not in her heart or her bones, as romantic as that would be. That keek only happened in fairy tales. No, the earpieces had vitals monitors built in. She could check his stats from her holo . . .

Except, of course, the earpieces were dead.

There went that plan.

And there went the idea that she'd know if he died, too. No. She should have known it wouldn't work like that, not here, not for her. She'd find out later, just like everybody else. And knowing her luck, there wouldn't even be any privacy for her to vent that first ugly rush of grief. She'd probably be in a hospital bed in a public ward, hooked up to a saline drip.

But he wasn't dead. He *wasn't*.

"Oi," Addy muttered.

"What?" She'd been twisting her rings in practised motions around her left ring finger. She stopped the movement, choosing to unsling the gun and check the charge on it as an alternative way of keeping her hands busy.

"Nothing."

Maunga cast a skeptical glance at her.

"Well nothing *now*," she added, hollowed eyes darting down at Maunga's left hand.

Huh. Good catch, kiddo. "Thanks."

Addy didn't look at her, but she caught a flicker of an eye roll. "Welcome."

They walked on. There was a distinct lack of doors on both sides. The room in front of them remained as endless and shrouded in mist as ever. It felt unnatural. Artificial. But at least the floor stayed stable. No pesky rows of tiles dropped out from under their feet and there were no signs of more octomen.

"Does this, uh, remind you of anywhere?" Addy asked.

Maunga threw another look around the room. Nope. Looked like any other room here. "The pillars are new, but other than that I can't see . . ."

"The cave. On the mountainside."

What was she talking about? "You've never been out of the city, Addy."

"In the TheraRPG session. Remember? Seth took me there. To meet you."

"Oh, that." It did ring a bell, come to think of it. "Yeah. I guess I can see it. The pillars, and the cavernous space."

"I asked him," Addy started. Paused. Kept going. "I asked Seth if truth was the cave on the mountainside or if it was coming out of the cave to see the world with fresh eyes. Said I'd heard it both ways."

She wouldn't have picked Addy for an amateur philosopher. "And?"

"He said it was neither." Her eyes were soft, crinkling in a familiar look of affection and grief. Maunga knew it well—she'd seen it in countless faces over the years as people spoke of lost friends or lovers. "He said that truth was the person in the cave." Addy looked away and shrugged. When she spoke again, her tone was matter of fact. "And then he brought me to you, and it explained . . . oh, so many things."

"Interesting."

"Is it?"

"Mmm. The idea of truth being a person, or embodied by a person, at least . . ."

"But the person still has to inhabit a place. So in a way, the truth is still the place; it's the place where the person is."

Maunga hefted the gun. "You think there's a truth waiting here for us?"

"I think we've been railroaded here for a reason," Addy said. "*A* truth? Not *the* truth?"

"There's never only one truth."

"Hmm. Don't know if I agree with you on that one."

"One man's truth is another man's white lie," Maunga said. "Everybody sees the world differently. It colours our perceptions and our values."

"Oh?"

"The existence of more than one truth doesn't negate the others. It's non-binary, like your pathfinding. Hundreds of truths exist simultaneously. One might apply only to one person at one particular time; say, if I said, *I am cold.* It might be the truth for me because I feel cold, myself, but it might not be true from anyone else's perspective because they could put a hand on my arm and I'd feel hot. Other truths exist for everyone, everywhere, all the time—*the sun is hot, the sky is blue, I think therefore I exist*—in some form or another."

Addy nodded. "Unless the sun doesn't feel hot, or the sky is overcast, or they don't, in fact, think. Self-perception."

"Exactly."

"Spot the psychologist."

Maunga glanced at her, but her eyes were bright over the rim of the mask. She'd been teasing. And there was something else in her expression, something lean and hungry and only temporarily surface-sated. Knowledge, Maunga thought. Addy thirsted for it.

It wasn't surprising. She'd always been a high achiever, driven to learn and learn and learn. Clearly an intrinsic motivation, then, not extrinsic. Was she like Theo, where the satisfaction lay in a complex problem solved? Or was it something else? Did she love learning for the satisfaction of a high grade? No, that wasn't Addy. She liked the high grade, but only as a reflection of a job well done, a lesson learned and put into practice. It was the learning itself that was its own reward; knowledge acquired and understood through and through, another gap filled in her mental library.

Ars gratia artis, indeed. Art for art's sake. Or, more properly, *scientia gratia scientiam*. Knowledge for knowledge's sake.

At least, that was Maunga's working theory at the moment. She'd been through more than a few in the last six years trying to figure Addy out, using what she knew of her, comparing and contrasting her to Theo. She was open to alterations.

Ahead of them, the room came to an eventual end. The walls swung out and around to encapsulate the dead end in a perfect circle. The pillars trotted out and around with them, framing the central stage.

And a stage it was. An unbroken circle of bright crimson stained the floor, harsh and garish to Maunga's eyes after the past hours of muted white and grey and black. In the centre rose a platform, again a perfect circle, in darker red; it was wide and shallow, an easy step up from the floor. And in the middle of the platform . . .

Oh, keek.

It was the mother of all octomen. It stood a full head taller than the others they'd seen, broader by far in the shoulders and hip, thicker through the legs—er, tentacles. Its face was narrow through the nose ridge and angular down the cheekbones. Like the others, the faceplate was blank where eyes and ears and mouth would be on a human. No hair, of course. Just sleek metal, seamless and malevolent.

It was unarmed, she noted. Good. One less thing to worry about. She lifted the gun and took aim—

And it spoke in a low, clear voice.

"Welcome."

Beside her, Addy drew a sharp breath.

Maunga lowered the gun. It was one thing to shoot an unarmed robot on sight. Quite another to do it after said robot had talked to them. He was male, if the voice was anything to go by. Mind you, that was no guarantee. She'd known a few low-voiced females in her life, not to mention high-voiced males. But the tone and timbre sounded male.

"Please," he said, "step forward. As you see, I cannot move from this place, and I would like to see you better and to speak with you more easily."

"Who are you?" Maunga asked. It seemed more polite than asking *what are you?* She didn't move. Anything could be waiting for them under that floor, and she didn't trust his claim about being unable to move. The other octomen had been able to slither around just fine.

"I am the master of this facility."

She doubted it. A minion with delusions of grandeur sounded more likely. But she humoured him. "Do you have a name, master of this facility?"

"You can call me Stafford."

Oh, please. He was clearly styling himself after Caroline. She was named for one of Te Maru's more memorable spots, like many people in the city. There were any number of Carolines and Benvenues and Frasers. They'd been named after Caroline Bay and Benvenue Cliffs and Fraser Park. And he'd chosen *Stafford*. Stafford Street, with its Edwardian building facades and pedestrian-only access, was one of the main shopping drags; it had been *the* main shopping drag before the Council converted the disused industrial grounds at Ashbury. These days it wasn't quite so popular. It still did good business, but it wasn't the roaring centre of commerce that he clearly pictured it as.

"Sure," she said. "Stafford. Let's go with that."

"You must be Maunga Richards. Married to Theo Te Ngawai. Who is, of course, the brother of your companion. Adelaide Te Ngawai."

Addy's chin lifted. "What's it to you?"

"I've been watching you for years. My brothers and I had bets going about how long it would take you to break. When you didn't, we switched to betting on how long it would be before Caro got so annoyed with you messing up her results that she killed you."

"Hasn't happened yet."

"Mmm." That blank face didn't move, but he sounded distinctly smug. "That's because she's not here anymore."

Maunga blinked. Had Addy been right about Caroline moving on to other projects? "She's not?"

"No. She's indisposed. She left me in charge."

Well. Maunga supposed even unethical scientists fell sick every once in a while. "Bummer. Guess we can't have a nice catch up over coffee with her after all."

"No," he agreed. "You can't."

An awkward silence filled the air.

"Did you bring us here?" Maunga said after a minute.

"I did."

"Why?"

"To see you. To talk with you. Both of you."

That was informative. "Again, why?"

"Can you help us?" Addy said abruptly. "We need an antidote. My brother's been poisoned."

"I know," Stafford said.

"So?"

"No."

"Why not?"

"I have no interest in helping your brother. Or you," he added, his face turning to Maunga. "It was bad enough that Adelaide ruined my tests. Even worse was you two dropping in here like a gale-force wind from a landfill site. This is supposed to be a controlled environment."

Oops. Maunga shrugged. "If you're expecting me to say I'm sorry, you'll be disappointed. I'm not apologising for coming here to rescue Addy."

"I didn't think you would."

"That's alright, then."

Another pause.

"So, uh," Addy said, "what did you want to talk about?"

"Your brother is dead."

The world froze.

"Liar." Addy's voice came from a vast distance away, muffled and shaken.

"The poison, combined with the excessive amount of medication she gave him . . ." His head turned back and forth between them, and for a moment Maunga thought she saw a sharp smile flickering on his faceplate. "It was too much."

Addy shook her head. "You're lying. He's still alive."

The words floated across to Maunga, wavering in the silence. She felt frozen; not just motionless but cold, colder than cold, cold as if she'd never be warm again. Dead. He was dead? He couldn't be dead. She'd know. Surely, she'd know.

But she wouldn't know, would she? It didn't work like that. There was no magic knowledge that came to her when he stopped breathing, no clenching in the pit of her stomach. Just Stafford's words, false and hollow, and this empty ache where her heart used to be.

She didn't believe him. But at the same time, she couldn't help believing him.

Theo was dead. Theo was not dead. Theo was dead.

Which was it? She didn't know. Wouldn't know until they got back to him. Schrödinger's husband, she thought, feeling an irrational urge to laugh. And then the anger rose, swift and hot, all-consuming, and the gun came up. She fired off half a dozen rounds without blinking.

The bullets hit Stafford's torso, lost their momentum without making a dent in his chest-plate, and clattered to the ground.

He laughed. "You're so predictable. Shoot first, ask questions later."

"Was that everything you wanted to tell us?" The anger fell away as swiftly as it had come, leaving an eerie calm that lit the blood in her veins with fire, sharpened her mind, and steadied her hands.

"Yes." Again there was that vague suggestion of a mocking grin. "I wanted to see your faces when I gave you the news. It was worth it."

"So we can kill you now?"

"Not if I kill you first."

She didn't know why he was doing this, but she didn't need to know. He'd been right: shoot first. Survive now. Find out why later.

Maunga threw herself left and rolled behind a pillar as Stafford lashed out with a tentacle, blacker and thicker than any she'd seen on his brothers. It came down hard, hard enough to bruise or break a bone, but Addy's spot held only air.

"That's right, my little lab rats," Stafford called. "Run and hide." His voice bounced off the round walls, hit the pillars, and bounced again until it reverberated through the room, seeming to come from every direction at once.

Maunga threw a desperate look back the way they'd come, but the walls had closed in, sealing them in this perfect circle of white pillars and red flooring and a lone, crazed, homicidal octoman. If only he was as easy to get rid of as the others had been. Maybe she could sneak around to the back of him and fire some rounds at the nape of his neck. That should do some damage.

She risked a glance around the pillar at Stafford. His head was turned away, tracking something almost at a right angle to where Maunga was. Addy must be on the move. Maunga tightened her grip on the gun and darted out from the safety of her pillar, across the open space, and ducked down behind the next.

Nothing. He hadn't seen her. Or—her heart pounded frenetic double-time—or had he noticed? Was he slithering silently closer on those slimy black appendages right now? Would his head pop around the side of the post right in front of her? Or would he simply wrap a freakishly long tentacle around it, crushing her against it?

There came a whistling sound of movement and a loud *thwack* from across the room. She ran for the next pillar, looking across the circle as she went. Stafford hadn't moved from his stage. Maybe it was true what he'd said about not being able to. He had thrown out two tentacles in tandem, bringing them down on either side of a pillar. Addy was nowhere to be seen. She must have slipped out from behind it before he made his move.

Good girl. Maunga kept moving. She paused at the next pillar to catch her breath, head tipped back against it, trying to breathe as quietly as possible in case Stafford had some sort of enhanced hearing implant. She wouldn't put it past him. He seemed able to see just fine without eyes; a lack of physical ears wouldn't stop him hearing.

She ran on, straight past the safety of the next pillar, and was halfway to the post beyond it when a tentacle slapped down at her feet with enough speed and force to make her jump. She yelled, brought the gun up by reflex, and put three shots into the ugly thing. To her surprise, Stafford bellowed in pain. The tentacle retracted. She finished her run, shooting blindly at the retreating tentacle before slipping behind the pillar.

Too close. That had been too close. Five centimetres to the

side and it would have come down on her feet; ten and it would have had her head. Far too close. He could move *fast*. But she was close to her goal, and she knew the tentacles could be wounded now. That was something.

"Maunga!" Addy yelled from the other side of the room.

"I'm alright!"

"Great! A little help here, please!"

Maunga peered around the side of the pillar.

Keek.

He'd done the double-tentacle trick again, but this time he'd caught her. Back pressed against her chosen pillar, eyes wild, Addy lashed out with a bare foot at the nearest tentacle as it inched closer. It had no effect beyond making a squishing sound and coating her foot in black goo. *Nasty.*

Maunga sighted and squeezed the trigger. One—two—and the first tentacle writhed and pulled back while Stafford screamed. Three—the second tentacle flinched—four—*look out!*

She dropped into a roll, came out of it, and shot wildly at the tentacle that was heading her way. It was too fast or she was too slow; it dodged, and she ran. Fired again twice in the four steps that took her to the pillar. Ducked behind it.

"On your left!" Addy called.

She twisted to meet the tentacle head-on and squeezed six rounds into it as it bore down on her. The first shot missed. The other five hit home. Stafford shrieked and the tentacle retreated, but a fresh one was already heading her way.

That became the rhythm for the next few minutes: shoot and run, shoot and hide, and shoot and run. The gun showed no sign of overheating. Its ammo seemed to be unlimited. She got Addy out of a spot of bother a few times, and Addy repaid the favour by calling warnings. Her frustration mounted. Sure, they weren't being massacred yet, but they were tiring fast. Delay tactics, that's all it was. Stafford was waiting until they were too exhausted to fight anymore.

They'd have to take him out before then.

She spotted Addy darting between the pillars not far in front. The knife strapped to Maunga's thigh slapped against her leg as she ran to catch up. She hadn't forgotten it. She shifted the rifle to hold it in her left hand, slipped the knife out with her right, and held it ready to throw. Bless her combat instructor for making sure she could throw almost as well with her off-hand.

Wait for it. She squeezed off a shot, deterring the tentacle that had been sneaking her way. "Addy! Heads!"

The knife flew true, spinning through the air to impact with a *thwack* in the pillar two handspans above Addy's head. Addy yanked it free, shouted her thanks, and darted off again to weave in and out of the pillars until she was halfway around the room.

The tentacles followed her, leaving Maunga in relative peace for a few seconds. *Excellent.* And she was in about the best spot she could be. Thanks to Addy's distraction tactics, Stafford was looking away from her with his back—and the back of his neck—a perfect target. Even better.

Maunga shifted the gun back to a two-handed grip and spun the power dial up to its maximum of sixteen. He wouldn't know what hit him. But she'd have to be quick.

She stepped out from behind the pillar and planted her feet. The stock hit her shoulder, nestled tight, and she brought the gun to bear. Addy was running left again, out of the firing line. *Good.* Safety off.

She drew a breath, held it, and fired on the exhale. *One. Two. Three.* They hit spot-on at the nape, knocking Stafford forward and off balance. A tentacle whipped out, heading straight for her. She ran, doubling back to her last pillar and on to the pillar past that, hearing him roar with pain. It hadn't been enough to kill him. With any luck, it had injured him and made him think twice about toying with them.

Dodge and run, duck, twist around the oncoming tentacle, and run, and run. Across the room, Addy stabbed at a tentacle that had wrapped itself around her leg; Maunga made it to the relative shelter of a pillar and leaned out, gun ready, to see the tentacle retreat, oozing blackish liquid from a dozen holes. Oil? Blood? She couldn't tell. *Thattagirl.*

Stafford shouted at them, oaths and curses melding together in an inarticulate jumble. Maunga dashed for the next pillar, aiming to work her way around the room to Addy.

Thwack.

She felt it an instant before the sound hit her ears. A tentacle struck her broadside, throwing her hard against the pillar she'd just left. Her shoulder hit first with a jarring shock, setting the nerves screaming; she yelled in pain and surprise, fought to lift her arm, and yelled again as the tentacle wrapped around her bicep.

It squeezed. *Hard.*

This time she screamed. Skin twisting, bones grinding, damaged nerves flared and sang in chaotic symphonies. Black spots flickered at the edges of her sight. But it wasn't broken, and she still had her left arm free. One-handed shooting was never ideal. It would do.

She lifted the assault rifle and shot blindly, felt the recoil run up through her elbow, throwing it back to smack against the pillar. The tentacle loosened and fell away, spraying slimy blood down her. She was free.

She gulped air and ran, vaulting over the retreating tentacle, weaving in and out of three pillars before pausing and looking back.

The tentacle lay lifeless in a loose coil at the foot of the pillar. She'd left the gun on the highest power setting, she realised—the overpowered shot had severed the slimy limb. The blunt end was leaking blood, an ugly dark stain on the white tiles. More blood poured from the stump of the damaged tentacle as it pulled back toward Stafford. He was screaming again.

Maunga gritted her teeth against the grinding pain and tried to move her injured arm into position to brace the gun. Keek

keek keek *no*. Not happening. She gasped and trailed off into a whimper. Sucked a lungful of air. Sweat poured down her face, stinging when it hit her eyes. She blinked it away and tucked her arm against her side. One-handed shooting it was.

"Addy!" Her voice was hoarse with pain. "Go for the tentacles! Hit him with everything you've got!"

The end was in sight.

She flicked loose tendrils of hair out of her face, shifted her grip on the gun, and moved out from behind the pillar. Brace, aim, fire.

The first shot went wide. The second struck true, severing the nearest tentacle near the base. She could see Addy off to the side, hacking her way through one tentacle as another fell loose at her feet. The third shot hit home and then her hand slipped on the sweaty grip. The fourth glanced off.

Keek. Four tentacles at once were snaking her way. She tightened her grip as best she could with only one hand and picked them off. One down. Two down. Three down, the shot hitting the seam where it joined Stafford's torso; that was bound to hurt. She shot the fourth when it was half a metre away. The severed tip flew through the air, slapping her face before falling to the ground. She felt sticky blood leave its mark and flinched back, but she didn't have a hand free to wipe it away.

She kept shooting, sparing a thought to hope the power pack didn't give out under the strain of so many overpowered shots. Tentacles fell loose one after another. Half of them were little more than bloody stumps now. Severed limbs littered the floor, black snakes and dark blood falling every which way. Stafford was still fighting, but she could see him fading, starting to curl in on himself under the combined attack.

Less than a handful left now. Time to finish it.

"Addy! Get clear!"

Addy slipped free, dealt one last blow to a tentacle that tried to follow her, and slunk across the room to take cover behind a pillar a quarter-turn from Maunga. *Good.*

Maunga started picking off the last few tentacles, exposing the mess of circuitry and welding that lay beneath. It had been true what Stafford said about not being able to move; he'd been welded to the floor in what was possibly the world's most inefficient model of Management Centralisation ever seen.

Not that she minded. It made her job a whole heap easier.

Six to go. The tentacles lay lax, that blank face staring her down in silence. She met him glare for glare.

Five to go. He knew he was beaten. He had to, by now.

Four to go.

And then a ghostly form flickered into life behind Stafford and fastened a slim arm around his neck joint.

"Goodness," said a smooth, hated voice. "You *have* made a mess of things in my absence, haven't you? You can come out," she added. "He's safe."

"Yeah," Addy called, "but are you?"

Caroline laughed. Her black pixie cut was as immaculate as ever, her clothes clean and creaseless. "I'm dead. Yes, I'm safe. For everybody except this one, that is." She gave the shoulder in front of her a pat.

Maunga stepped out. So that was what Stafford had meant by 'she's indisposed.' It was a rather more permanent state than they'd suspected.

"You're dead?" Addy padded out from behind her post and walked around the circle to join Maunga.

"Unfortunately." Caroline sounded resigned. "This whole project just didn't work out very well. First you start ruining my test results, then he—" another pat, rather harder than the last "—gets ideas above his station and murders me. No, it hasn't worked out."

"How are you here if you're dead?" Maunga suspected she already knew.

"I had safeguards in place, not to mention a ghost in the system. I might be dead, but I can still continue my research . . . with what little results I've got that aren't skewed beyond usability."

"You're one—" Stafford gasped "—to talk about ruined results!"

Caroline smiled. "You killed me. The least I could do was help Adelaide ruin your results."

Interesting. But it didn't solve the most pressing issue. Keek, her arm hurt. "We need the antidote."

"He's already got it," Caroline said. "I gave it to him."

What? "Why?"

"I like his brain; it would be a pity if he couldn't use it anymore. And he reminds me of . . . well, me. We think alike. Pointless death is never part of the plan." Her eyes flicked upward, narrowing in concentration. "He's close to getting that exit open." She looked at Addy. "I won't offer an apology for your experiences here."

"And I won't extend my condolences for the loss of your results," Addy returned.

Caroline turned back to Maunga. "If I were you, I'd leave now."

"Why?"

"Because I'm destroying this place once I've dealt with this moron. I'm dead. The project is finished. The facility has no purpose anymore."

"That's it?" Addy asked.

"That's it." Her eyes darted upward again. "Don't bother going to the office where you left him. He's at the top of the stairs."

"How do we know you're telling the truth?"

"What reason do I have to lie? You might want to run."

Walls snapped up around the stage, hiding Caroline and Stafford from view. A quarter-turn around the room, a doorway opened, tall and wide, with a white passage beyond.

Maunga and Addy ran.

CHAPTER FIFTEEN

They came to the green wall after a single corner in the white passage. The ground trembled beneath Maunga's feet. She led the charge through the gap in the base and up the first flight of stairs. Addy's bare feet were quiet at her back, but she could hear her panting easily enough.

Keek, she hurt. Every step sent grinding pain through her injured arm. She'd slung the gun strap over her shoulder; she couldn't hold it two-handed, and it was too heavy to carry with one hand while they ran. The rifle bounced up and down against her back, hitting hard.

Up, and up, and up. The stairs felt endless. Addy lagged behind as they came to the third landing. By the fifth, she was a full flight behind. Maunga stopped to dry heave over the side when the pain grew too much, and by the time she settled, grimacing at the empty aftertaste of acid and bile, Addy had caught up.

"C'mon," Addy gasped. "Nearly there."

Maunga forced her legs to move again. Up and up. Would this never end?

And then she rounded the last corner, Addy padding along beside her, and saw the landing ahead, and the door, and the familiar head of messy curls.

Theo.

There was a heart where the hole in her chest had been, pounding too fast, too loud, blood racing through her veins. Caroline hadn't lied after all. He was alive. She caught her breath on a sob. He was *alive.*

She dashed up the stairs, heard him muttering under his breath, and his name tumbled from her lips. "Theo!"

"Got it!" He gave a final jab to the keypad. The door clicked open. "Hexadecimal. Maunga, good timing." His other hand held his pocketknife, blade weaving into a sharp silver blur as his hand trembled. She'd bet the slanting calculations scratched into the wall beside the door hadn't been there an hour ago.

Theo's eyes were fever-bright, face pale under brown skin with a sickly greyish tinge. His hands were blotchy red at the wrists with white knuckles and blue nails. They spasmed at his sides, but he either didn't notice or was past caring. Tear tracks stained his cheeks. She caught the tang of vomit on his breath and winced. How was he upright? By rights he should be flat on his back in a hospital bed.

He pushed himself up off his knees and stopped, swaying. She caught him a split second before he collapsed, grunting as his weight bore down on her shoulder.

"Thanks," she gasped as Addy got an arm around him from the other side. Together they lowered him to ground. "Theo? You with me?"

He mumbled something inarticulate, lashes fluttering.

"Theo!"

"'m fine," he whispered.

"Yeah, you look it," Addy said.

"Liam."

"What?"

"Liam." He stared past Maunga into space.

He was delusional. "Liam's not here, Theo."

"Liam," he said again. "Addy. Maunga."

"I'm here," Maunga and Addy said in unison.

"Maunga." A loopy smile crossed his face. "Addy. Maunga. Addy."

Maunga threw a despairing look at Addy. They'd never get him through the exit, not in this state. He didn't have a hope of walking under his own power, and they were both too far gone to be able to carry him. What was behind the door? She kicked a leg out to catch the handle, throwing the door open wide.

More stairs. These were the dingy, abandoned-industrial sort, like the ones they'd used on the way down from the school.

No. Not a hope.

"Can you stand up?" she asked Theo.

No reply. He was staring past her again, eyes glazed, brows furrowed.

"Theo." If they could get him up, at least, maybe they could plan where to go next. The rumbling from below grew louder. She thought she felt faint tremors once or twice. They didn't have much time.

A spark of recognition lit his eyes.

"Theo, can you stand up?"

"Mm." He rolled onto his knees. Braced a hand on her shoulder—the good one, thankfully, or she would've been down and screaming right alongside him. Addy wriggled around to pull his other arm over her shoulders and between them they half-lifted him into a standing position. He drooped, leaning against Addy, his bearded chin resting above her ear.

"Liam," he muttered.

"Yeah, mate. I'm here."

Maunga jumped as Liam appeared from the dingy stairwell. He proffered a bottle. His eyes were soft even if his tone was strict. "Drink it all."

To her surprise, Theo reached out a trembling hand and took the bottle without protest.

Liam dug a hand into his pocket and withdrew a sealed pee-pot. "Aim for that when you're done. We'll send it to the lab to get tested."

"Thanks," Theo rasped.

At least he was semi-coherent again. That was a good sign.

"There's an ambulance waiting up top," Liam said. "The

crew's on their way down now. Hospital for the three of you. No arguments."

"No argument here." Maunga raised a hand in surrender. Hospital meant sleep. And painkillers. And safety.

No, she had no argument with that.

None at all.

~

Maunga woke slowly. Her bicep felt distantly sore, like someone had taken the pain out and wrapped it in cotton wool. She inhaled, wrinkled her nose at the too-sterile smell, and let the breath out. Hospital. Okay. She was safe. She could go back to sleep now.

But she couldn't. Something was missing.

Theo.

He'd made it out of that hellhole with them, alive and mostly upright and semi-lucid. Where was he?

"Maunga." Te Kaha spoke in her ear, deep and calm. "It's okay. Theo's right here."

She turned her head, saw the lump on the next bed, and relaxed. So he was. "Addy?"

"On the other side of Theo. Need a hand sitting up?"

She shook her head and peeled back the sweaty tangle of sheets, trying to marshal her thoughts. "Anything to report?"

Te Kaha shrugged. "Theo's been sedated the whole time. They've taken his sample away to the lab. Once they've got results they can start combating the poison. In the meantime it's standard stuff: saline drip, oxygen, morphine, and so on. Addy's refusing to be sedated, so it's light painkillers and whatever sleep she can grab naturally."

"Diagnosis?"

"Chronic undernutrition, chronic fatigue, chronic insomnia, any number of non-chronic issues."

Maunga glanced over Theo's sleeping body. Sure enough, a glint met her eyes. Addy was awake and staring at the ceiling.

"My arm's not broken?"

Te Kaha shook his head. "Deep tissue bruising. They were worried there could be hairline fractures, but the scans came back clear."

"Good," she said, yawning again. Maybe she was more tired than she'd thought. All she wanted to do was sleep.

But first . . . "I need the loo."

"Want a hand?"

She felt as weak as a kitten. "Please."

Together they shuffled to the bathroom. Te Kaha gave her privacy and promptly escorted her straight back to the bed.

"There," he said, supervising her slow movements. "You've got no excuse to move until morning, now."

"Doesn't—mmm—worry me." *Another* yawn? Where were they all coming from? "G'night."

He might have answered her, but she was already asleep.

~

Maunga was the first to be released. She went home, had the longest shower of her entire life, then packed a bag for Theo and headed straight back to the hospital. A short stop on the way took care of Addy's supplies. She was back three hours after she'd left to relieve Challa of bed-sitting duty.

"You're sure?" Challa asked. "Normally I'd stay, but I'm still on the clock, and work needs me."

"So get going." She softened the words with a smile.

Once Challa was gone Maunga let the smile slide off her face. *Alone. Good.*

Exhaustion would be normal, the discharge medico had warned her. She wasn't surprised it had caught up with her. She just hadn't expected it to be so soon, mere hours after she was freed from the constant low-level stress of scans and meds and hourly checkups.

And now she was back.

As uncomfortable as she might be here in the hard visitor's chair, as much as she wanted nothing more than to crawl under the duvet at home and steal Theo's pillow and sleep for a thousand years . . . she wouldn't.

Some things were more important than her weariness and insecurities.

Her husband slept in the hospital bed beside her, being treated for severe poisoning. His insides were on the mend, but they were by no means healed. Her sister-in-law lay in the second bed, knee-deep in a programme designed to slowly normalise her system after years of strain. Even after that, they had a long road ahead of them. She would have insomnia. Nightmares. PTSD. A host of other issues to work through.

Maunga couldn't stop the tears welling up. It was the release of weeks of constant tension; the slackening of a line that had been stretched taut for far too long. She reached for Theo's hand. It was comforting just to be here with him, watching the rise and fall of his chest as he breathed freely and without pain.

The tears came. She laid her head on the bed at his hip and let them fall.

~

Theo woke to a weight at his hip. He inhaled, caught the familiar scent of lime, and frowned. Maunga. The sound came to his ears next. Crying. Why was she crying? How could he fix it?

He managed to lift a hand. Combed his fingers through her tangled hair. "Hey," he mumbled. How long had it been since he'd last spoken? Days, maybe. He was just so *tired* all the time.

His eyelids felt like someone had outlined them in gritty sand and weighted them down with bricks; he forced them open and found Maunga staring back at him. A white bandage peeked out from under the short sleeve of her shirt. Good to see she'd followed the medico's orders on that one.

"Hey." She sniffed. Another few tears broke away to trail down her cheeks.

"What's wrong?" The words slurred as they left his mouth.

She shook her head. Or was it a nod? It was hard to tell. "Nothing."

"You don't . . . cry over nothing."

"Tension and release," she murmured, moving her head further up the bed to nudge against his shoulder. "Basic physiological reaction to stress. It'll pass."

Nothing that he needed to worry about, in other words. He brushed his fingers clumsily over her cheeks. "You'll be alright?"

"I'll be alright."

Despite the exhaustion lapping at him, despite the fresh tears falling from her eyes and dripping onto the sheets, he could hear that old layer of conviction underpinning her words. She'd be alright. They'd be alright. With a bit of time and sleep and love and care.

"Good."

He closed his eyes and they lay in silence, her hand on his chest, his fingers in her hair, and listened to each other breathe.

CHAPTER SIXTEEN

It was another week before the medicos deemed Theo fit enough to be released from hospital—a week of hazy numbness when the painkillers worked and wracking pain when they didn't, of lethargy and tiredness and gradually feeling like himself again.

During that week, Maunga visited as often as she could for as long as she could. She'd curl up next to him during the early morning hours, sneak food in when she came back after lunch, stay far past when night visiting hours ended.

Now that she'd been released and Theo and Addy were both on the mend, there was less of a need for the round-the-clock company that Challa had so thoughtfully organised. But he didn't ask them to stop. He liked the company, truth be told. Liked Tuku's mischievous tales and Liam's quiet medical checks, Kim's everlasting optimism and Te Kaha's solid warmth—and, of course, his coffee. Tarata brought science journals from the stacks at Breach. Manatu dropped in after work a few times to see how things were going. After he was released, they kept up the visits to the hospital room, relieving him from Addy-duty in much the same way that they'd relieved Maunga from Theo-and-Addy-duty. He still spent a solid eight hours there most days—once as little as four, once a full eighteen when Addy was reacting badly to new medication.

Five days later, Addy herself was discharged.

"You can stay at our place if you want," Theo said, careful to phrase it as an offer and not an order.

Addy nodded. "Thanks. I'd like that."

The arrangements were made and diplomatically handled on all sides. There was no way he was letting Addy out of his sight, not after losing her for so long, and he suspected she felt something of the same thing, albeit tempered by a natural feeling of isolation.

He'd discussed it at length with Maunga, worried that she might not want Addy intruding on territory that had always been exclusively *theirs*. Her reaction had been characteristic.

"Don't be daft, Theo, of course she can stay with us, and for as long as she needs to. Or for as long as you need her to," she added with a knowing look.

"You don't mind? I can't let her go to Mum and Dad's, not straight out of the hospital. I've warned them about the situation, but I still need to visit and give them the full explanation in person. A lot will depend on how they react to that. They're not going to be happy about me keeping them in the dark for years, to start with, and . . ." He hesitated. "I don't want her to go before she's ready."

"And she's not ready. Nowhere near it. She needs you—needs both of us. And you need her."

So it was settled. They tidied the spare room, cleaning out the clutter and making it feel more like home. They picked out a new duvet cover, added a few books and pictures. Nothing too overt. Nothing too threatening. Nothing that said, *This is your home forever,* because it wasn't true, and nothing that said, *This is the equivalent of a motel room,* because that wasn't true either. It was her temporary home for as long as she needed it, simple as that.

Maunga waited with the car—their comfortably worn Ford, not the rental Jaguar—while Theo went to the ward to find Addy up and dressed. He escorted her through the discharge station and then helped her with what little belongings she had in hospital storage. Theo shouldered the duffle bag with her toiletries and new clothes. Addy lifted a hand toward the canvas sack from the testing facility, paused, and lowered it again, empty-handed. Theo picked the sack up without a word.

"Maunga's out at the car," he said.

Addy rubbed a hand along her thigh and nodded. She walked beside him in silence and maintained her silence all the way home.

He didn't push. Maunga must have noticed the glances he kept sneaking in the rearview mirror. She reached over and squeezed his hand, and then grinned at his automatic response of, "Hands."

"Yup," she said cheerfully. "Two of them."

They got Addy inside without any trouble. Theo ushered her upstairs, meaning to drop her things in her room before showing her the rest of the house. But the cracks appeared as soon as she stepped through her bedroom door.

"This is your room." He nudged the door open with a shoulder and led the way in. "Pretty basic but it should have everything you need. If there's anything we've forgotten, please ask. It's yours, Addy. We want it to feel safe for you, okay?"

Silence answered him.

"Addy?" He dumped the bags on the bed and turned back to her.

She had frozen in the doorway, eyes staring blindly around the room. One hand gripped the fabric of her trousers and released it, gripped it and released it.

"Addy." Theo was in front of her in two strides. "What's wrong?"

She blinked. Shook her head. The glazed look dissipated, a fog lifting off the ocean at dawn, leaving her in the here and now.

"Do you—" Her voice cracked. She started again. "Do you know how long it's been since I've had anything to call *mine*?"

"Too long." Anger washed over him, and then grief, and the overwhelming weariness that dogged his footsteps these days. "I know."

She moved past him to stand by the bed and raised a shaking hand to splay her fingers on the deep blue covers. She spoke without looking around. "You probably had plans for this afternoon. Sorry. Would you mind if I, um . . ."

"No problem. Take all the time you need. We'll be downstairs.

Tea won't be for a couple of hours. I'll call you when it's ready if you're not down before then."

"Thank you."

He hesitated, looking at her back, the crisp lines of the new clothes, the way she huddled into the folds of her too-large jersey and drew the cuffs down over her hands. He wanted nothing more than to sweep across the room and wrap her in a hug, but her body language screamed to be left alone, and her words only confirmed it.

So he left, closing the door behind him, and made his way downstairs.

Maunga was standing at the coffee machine, pouring the shots for their usual mid-afternoon drinks. He wrapped his arms around her from behind and dropped a kiss on the bare skin of her neck, grinning at her reflexive shiver.

"That was quick." She reached for the milk jug. "Everything okay up there?"

"Yeah. I think."

"You *think*?" Maunga readied the steamer. "Hold that thought. There're a few biscuits in the tin if you want to take them over to the sofa. I'll bring the coffees in a sec."

In another few minutes they were nestled on the sofa, mugs in hand.

"Mmm." Theo sipped his coffee. "Good coffee, thanks."

"Isn't it always?"

"It's . . . more good . . . than usual."

Maunga quirked a grin. "I think the word you're looking for is *better*."

"Yeah, that."

"Is she okay?" Maunga flicked her eyes up at the ceiling.

"Hard to say. She's functioning fine, in the most basic sense. I showed her the room and she sort of—froze. Went away in her head for a bit."

"Gosh," Maunga said with heavy irony. "I wonder what that's like to watch."

He acknowledged that with a tip of the head. "She came back fine when I said her name the second time."

"What triggered it?"

"Keeking Caroline."

She made an impatient noise in the back of her throat. "What, *specifically*?"

He related what had happened upstairs.

"And?"

"She froze up. Did the—" he clenched his hand in demonstration "—the stressing-anchoring thing." He huffed a breath and frowned into his coffee cup. "It's been years since she's owned anything herself, I know that. I'm painfully aware of it. Some of the best years of her life, they should have been. Anyway. She just—she wanted some time to herself. So I left her to it."

Maunga nodded. "You did the right thing."

"Doesn't make it easy."

"Of course it doesn't. But she needs that space. She needs to be able to find some sort of independence again."

"I know," he said. "I mean—she's independent now, but it's—it's the wrong independence. If that makes sense. She's too isolated, too unwilling to ask for help. Because she's gone so long without having that option. If we let her go now, she'll be . . ." He floundered. He couldn't find the words for it. "I don't know, it just, it wouldn't be anything good."

"Exactly. We support her, we help her through this, we help her find her feet again. And it's not to say that she'll be moving out next week. She needs you almost as much as you need her, right now."

"Almost." The word rang hollow. "But not quite."

"Hey." Maunga sat up to face him front-on, mouth set in a determined line. "We found her, Theo. We brought her home."

"Now we fix her," he said. His heart lifted, just a little.

"Now we fix her."

He drained his coffee. "What do you want for tea?"

"Pasta," she said and then, after a moment, "Yeah. Lasagna. With lots of cheese. And fresh garlic. There's a whole bulb in the pantry."

"Sounds good." Theo went to start preparations.

~

By the third night after Addy came home from the hospital, Theo was a ball of tangled worry and strain. By all accounts Addy was making progress: she ate two meals a day at something approaching half-sized portions, even if she scoffed the food down in record time; she devoured books and news holos during the day, or played endless word games with him, or sat in comfortable silence with Maunga; she went to bed early and appeared downstairs in time for a late breakfast.

But the shadows under her eyes were deepening. Her hands shook when she thought they weren't watching and she'd started flinching at sudden movements or noises again.

"I don't think she's sleeping," Theo said, pacing up and down their bedroom floor in bare feet. It was after midnight. Tonight, like the last two nights, they'd heard nothing from Addy's room since she'd said goodnight: not a peep, not a whimper, not a stifled scream from one of her recurring nightmares. He crossed to the open bedroom door and leaned out, peering down the hall to where Addy's door stood firmly closed. Nothing.

"It would explain the bruising under her eyes," Maunga said. "And the yawning."

"Yawning?" He hadn't noticed her yawning.

"I've caught her a couple of times by coming into a room suddenly. She only lets them loose when we're not there."

He couldn't bear this. "I'm going to check on her."

"No, I'll go." Maunga slipped out of bed and threw on a jersey—one of his, he noted—over her pyjamas.

"We could both go."

She shook her head. "Too threatening, both of us invading her space at the same time. Especially at this time of night."

"So why don't I go alone?" He wanted to check on Addy. Needed to check on her.

"Theo. You're her brother."

"And?"

"She's going to know you're checking up on her and she's going to think it's because you're obligated to. Because you're family."

"So are you," he said. "Family. And checking on her."

"It's . . . not the same." She was already halfway to the door. "Will you trust me with this?"

Did she even have to ask? "Always."

"Thank you. Don't wait up for me." She slipped out the door and was gone.

Don't wait up. Yeah, right.

He'd never get to sleep now, not with wondering what was going on down the hall. The two women had seemed to reach some sort of truce in these last few weeks; they weren't the best of friends, but they could tolerate one another and even enjoy each other's company in some small way. Was it a strong enough bond to survive Maunga invading Addy's territory in the middle of the night? He didn't know.

He could bet he'd find out soon, though.

More than an hour later, Maunga snuck back into their bedroom and closed the door behind her.

"How was it?" he asked, looking up from his book.

Jaw tight, she shook her head and stripped off the jersey before sliding in beside him. "She'd been using the keeking noise shields."

"What?"

"Yeah, that was my thought, too. She, I quote, didn't want us to worry, unquote."

He snorted. "I—I can't even—*how?* How could she think that was a good idea?"

"You know how."

"Caroline."

"That's the one." Maunga stretched her neck out one way and then the other, wincing. "So I walked in there to find her holed up behind the shields, crying and literally biting her hand to keep from screaming—thank you," she said as he shuffled in behind her and started massaging the tension out of her neck muscles. "And she was horrified to see me, of course. Or she was once she'd calmed down a bit. We got that straightened out, and I've confiscated the shields for her own good."

"Doesn't explain why it took you over an hour to get back here."

"Ah." She looked down and away, a dull flush climbing her cheeks.

Theo tipped his head to study her, intrigued. Maunga, embarrassed? That happened once in a blue moon. "Spill."

"Let's just say standard office hours don't apply for family."

He choked back a laugh. "You gave her a counselling session?"

"Of a sort."

"In your pyjamas. In the middle of the night." Now that he knew to look for it, he could see the remnants of client-brain fading from her expression.

"To be fair, she was wearing her pyjamas, too. I believe in meeting people where they're at—and if that means a counselling session in pyjamas in the middle of the night, then so be it."

A teasing jibe crossed his mind, something along the lines of *hope you don't let your male clients do that.* It died before it came anywhere near his lips. Some things weren't even worth mentioning.

He dropped a kiss on her head instead. "You're one amazing woman, you know that?"

"I know," she said, snuggling under the blankets with a sleepy smile. "But thank you."

~

It wasn't just Addy who had bad nights.

Theo woke with a dry mouth and racing pulse, gasping for breath. He kicked the blankets off and rolled out of bed, rubbing trembling hands over his damp face. Maunga was nowhere to be seen. She'd gone back to a half-time case load last week; had she had an early morning emergency call?

He crossed to the window and threw the curtain back. The city lay below, quiet in the grey hush before dawn. He traced the lines of the streets with his eyes, mapping it mentally, naming roads, picking out friends' houses, the university, his old high school. The familiar routine was designed to calm his frenetic thoughts, replacing the what-ifs with the these-ares, the unknowns with the knowns.

It wasn't enough this morning.

He turned away and fell full-length onto the bed. Grabbing Maunga's pillow, he rolled onto his back and slipped it under his head. It was still warm. But she was gone, and she'd been gone in his dreams, too, in those awful realms of doubt and ghosting pain.

The thoughts chased one another around in his head, *she was here, she's gone, what if she's hurt,* piling up until he could scream from frustration. Her side of the bed was still warm. She'd been here only minutes ago. No message waited on his holo; she was still in the house.

He didn't need to worry.

But he couldn't stop the circling thoughts. By the time she came back, his mind had moved on to playing music, an endless loop of melodies that mingled love and grief in equal part. He couldn't remember the words.

"Oi." Her voice was soft. The hand that prodded the ticklish arch of his foot was equally gentle. "Alright?"

"There's too much mind in my brain." He didn't look away from the ceiling.

"Anything I can do to help?" The bed sank as she sat beside him.

"No. Yes. Just being here helps."

"How bad is it?"

"Better now. Mostly. I dreamed you were gone, and then I woke up and—you were gone."

She didn't apologise. He didn't expect her to. "A client called."

"I figured." Only a few things would take her to the study at this time of the night. He turned his head to look at her. "Suicide attempt?"

Not quite, said her eyes. "Confidential," said her mouth.

He nodded. He'd learned to be content with that answer over the years.

"Are you going back to sleep?" she asked.

"Don't know."

"Well, I am. Can I have my pillow back?"

"Mmm, I don't know . . . it's a very comfortable pillow."

"I'm aware." A moment later it flew out from under him, and his head hit the bed. "Thanks," she said, holding the pillow up with a grin.

"Welcome."

"Now scooch over."

He scooched.

~

"Anti-fragility," Maunga announced one night at the dinner table.

Theo and Addy looked at each other blankly.

"Sorry?" Theo asked.

"Anti-fragility," she said again, as if that explained everything.

"You might need to expound on that," Addy said.

"Okay." Maunga rubbed her hands together, eyes alight, and then lifted her wine glass and waved it at them. "What would happen if I hit this with a hammer?"

Theo winced. The glasses were antique crystal from his grandmother. "Please don't."

"It would break," said Addy.

Maunga pointed at Addy. "It would break. Exactly. Which makes it . . . ?"

"Breakable?"

"Expensive crystal with priceless sentimental value?" Theo suggested.

That earned him a *look*. "Fragile," said Maunga.

"Oh. Fragile. Right."

"We knew that," said Addy. "Fragile. Yes."

"If I hit it with a hammer and it broke, it would be fragile. What about if I hit it with a hammer and it *didn't* break?"

Hmm. Now there was an idea. "I don't think technology's quite at that point."

"But what would it be?"

"Um," said Addy. "An unbroken wine glass?"

"A miracle of glassblowing," said Theo.

"Or a poor quality hammer," said Addy.

"Strong," said Maunga. "It would be strong. So if it breaks, it's fragile, and if it doesn't break, it's strong, right?"

"I think we just established that."

"What if it not only doesn't break, but it gets even stronger?"

What? He didn't get it. Judging from Addy's blank look, she didn't get it either. "Sorry. You've lost us."

Maunga put her glass down by her left hand. "Call this fragility, okay?"

"Okay."

She slid the glass up to her right hand. "And this is the opposite of fragility. You'd think this would be the strong point, right?"

"Right," said Addy.

Maunga slid the glass back down to halfway between her left and right hands. "What if this is the strong point? Strength isn't the opposite of fragility; it's just the *absence* of fragility."

Aha. Theo finally clicked to what she was saying.

"On the one hand you have fragility," she said, patting the table at her left, "which is when you hit a wine glass with a hammer and it shatters. In the middle, with the absence of fragility, you have strength, which is when you hit the glass and it doesn't break, but it doesn't do anything else, either."

"With you so far."

"And on the other hand, you have the *opposite* of fragility." Maunga patted the table at her right. "Not the absence, but the opposite, which we call *anti*-fragility. Which is what happens when you hit a glass with a hammer and then the glass picks up the hammer and hits you right back—or something to that effect. The glass gets stronger as a result of the shock, anyway."

Addy understood that time. He watched it sink in.

"So what you're saying," Addy said, "is that those six, seven years with Caro . . . what, they turned me into a wine glass that can pick up a hammer and hit someone back?"

Maunga made a soft noise of frustration. "Not exactly. But yes, that's the gist of it. I'm saying that most people—90 percent or more—would have broken in that testing facility. You didn't. Under the stress of seven years of absolute hell, you—keek, it's incredible—you became *stronger*."

"I had to." A frown knitted Addy's forehead. "I don't know, I just knew I had to survive, and I had to stay myself while doing it. It wasn't a choice. Not consciously."

"Of course it wouldn't be conscious. But it happened nonetheless." Maunga leaned forward. "Most people would have died in those conditions, Addy. Almost anyone else. Theo would have, most likely. I would have, almost certainly. But you didn't. You survived, and you grew stronger."

Addy shrugged and looked away. "I just did what I could to stay alive. I don't reckon it makes me anyone important." She laid the faintest stress on the last word.

Her choice of words was clearly significant. Maunga grinned and shook her head. A flurry of emotion played across her face:

wonder, fascination, professional interest, a shade of bemusement, and then a large dose of affection. "Yeah," she said. "You don't. And there's the rub."

~

"Would you have killed Caroline?" Theo asked Maunga one night when the two of them were out for a walk after tea.

"No." She didn't look surprised by the question.

"If she wasn't already dead, I mean."

"I know. And no." She stepped around a branch that had fallen onto the path. "What do I value, Theo?"

Another trust test. He'd been missing them. "Loyalty."

"And?"

"Patience. Hard work. Honesty. Genuineness. Justice. Equality—"

"That's the one."

"Equality?"

"Yeah but nah. The one before that."

"Justice."

"Justice," she said. "Exactly."

They cut left across the grass of the rugby field. He waited.

"Quite aside from the ethics of it." She stopped and started again. "No. Killing her wouldn't be just. And I don't mean only for us, I mean for everyone, all those people who had Vox Pox, all their families, the ones who couldn't—couldn't handle it—"

"Like Seth."

"Like Seth. Does that make sense? It might be—oh, not justice, not really. Call it revenge, I suppose—it might be revenge for us and for Addy, but it wouldn't be justice for everybody else Caroline hurt."

"Yeah. That makes sense." He couldn't hide the relief that slipped into the words.

Maunga caught his hand and squeezed it. "She would have

been up in court, Theo. Eyewitness accounts. Hard evidence. We've got Addy's written account. I would have stood on the witness stand and spilled my guts: told them about Seth's suicide, the blackmail, everything. She would have gone away for a long, long time."

"You wouldn't have killed her."

"I wouldn't have killed her."

He nodded, absorbing the words, the truth behind them. "Thank you."

~

The soft chime of the alarm woke Theo in the small hours. Maunga groaned and turned over onto her back. He watched her eyes blink open to gaze at the ceiling.

"Six days," he mumbled. "Since the last one."

"She's making good progress."

"Wonder who she wants this time."

He turned his eyes to the small holo plate they'd fixed to the ceiling above the bed. *Theo,* said the glowing block caps in green on the left, and *Maunga,* in yellow on the right. The signal lights below each name were still dark. Addy had hit the general alarm to wake them but not a specific call button yet.

Sometimes she didn't ask for either of them. It was enough for her to know that they were there, ready to respond if she needed them. Usually she'd call one or the other of them: Maunga if she needed to talk, Theo if she needed a shoulder to cry into. He offered a listening ear, of course, and he knew Maunga had offered a hug more than once. But they never pushed. Always, always, it was only what Addy was comfortable with in her space.

In the daytime, in the more neutral areas of lounge and kitchen and the city outside, they could afford to push her harder, tease her more, stretch her boundaries. But nights were vulnerable, and her room was her territory. They respected that. Always.

The chime sounded again. The light under his name came on. Theo slid out of bed and reached for a shirt.

He kissed Maunga on his way out of the room. "Don't wait up," he murmured, and heard a sleepy mutter in reply. She was already halfway back to sleep.

It was like he'd walked into the picture of the two of them from before Addy left, except for the small fact that they'd both aged more than seven years in the interim. He found her curled tight in the corner where her bed met two walls, knees to her chest, arms wrapped around them, her tearstained face staring down the darkness in grim defiance.

"Addy?" He slid onto the bed with the ease of long practice, setting his back to the wall and opening his arms. "I'm here."

Her jaw trembled. He could see the moment she broke. The dam burst and she threw herself into his arms, head buried in his chest, shaking hands digging into his shirt and scratching through the material to his ribs below.

He tucked her head more securely under his chin. Stroked a hand over her hair, which was almost down to her chin in places now. Rubbed her back. He didn't say anything. There was nothing to say on these nights. He'd grown used to the echoing ache in the hollow space where his heart lay. Grown used to hiding his own tears at the thought of what she'd been through, the sight and sound of what she was still going through—what she would, in all likelihood, go through to a lessening extent for the rest of her life. He'd even grown used to falling asleep with his fully-grown, adult little sister in his arms, and waking up to a stiff neck and pins and needles.

Pain was the price you paid for love. He'd known it for a long, long time.

But it didn't make the love any less worth it.

If anything, he thought, tucking Addy closer and feeling her tears soak through his shirt, the pain made it more worth it.

Because it meant something.

~

"I reckon she's getting ready to move out," Maunga said one day when Addy was out shopping with Challa.

Theo started. "You do?"

"What, you don't?"

The possibility hadn't even crossed his mind. "Don't know. Hadn't really, uh, thought about it in a while."

"Mmm." He could see she wasn't fooled by his dodge. She went on. "Liam said she's fully recovered, physically, as much as she'll ever be. Psychologically she's been a functioning member of society for weeks now. Hasn't had a bad night in more than a month, and even then it's been, what, six weeks since she called us in?"

"Seven."

"Tuku's volunteered her spare room down on Rakiura, but I don't think Addy's of a mind to trade one married couple for another, and I doubt she'd leave the city."

"No," Theo said. "She loves it here."

"So I had a quick chat with Challa—"

At a guess, he'd say Addy and Challa's friendship was even stronger now than it had been when they were children. "And?"

"Her flatmate's moving out in two months. She'll have a room free then."

Hmm. "Anyone else in the flat? Other women? Strange men?"

"Just Challa. It's a little two-bedroom place down near Cemetery Hill."

That was the unfashionable end of town but that wouldn't matter to Addy, not when it was only a few blocks from the ocean. And it was a safe enough neighbourhood. You wouldn't catch a city lawyer living there, but it was a far cry from the state housing blocks to the west. Artisans and bohemian types, he thought. The quiet-livers. People who preferred to be a bit more isolated from the city rush and who didn't need a quick commute to work every day. Less participants in city life and more observers of it. Like Challa with her journalism.

That would suit Addy down to the ground.

"She doesn't have a job yet," he said neutrally. Whether she was *ready* for one or not, he wasn't sure. It wasn't his call to make.

"She's got savings, doesn't she?"

"Yeah. Technically she's had access to her trust fund since her eighteenth. It's been sitting there accumulating interest."

Maunga nodded. "That should last her until she's ready for a job."

"Easily, I should think. A couple of years at least. More than that if she's careful with it. She lives pretty quietly; I doubt she'll go on a spending spree the day she moves out."

"Challa said the flat's already furnished. She'll need a bed, but that's about it."

He swallowed a surge of bittersweet feeling. He liked having Addy around. He'd gotten used to it. Perhaps too much, now that he thought about it. Maybe Maunga was right. Time for Addy to spread her wings.

"Alright?" Maunga asked, eyes soft.

"Yeah," he said, and found it was the truth. "It'll be a change, but a good one, I think."

He heard a noise at the front door. A moment later there came the triple-tone chime of it opening. Boots thudded on the polished wood floor, and then it closed again.

"Hello?" Addy called from the front hallway. "Anyone home?"

"In the lounge," he yelled.

"Give me a hand?"

"Keek, what's she gone and bought now?" he said to Maunga.

"More books?" Maunga suggested.

"She'd better not have. Those shelves are overflowing as it is."

"Theo!"

"Coming!"

Maunga grinned. "Yeah, go and carry her books like a proper big brother."

"Shush, you." He kissed her on the way past. "I bet Challa's been encouraging her again. They're a right pair, those two. When I get my hands on that woman . . ."

"Theo! Come on! My arms are about to fall off!"

"Alright, I'm coming!"

With Maunga's laughter chasing him from the room, Theo strode down the hall to his sister's rescue.

CODA

The voiceless we have heard, and on this day we vow
To trace the spectral pulse of your wounded heart—
It matters not the time, it matters not the price—
To find you, O Voiceless, and make you well.

E.G. WILSON

E.G. Wilson grew up on the adventures of Bilbo Baggins, those Pevensie kids, and the Swallows & Amazons. Further inspired by Sherlock, Firefly, and Tolkien's Legendarium, she turned her hand to writing stories of her own and has never looked back. Introduced to National Novel Writing Month in 2012, she has completed the challenge every November without fail. Wilson lives in South Canterbury, New Zealand. She loves mountains, hates broad beans, and never wears matching socks. In high school, Wilson was voted *Most Likely To Re-Write The Lord Of The Rings* by her classmates. She thinks *The Lord Of The Rings* is just fine the way it is.